A SURPRISE FOR THE SINGLE DAD

JEN GILROY

HEARTWARMING

Recycling programs for this product may not exist in your area.

ISBN-13: 978-1-335-46049-3

A Surprise for the Single Dad

For questions and comments about the quality of this book, please contact us at CustomerService@Harlequin.com.

Harlequin Enterprises ULC
22 Adelaide St. West, 41st Floor
Toronto, Ontario M5H 4E3, Canada
www.Harlequin.com

HarperCollins Publishers
Macken House, 39/40 Mayor Street Upper,
Dublin 1, D01 C9W8, Ireland
www.HarperCollins.com

Printed in U.S.A.

"Don't you want to see inside?" Laura held out a key.

"Nah. I remember what the place looks like, and I don't expect it's changed much," Trevor said. "Besides, if Danny's okay with it, so am I."

"You're a good uncle." Laura's gaze never left his. "And while I wish you hadn't had to come back to Strawberry Pond for the reason you did, it's good to have you home."

Trevor's heartbeat sped up. "It's good to *be* home." For the first time in twenty-four hours, he meant it. "Here." He held out his hands so Laura wouldn't slip as she clambered up and over the snowbank. Through his gloves and her mittens, their hands connected, and he felt a zing in his palm and up his arm.

He stood still for several seconds. If it had been any other woman, he'd have said that brief "zing" meant something, but it couldn't. Not with Laura. His best friend since kindergarten.

Dear Reader,

A Surprise for the Single Dad is the second book in my Strawberry Pond miniseries, following *The Hero Next Door*, but it also stands alone. Although Strawberry Pond is fictional, New Hampshire's White Mountains, where this series is set, is a beautiful part of the world and inspires me in all seasons.

In *A Surprise for the Single Dad*, veterinarian Trevor Kaminski and real estate agent Laura Sullivan are childhood friends. While Trevor's never met the right woman to make a family with, Laura's always been happily single. However, when Trevor returns to Strawberry Pond and becomes a dad to his orphaned teenage nephew, have the love and family Trevor and Laura need been right in front of them all along?

For me, friendship is part of the foundation for romantic love—a friendship I'm blessed to share with my own husband. As always in my books, this story has other kinds of friendship too, including with animals, along with multigenerational families and cozy small-town and rural life.

I enjoy hearing from readers, so visit my website, www.jengilroy.com, and message me there, where you'll also find my newsletter sign-up and social media links.

Enjoy!

Jen

Jen Gilroy writes sweet romance and uplifting women's fiction—warm feel-good stories to bring readers' hearts home. A Romance Writers of America Golden Heart® Award finalist and short-listed for the Romantic Novelists' Association Joan Hessayon Award, she lives in small-town Ontario, Canada, with her husband, teenage daughter and floppy-eared rescue hound. She loves reading, ice cream, ballet and paddling her purple kayak. Visit her at jengilroy.com.

Books by Jen Gilroy

Harlequin Heartwarming

The Montana Carters

Montana Reunion
A Family for the Rodeo Cowboy
The Cowgirl Nanny
A Rancher's Return

A Strawberry Pond Romance

The Hero Next Door

Visit the Author Profile page at Harlequin.com.

For my husband, with love and happy memories
of our “second honeymoon” in
New Hampshire’s White Mountains.

CHAPTER ONE

FROM HER FRONT-ROW SEAT, Laura Sullivan glanced around Strawberry Pond's community center, filled on this early January evening with friends, neighbors and family. Although the "Save the Animal Rescue" meeting she and several others had organized was last-minute, despite the frigid weather, her New Hampshire hometown hadn't let them down.

She shrugged into the cozy red fleece jacket she'd left on the back of her folding chair and returned her attention to the speaker. Anne Sullivan, Laura's aunt by marriage, had supported the rescue as long as Laura could remember.

"We only have just over two months." The overhead lighting glinted on Anne's silver-gray hair as she referred to a sheet of paper she'd taken from a blue folder. "In mid-March, that's when the animal rescue's lease ends. The new owner plans to sell the building and accept an informal offer, which was made before any For Sale sign went up."

Voices murmured and then rose in volume as Anne answered several questions from those in the audience.

Laura folded her hands in her lap to try to keep from fidgeting. If the building that housed the rescue had ever been officially for sale, as a real estate agent she'd have been one of the first to know. But it hadn't, so she'd only found out about the upcoming sale along with the rest of the town when Fred Sinclair, editor of the local newspaper, *The Strawberry Pond Gazette*, broke the story on yesterday's front page. Still, maybe they shouldn't be so surprised. After the building's owner had died a few months earlier, leaving no close family, it was understandable that the estate beneficiary, an out-of-towner, would want to sell.

"I spoke to the seller by phone earlier today." Anne raised a hand and the room quieted. "She appreciates our concerns and said that if the town can match the offer that's been made, she'd sell to us instead."

More chatter broke out, and Laura looked out one of the community center's tall casement windows. Illuminated by a streetlight, snowflakes spun like graceful ballet dancers as they tumbled to the ground. High snowbanks lined both sides of the street between well-kept white clapboard and brick buildings, many still housing the same families and businesses they had since Laura's childhood. While many things had changed in Strawberry Pond in the last forty years, the most important ones hadn't. That's why Laura couldn't imagine living anywhere else.

"What did I miss?" Her friend Josie Ryan-Tremblay, who ran a dairy farm near town, slid into the seat Laura had saved for her. In a low voice, Laura recounted what Anne had said, and Josie's forehead, beneath wavy strawberry blond hair, creased into a worried frown. "How can we raise several hundred thousand dollars by the middle of March?"

"I don't know but we have to try." Like many other townspeople, Laura had adopted her own pets from that rescue, and the compact premises, one street back from Main behind the post office, was a cherished part of their small-town life.

"Sure we do." Josie's voice was firm. "Heath couldn't be here, he's working in Boston this week, but I spoke to him earlier and he's on board to advise and support on whatever's needed." As Josie smoothed her hair, a new yellow-gold wedding band sparkled beside her ruby engagement ring.

"Great. With Heath being a financial analyst, his skills will be superhelpful."

After a Christmas wedding where Laura and another friend, Alana, had been bridesmaids, Josie and Heath were settling into marital bliss.

While Laura was thrilled for them, she'd never wanted to marry. She was happy on her own, and as the oldest of eight brothers and sisters, she had more than enough relatives to want to add any more to their weighty family tree. Unlike her siblings and friends, all Laura wanted to be when she grew up was her own person. Now, between her real estate business and buying a horse farm a few years before, she'd achieved that goal and more.

"Laura? What do you suggest?" Anne's voice broke into Laura's reverie.

"About what?"

"Fundraising ideas." Anne peered at her from behind tortoiseshell glasses. "You already said we need to think big."

"I've put together a project proposal and—" Laura stopped and turned around as the community center's outside door opened with a clatter. Fred Sinclair, the newspaper editor, entered in a swirl of snow, followed by Trevor Kaminski, Laura's childhood and teenage best friend.

"What's the news, Fred?" The mayor spoke into Laura's pause and stepped up beside Anne. Meanwhile, both men had stopped to stamp snow off their boots.

While Fred made his way to the front, Trevor slid into an end seat several rows behind Laura and gave her a small wave.

As she returned his greeting, Laura's heart squeezed. They hadn't lived in the same place since high school, but earlier today Trevor had returned to Strawberry Pond from California for the saddest of reasons—to take on guardianship of his orphaned thirteen-year-old nephew.

Fred Sinclair now had everyone's attention. He beamed and, with his fringe of white hair and jolly expression, he resembled the inflatable Santa Claus that Laura had on her lawn for the holidays. "I didn't want to say anything before so as not to get your hopes up, but as soon as I heard the animal rescue was in peril I called Sarah Brennan—now, of course, Sarah Fournier."

Jack and Sarah Fournier's marriage had been the talk of Strawberry Pond all fall. As her widowed mom had said on one of Laura's weekly visits to the farm where she'd grown up, "It goes to show that even the most confirmed singletons can find love." Then she'd given Laura a pointed look, which Laura had done her best to ignore. Despite brief moments of loneliness, maintaining her independence was more important than making a life with someone. Besides, everyone was lonely sometimes and it was better to be alone than unhappily partnered.

"As most of you know, the new Mr. and Mrs. Fournier are spending the winter in Florida, where Jack has a home, but Sarah wants to help. Since she adopted her dear Buttons from the rescue, it's a cause that's especially close to her heart."

Another low murmur went around the room. Buttons the basenji was the most pampered dog in Strawberry Pond and also the most mischievous. While Josie, who had a sideline in dog training, had done her best, Buttons remained a lovable scamp. However, the dog's sweet nature and cuteness mostly compensated for the destruction to screen doors, plants and porch cushions the curious canine often left in her wake.

"While Sarah has always been somewhat of a town benefactor," Fred continued, "now, she's outdone herself. On behalf of Buttons, she's offered us an exceedingly generous donation of one hundred thousand dollars to launch a fundraising campaign."

As the meeting dissolved into gasps, exclamations and chatter, Laura knew it wasn't the time to take everyone through her project plan. She exchanged a quick glance with Anne who raised her eyebrows, shrugged and nodded to confirm what Laura was thinking. Fred's announcement hadn't only derailed their agenda, but also ended the meeting. With townspeople breaking into small, excited groups, it'd be like herding cats to try to resume anytime soon.

Discussion about Laura's ideas for getting

the car dealership involved with a vehicle raffle, a large-scale corporate fundraising drive and smaller activities like a pet-themed bake sale, a pet photo session, an art festival and more could wait. While they still had to raise over two hundred thousand dollars, with Sarah Fournier's huge gift, all of a sudden, the goal didn't seem quite so overwhelming.

"Hey, you." Trevor appeared at Laura's side.

"Hey, Tuna." She greeted him with the childhood nickname only she, his mom and sister ever used.

"Lulu." His voice cracked before he wrapped her in a hug. "Long time, no see."

"Several years." As she returned his hug, Laura held him tight for an extra few seconds. While they talked by phone or had a video call every few weeks, it wasn't the same as being together in person. "I missed you." When Trevor had called before Christmas to tell her about his widowed sister's sudden death, she'd vowed to be there for him and his nephew, Danny, no matter what.

"I missed you, too." As Trevor stepped out of the hug, he looked Laura up and down.

Her face warmed, and she put a hand to one cheek, aware of Josie studying her from a group with Fred, Anne and the mayor. Trevor was older—they both were—and his brown hair had more silver strands. There were also a few more lines around his mouth and nose. But what was that unexpected flutter in her chest? He was her "best bud," the guy whose shoulder she'd cried on too many times to count, and whom she could talk to about almost anything.

"I'm glad you could make this meeting. With everything going on, I expected to see you tomorrow, not tonight." Had he slipped in late on purpose?

"Yeah. After spending time with my mom and Danny, I figured I had to face the town sometime. Better to get it over with." Although Trevor gave her an easy smile, the expression in his blue eyes was bleak. "It's the condolences that get me, you know? I still can't believe Renée's gone."

"I can't imagine." Laura spoke around a lump of emotion. She didn't want to think about the pain of losing one of her own siblings. "So can we count on you to get involved in the 'Save the Animal Rescue' project?" Best to change the subject so Trevor wouldn't feel even more uncomfortable than he undoubtedly did. "As a veterinarian, it should be right up your street."

"Well, I'll donate to fundraisers and such, but I can't get more involved than that." His voice held both weariness and tension. "Danny has to come first. He's dealing with the loss of his mom, moving to a new town and starting at a new school. My turning up, an uncle he only knows from vacations to be his guardian… I've got my new job as well. Sure, I worked at the clinic here in high school but it's different coming back as a vet rather than cleaning kennels." Trevor squeezed Laura's hand, and there was that flutter again, stronger this time.

"It's a lot. I understand." But how could she? As much as she might try to put herself in Trevor's shoes, she couldn't. She hadn't walked that path so all she could do was offer support like she'd promised. Yet, as Trevor turned away to speak with their third-grade teacher, Laura's breath caught for an entirely different reason.

Either he'd changed, or she was seeing him through fresh eyes because something about him was sure different. If it had been anyone else, she'd have said he was an attractive man, but that was ridiculous. He was Trevor, Tuna, the guy who'd seen her in all the different seasons of her life through bad hair, bad dates and from riding a tricycle to mastering a two-wheeler and then driving a car. In high school, she'd decided she couldn't be attracted to him romantically. After all these years, that wasn't about to change.

"You said there's one more rental property to see before we lose the daylight?" The day after he'd arrived back in Strawberry Pond, and following all the well-meant but nevertheless uncomfortable expressions of sympathy at the town's "Save the Animal Rescue" meeting, Trevor sat in the passenger seat of Laura's sporty SUV and flipped through the folder of rental properties she'd given him earlier. "I can't find the listing." After last night, it was good to have something practical to concentrate on, and there was nothing more practical or immediate than finding a place to live.

"That's because this one's a surprise." Laura gave him a sideways glance as they stopped at the exit to a mountain subdivision outside town.

"O-o-okay." Trevor drew out the word as they waited for a group of young guys, carrying snowboards and wearing fluorescent green, yellow and orange ski jackets and snow pants, to cross the road. While January was the worst time of year for him to move from Southern California to northern New Hampshire, it was sure great for winter sports. Under other circumstances, Trevor would be careening down one of the nearby mountain runs on skis or his own board, bringing Danny with him. Instead, he was grounded, literally and figuratively. However, even though he hardly knew his nephew, he'd do his best to make a new family and home with Danny.

"Don't panic. I think it'll be a good surprise. This last house is right in Strawberry Pond and within walking distance of Danny's new school and the veterinary clinic." When the intersection cleared, Laura drove the SUV through it and turned right.

"Wicked." From the back seat, Danny leaned forward between them.

Trevor raised his eyebrows at the boy. "If you say so."

"Wicked means what us 'oldies' would call great, cool or wonderful." Laura's voice was threaded with amusement as she looked over her shoulder at the boy. "Right, Danny?"

"Yeah." Danny gave her a tentative smile before fiddling with his phone to change the music playlist, a thick piece of blond hair falling over his face.

"I have nephews and nieces, several of them your age. It's hard not to pick up stuff when I'm around them. I like trying to keep up-to-date with the kids." Laura chuckled as she drove the SUV along a narrow, snow-covered country road.

Trevor stared out the window again and swallowed a sigh. As a veterinarian, he understood animals, but kids, not so much. Since he'd arrived at his mom's house yesterday, his own childhood home and where Danny was staying temporarily, the boy had only said a few words to him. Not surprisingly, he was traumatized by Renée's illness and death, but Trevor was the adult and somehow he had to find a way to reach him.

"If you need anything for school on Monday, clothes or binders or other supplies, Danny, I can help." Laura kept her eyes on the road but again she'd thought of what Trevor hadn't.

"That'd be great." When Trevor looked back at his nephew again, Danny's head had emerged from the confines of his parka hood like a turtle from its shell. "Mom did that kind of stuff with me and now..." His voice trailed away.

The unfairness of Trevor's sister being taken when the son who was her world still needed her hit Trevor again with the force of a slap. At forty, he'd also expected to have a family of his own but somehow he'd never met the right woman. Now, after his sister's sudden passing, Trevor had an instant family and no idea what to do or even where to start.

"Don't worry. We'll figure out what you need, no problem." Laura smiled into the rearview mirror. "Won't we, Trevor?"

"Of course." While he was a spur-of-the-moment, go-with-the-flow kind of guy, Laura was the organized planner. Yet ever since they'd met on the first day of kindergarten, and he'd shared his snack with the little blond girl who'd forgotten hers at home, they'd been fast friends. Now, when he was struggling, she had his back, like always.

"After seeing this property, why don't we get pizza so your mom doesn't have to cook?" Laura darted another glance at him, and the softness and compassion in her brown eyes almost broke him.

"Yay." One of Danny's hands bounced against his leg in time to a rap song Trevor didn't recognize.

"Good idea. That's really thoughtful. I'll text Mom to let her know." Trevor's mom seemed to have aged ten years or more in the past month alone, and that was only from when he'd seen her on video calls. Now, in person, she looked even worse. Parents weren't supposed to outlive their children, and since his mom was already older and dealing with ill health, Trevor worried about her.

"I'm taking this route to the last rental property because we'll drive by my farm," Laura said, breaking what was becoming an awkward silence. "You can't see much of it from here, but I'll invite you two over for dinner soon."

"Uncle Trevor said you have horses." Danny turned the music off and leaned forward again.

"I do. Two of my own, a boarding stable and a few for sale." She smiled. "I started out small, but I want to continue growing my real estate business and horse farm. One day, I'd like to farm full-time. See?" She gestured to a farm gate etched in fresh snow. "Sugarbush Knoll Stables is mine."

"Awesome." Danny gazed out the window until the gate disappeared from view.

"Good for you. I always knew you'd have your farm, and I can't wait to see it. Pictures aren't the same." Trevor seconded Danny's praise. While Laura was determined, goal-driven and hard-working, she was also a loyal, caring and steadfast friend. And today, with her honey blond hair pulled up into a high ponytail and wearing faded jeans, a jacket and a green sweatshirt with a mountain silhouette, she looked a lot like the young girl Trevor remembered. "I know this road. It comes out along Strawberry Pond's Main Street, right? Didn't we used to ride our bikes along here?"

"We sure did." Laura slowed the SUV as they rounded a curve, and a red-painted covered bridge came into view. "Different from California, isn't it?" As they rumbled across the bridge, she gave him a teasing smile.

He nodded. Strawberry Pond was *much* different than California and not only in terms of geography. Now, Trevor was caught between those two worlds, as well as between the man he'd become and the memory of the boy he used to be.

"Uncle Trevor has palm trees and a pool in his backyard," Danny said. "I remember from when my mom and I visited."

"You never came to see me in California." Except for real estate conferences in New York City and Atlanta, and a few long weekends in Montréal, as far as Trevor knew, Laura had never travelled much beyond New England.

"My life's busy here." She shrugged. "I'm not like you, flying around everywhere."

Was there a hint of defensiveness in her tone? If so, why? Laura had always seemed happy with her life and choices. From behind the sunglasses he'd donned to filter the bright, January sunshine, Trevor gazed around Strawberry Pond's busy Main Street. Although he'd left town more than twenty years ago for college and only returned for brief visits, "The Pond" as some of the locals called it, never changed much. Although he hadn't truly recognized it before, from Stella's Jewelers to the bowling alley, a toy store, state bank and Kaminski's Sporting Goods, which one of Trevor's cousins still ran, this dot on the map was one of the few constants in his life.

"See, Danny? There's the Strawberry Spot Diner." He gestured to the big, red strawberry perched on the snow-covered roof. "Laura and I used to hang out there when we were in high school." Laura was part of that constancy, too, and from late-night phone calls for support to practical advice, in the past month especially, Trevor didn't know what he'd have done without her.

"Yeah. Mom took me there last summer when we spent the Fourth of July weekend with Grandma."

Danny's voice caught, and Trevor mentally kicked himself. He was trying to stick to what he thought would be "safe topics," ones that had nothing to do with Renée. However, although Danny and Renée had lived several hours away in Manchester, New Hampshire's largest city, Strawberry Pond still held memories of his mom. Maybe Trevor needed to take a different approach to them being here.

As they turned off Main onto a side street lined with historic homes, the SUV slowed. "Here we are. Hale Street." Laura's voice was upbeat as if, like Trevor, she, too, wanted to avoid anything distressing.

"The Brennan house?" Trevor leaned forward as Laura parked in the driveway of a classic New England Colonial, which sat on a large lot halfway along the street on the left. "Sarah Brennan's house?" As kids, he and Laura had walked home from school past this house and Miss Sarah, who'd seemed old then but was likely only in her early fifties, had always waved and sometimes invited them in for a glass of lemonade or cocoa and fresh-baked cookies.

"Sarah Fournier, remember? Last night's town meeting? Wintering in Florida?" She gave him a half smile. "She wouldn't rent to just anyone but she remembered you, and well..." Laura's smile slipped and she inclined her head toward Danny, who was already out of the SUV and halfway along the snow-cleared walkway to the front porch. "She's got a management company taking care of the property, but it would be better if someone lived here all the time, so the rent reflects that."

As Trevor and Laura left the vehicle, she named the monthly payment, which was comparable to the other, less desirable places they'd looked at today or he'd seen online. Going to stand at the bottom of the front steps, Trevor's gaze swung from Laura to the wide porch and then the upper story with its symmetrical windows, bookended on one side with a turret room and cupola. The latter, a late-Victorian flourish added by a previous Brennan, was quirky but somehow worked.

He turned in a slow circle. This house was special, and from what he remembered, it had a warm and welcoming feeling. Although he'd rented out his house in California, and for now, wanted to rent here, Danny especially needed a nurturing home, not any four walls. Although it would be too much for his mom to have Trevor and Danny live with her permanently, the Brennan house was nearby. Danny would be able to see his grandma often, and Trevor could keep an eye on his mom and help her when needed.

"Laura, Uncle Trevor." Danny gestured from behind a snowbank, where he'd left the cleared path to explore. "There's a huge backyard perfect for kicking a ball around. I looked through one of the windows and there's a big room with a TV and enough space for me to set up my gaming stuff. There's also no houses behind so it's all woods. Come see." His voice vibrated with excitement. "Can we live here?"

"Sure, let's take it." Trevor moved to follow Danny. "What?" He looked back at Laura.

"Don't you want to see inside?" She held out a key and gestured to the front door.

"Nah. I remember what the place looks like, and I don't expect it's changed much. Besides…" He stopped and the almost ever-present emotion threatened. "If Danny's okay with it, so am I."

"You're a good uncle." Laura's gaze never left his. "And while I wish you hadn't had to come back to Strawberry Pond for the reason you did, it's good to have you home."

Trevor's heartbeat sped up, but it wasn't from the familiar grief, stress and worry of the last month. No, this reaction was different. “It’s good to *be* home.” For the first time in twenty-four hours he meant it. “Here.” He held out his hands so Laura wouldn’t slip as she clambered up and over the snowbank. Through his gloves and her mittens, their hands connected and he felt a zing in his palm and up his arm.

“Thanks.” Laura dropped his hands and then brushed past him, pulling on her white knit hat as she said something to Danny that Trevor didn’t catch.

He stood still in the snow for several seconds. If it had been any other woman, he’d have said that brief “zing” was attraction but it couldn’t be. Not with Laura. He was tired, jet-lagged from the cross-country flight and whirl of the last days and weeks, and his mind and senses were playing tricks on him. He was grateful to Laura for her help, nothing more. She was his friend, and he’d never do anything to jeopardize that friendship.

CHAPTER TWO

"HEY, DANNY." TWO DAYS later, Laura stood from behind a table at the front of the Strawberry Spot Diner and waved him over. She'd promised Trevor she'd meet Danny here since it was on the boy's way home from school, and Trevor was running late at the attorney's. "How was your first day?" She gestured to the seat across from her.

"All right, I guess." Danny shrugged and pulled off his hat, scarf and parka. After hanging his coat over his chairback, he dropped his backpack on the floor at his feet.

"Some of the teachers who taught your uncle and me still work there." Laura gathered up her scattered papers and slid them into a folder. Unlike Trevor, unless she was showing a property to a client, she could work from almost anywhere. "Your uncle knew you wouldn't have your phone on at school. That's why he texted me as well. Do you want a milkshake and something to eat while we wait for him? The Strawberry Spot has great milkshakes."

"Yeah, I had a milkshake here with my mom." Danny took the diner's laminated menu from its metal stand and unfolded it, covering his face. "Last summer." His voice was expressionless.

Laura studied the top of the boy's head. Did Danny *want* to talk about his mom? Death was one of those things nobody liked to talk about. She'd seen it often enough in her job, from selling a family home after a patriarch or matriarch's passing, through to a widow or widower downsizing. But sometimes the person who'd been closest to the deceased wanted to talk, and it was everyone around them who avoided the subject.

When she'd taken Trevor and Danny to see those rental properties and again on yesterday afternoon's back-to-school shopping trip, Trevor hadn't mentioned Renée. Maybe he was afraid of upsetting his nephew, but it wasn't good for anyone, kid or adult, to keep grief or other strong feelings bottled up.

Laura had learned that lesson all too well. As the server stopped by their table to take Danny's order of a cheeseburger, fries and a soda—no milkshake—the old pain of loss knotted in the pit of her stomach. She had to do something to help the boy, but what?"

"So do you have a favorite subject at school?" Laura nodded her appreciation at a second server who'd refilled her coffee mug.

Danny stopped midway from taking his phone from the pocket of his jeans. "Not really. I'd rather be outside." His gaze darted to his phone.

Laura worried her lower lip. On one of their late-night video calls before Trevor had moved to Strawberry Pond, he'd said that Danny needed a fresh start at school. He hadn't volunteered any information as to why and, at the time, Laura hadn't asked. Despite their close friendship, Laura didn't know Danny and she wanted to respect the kid's privacy. Now, however, Danny was part of her life.

She glanced around the bustling diner. It was never not busy, but now, it was filled with the high school crowd. Kids like she and Trevor had once been. Soon, Danny would be one of those teens. Or would he? With his head bent over his phone, he looked more like he wanted to shut out rather than be part of the world.

Another lesson she'd learned well. She took a sip of coffee. "Danny?"

"Yeah?" He raised his head and gave her a tentative smile. "Sorry. My mom never let me have my phone out when we were eating. It's…" He put the phone away. "I dunno."

When Laura was his age, she hadn't had a phone of her own—no kid did—but all of a sudden she knew what she needed to do. "It's okay, but I wanted you to know I kind of understand where you're coming from. I don't mean Manchester, although it's a nice city, but with losing your mom."

"You do?" Danny blinked and fiddled with a lank strand of hair.

"My dad passed when I was around your age. He had a heart attack. Unlike your mom, we didn't know he was sick, but it was quick. Like with your mom." Laura studied Danny's closed-off expression. "I never really got over losing him, but somehow I learned to live with it. Time healed, true, but all I'm saying is it's hard, and it's okay to be sad. If you want to talk about your mom—"

"I don't." Danny took his soda from the server with a murmured thanks and then slurped the drink from the straw.

"That's okay, too." For now, because Danny must still be in shock, but he needed to know there were adults in his life he could trust to help and guide him. "But in a few weeks or next month or whenever, you can talk to your school counselor, me or your uncle and grandma. Your counselor or family physician could even refer you to someone else, a grief counselor, for example, who works with teens who've lost a parent."

If Laura had been able to talk to someone like that when she was Danny's age, maybe she wouldn't have felt so lost and alone. However, she'd pretended everything was fine and had thrown herself into helping her mom on the farm and raising her younger siblings.

Was that part of the reason why, even so many years later, she was still afraid to truly open her heart or life to anyone else? No, of course not. Laura picked up her mug and gulped a mouthful of coffee. She wasn't prone to self-analysis and had always looked forward rather than back. Her life was fine and with Trevor in town again, it would be great. And as she got to know Danny, he'd be like another nephew.

"Here." She reached for the green-and-white-striped gift bag on the chair at her side and passed it across the table. "I got you a few things. Welcome-to-Strawberry-Pond presents."

"What are they?" Danny's head jerked up, and his deep-set brown eyes held a flicker of interest.

"Open the bag and see."

Danny pulled out white tissue paper and then his eyes widened. "No way."

"Yes way." Laura grinned.

"New headphones, a portable speaker and a gift card for games. Oh, and a beanie hat." Danny returned her smile. "Thanks, Laura. You're the best."

"My nephew near your age gave me tips to pick things he thought you'd like." She beamed at Danny as he stuck the beanie on his head.

"Hey, Uncle Trevor." Danny waved as Trevor came into the diner, shaking snow off his coat and stamping his boots on the mat. "See what Laura got me?"

"You shouldn't have." Trevor reached their table and slid into the empty chair next to Danny.

"I wanted to." Of course, Trevor would sit beside Danny. It was a way of making them seem connected, like a family. The chair beside Laura was also piled with her coat, laptop bag, purse and other things. So what was with that moment of disappointment Trevor wasn't by *her* side? "I also have something for you."

Laura retrieved another gift bag from beneath her coat and passed it to him. Except when they were kids going to each other's birthday parties and for their high school graduation, she and Trevor had never exchanged presents. They didn't need to because their friendship was marked in all kinds of other ways—movies, dinners and being there for each other, no questions asked. However, he was going through a tough time, and she'd wanted to do something nice for him, as well as Danny.

"Thanks, Lulu."

"You're welcome, but you haven't opened it yet. Go ahead." She smoothed her hair and then focused on their server arriving with Danny's food, so she wasn't looking at Trevor. She'd never been the least bit uncomfortable with him before. Where had this new awkwardness come from?

"Okay." He dug in the bag and found a pair of dog-patterned socks, an animal-themed mug made by a local potter, a veterinarian pin badge personalized with his name and a gift card for the local outdoors store. "It's too much. I don't know what to say."

"You don't need to *say* anything." She made herself give him what she hoped was an ordinary, friendly smile. "We're friends."

"We are. And thanks for everything. Sarah Fournier's house is going to be great for us." Trevor also focused on Danny's meal as if he couldn't look at Laura, either.

"Let me know if you need any help moving in." Friendly. It was all very friendly, but with an undercurrent that had her unexpectedly on edge. She drained her coffee and dug in her purse for her key fob. "I should get going." I have a 'Save the Animal Rescue' meeting at the car dealership. We're finalizing details for them to raffle off a car."

"What's Save the Animal Rescue?" Danny stopped with his burger halfway to his mouth and looked from Laura to Trevor.

"It's a town fundraising project, and I'm on the committee." As Laura briefly explained what it involved, Danny's eyes widened with what looked like interest and excitement.

"Can Uncle Trevor and me join in? I love animals."

"It's open to everyone but..." Laura darted a sideways glance at Trevor.

"We'll talk about it at Grandma's, Danny." Trevor's expression was bleak all of a sudden. "I have lots to do, and you've only started school and—"

"But you said I hafta make friends here, and everybody at school has known each other since they were like five. The only kid who talked to me the whole day was some guy who told me to hurry up and throw the ball to him in gym." Danny dropped his burger on his plate, and the top half of the bun fell off.

"I said we'll talk about it later." Now, Trevor's face was strained, and he tapped one index finger on the table like he did when nervous or upset.

"Sure, no problem." Laura grabbed her coat, purse and laptop bag. "See you later, guys." It also wasn't *her* problem because Trevor and Danny weren't her family.

As she joined the line behind the cash register to pay for her coffee and Danny's meal, she snuck a glance at his slumped shoulders and downturned mouth. It might not be so easy to keep her distance. Laura couldn't turn her back on anyone who needed help, especially a kid who'd lost a parent, as she had. Her heart hurt for Danny, and the grief, devastation and uncertainty in every part of his life he was surely facing.

Despite her new and uncomfortable feelings for Trevor, she couldn't turn her back on him, either. His friendship was too important to her, and she'd never do anything to risk it or make him doubt her. Friends were there for each other, no matter what. Right now, Trevor needed her support more than ever, and she wouldn't let him down.

So, Save the Animal Rescue or not, she'd have to figure out a way to deal with those pesky emotions…and maybe even bring Trevor and Danny together as a real family. If anyone knew about family, she did. But after having to take on too many adult family responsibilities too young, she also knew they came at a cost. One that for her had been too great. She'd be there for Trevor and Danny in whatever ways they needed, but she also had to protect herself and her hard-won independence. No crossing or blurring the line between friendship, romance and building a family. That's what she had to focus on.

"YOU'VE ONLY JUST arrived and now you're moving out." Several hours later, in the kitchen of the house she'd lived in for almost fifty years,

Cheryl Kaminski took the remaining plates out of the dishwasher and passed them to Trevor to put with the others in the cupboard to the right of the sink. "I know you need your own place, but I'll miss you, Danny especially." Having her grandson and now her son here had made the house seem less empty.

"We'll only be a few blocks away. You'll see us all the time." Trevor gave her a one-armed hug as he stowed a plate atop the rest of the set.

Once, with her husband and two kids at home and friends and neighbors often dropping in, Cheryl had used all those plates daily. Now, the stack of them sat there and, apart from one or two, collected dust. "For the next few months you'll be close by, but what happens when Sarah and Jack return from Florida?" At the best of times, Cheryl didn't like change. With Renée's recent death, she was even more afraid of losing her remaining family.

"Don't worry, Mom. No matter what happens, I won't leave you on your own again." Trevor took a tea towel to dry the dishes in the drainer—the wooden salad bowl and tongs she'd received as a wedding present and didn't put in the dishwasher.

Except, what if her son wanted to go back to California or somewhere else? Cheryl's whole life was in Strawberry Pond and always had been. She didn't want to move anywhere, let alone to the other side of the country. "You're a good son." She patted Trevor's arm. "A good uncle as well." But, over dinner, there'd been tension between Trevor and Danny. As soon as the meal was over, Danny had muttered something about homework and escaped to Renée's old room. "It'll take time for you and Danny to be comfortable with each other. Living together is different than a vacation visit."

"True." Trevor dried the salad tongs and avoided Cheryl's gaze.

"Did something happen with Danny at school?" Although Trevor wouldn't likely have recognized it yet, he and his nephew were similar, including not wanting to talk about problems or feelings.

"I don't know. He hardly said anything about school, apart from the other kids not talking to him." Trevor sat in a kitchen chair, rested his elbows on the table and dropped his head into his hands. "He heard about that 'Save the Animal Rescue' thing from Laura and wants to take part, but I think it's too much. I already told Laura so after the town meeting."

"That's what you and Danny were talking about in the living room while I was fixing the salad?" Cheryl had known something was going on but decided it wasn't her business.

Trevor nodded. "I told Danny I'd think about

it, but between school for him, my new job, a new place to live, Renée's estate and memorial service…it's a lot." He shrugged in an almost defeated way, which was unlike him.

"True." To his credit, Trevor hadn't mentioned becoming an instant father figure to Danny, and the stress, worry and "newness" that must certainly have brought.

If only Danny could've lived full-time here with her. However, what Trevor also didn't say, but which lurked between them, was that Cheryl was getting older. A few health issues, thankfully still minor, but ones that nevertheless needed monitoring, meant she didn't have as much energy as she once did. She'd relied on Renée being in the same state and her regular weekend trips to Strawberry Pond. With her daughter gone, she'd need support from someone, and who else but Trevor?

"So you think I'm right not to let Danny take part?"

"No, I didn't say that." Cheryl sat across from Trevor and studied her son's bent head. It had more silver-gray hairs than when she'd visited him in California last September. "Maybe being involved in the 'Save the Animal Rescue' project would be good for Danny and you as well. It'd help you both feel part of things in town." And Trevor would be less likely to leave. Although that wasn't Cheryl's primary motive, she also had to think about herself. Downsizing and leaving this house would be hard enough, but moving away from Strawberry Pond would be heartbreaking. "Danny likes animals so that could make a connection, a bridge, between you."

"I guess so." Trevor raised his head, and at the sight of her son's bloodshot eyes and new lines running between his nose and mouth, Cheryl reached across the table and took his hand.

"You could at least give it a try. When I was at my knitting group at the library this afternoon, Anne Sullivan said they're planning a pet-grooming session and photo-shoot event. There's also talk of a pet-themed bake sale and art show. I said I'd dig out one of my old recipes and make several batches of dog biscuits. The kind Benji liked." Although their poodle had died when Trevor was in college, she still missed that dog. "I'm sure Anne and Laura would understand if you had to back out, but if you don't try you won't know if it might help."

"No." Trevor's smile was pained.

Cheryl returned his smile. "I can also pitch in with Renée's service and lots of other things. Martha Ryan was at knitting group today, and after her son's death in that car accident, even though it was years ago, she understands the pain of losing an adult child. We had a good talk." Cheryl brushed a hand across her face as the tears that were always close to the surface threatened. "I'm not on my own and you aren't, either. If we need it, the town's here for us *and* Danny. But we have to take that first step and reach out. The Save the Animal Rescue might be just the thing."

As Cheryl knew from her husband's death, while that first step was the hardest, it was also the most important. Now, she had to set an example for Trevor and Danny. For herself and Renée as well. Before she'd moved away for work and then met and married a fellow from Manchester, her daughter had been part of lots of things in Strawberry Pond. She'd want the same for her son.

"I'll go talk to Danny." There was resignation in Trevor's eyes, but for the first time since he'd arrived back, they also held a bit of their once-familiar twinkle.

"Good. I'll call Anne and get more information about what the 'Save the Animal Rescue' committee's planning." Cheryl hesitated. "Unless you want to call Laura instead?" There'd been something different in Trevor's voice when he'd shown her the welcome-home gifts Laura had given him. Something that had made Cheryl wonder if he had new feelings for his "best friend."

"Sure, I planned to call Laura later, anyway. To ask her to help with unpacking in our new place and if she wants to go sledding with us on Saturday. Sledding was Danny's idea. He really likes Laura, and she's great with him."

When he said Laura's name, Cheryl heard that tone in his voice again and, before he got up from his chair and left the room, his cheeks had a faint pink tinge. She prided herself on minding her own business both with her kids and when it came to town gossip. But if Trevor indeed had new feelings for Laura, did Laura feel the same way?

Cheryl pushed her chair away from the table and looked out the kitchen window into the January night. She turned off the overhead light and, when the room was plunged into shadows, her eyes adjusted to seek the pinpricks of starlight above the nearby mountain ridge.

Even in darkness, she had to look for the light. Trevor and Laura were both single, and a mother could always hope.

CHAPTER THREE

"IS THAT YOUR last box, Danny?" On Thursday evening, Trevor gestured to a carton on the floor in the middle of the front hall at the Brennan house. Although he'd rented the place fully furnished, and left most of his own stuff in storage in California, he'd brought a few essentials with him and shipped several larger items. That load, including bedding, extra clothes, his coffee machine, sports equipment, family photos and other special keepsakes, had arrived a few hours ago. Now that he'd unpacked, he'd feel more settled and at home, and that persistent sense of unease would diminish.

"Yeah." Engrossed in his phone, Danny sprawled in a living room chair, one foot on the rug and the other dangling over the chair's arm. Except for some personal belongings, most of the things from Danny and Renée's Manchester apartment were also in storage, waiting until Trevor found a more permanent home.

"Then maybe you could…help?" Trevor stood

at the foot of the wide, curving staircase that led to the home's upper level. He hated the hesitancy in his voice but even after almost a week, he still felt like he was walking on eggshells around his nephew.

"I have homework." Danny didn't look up from his phone.

"So why aren't you doing it?" Trevor held back an impatient exclamation. "Laura already set up your desk and computer in the family room."

Danny shrugged. "I'll get to it."

"Hey, guys." Laura came down the stairs carrying a gray, industrial-looking toolbox. "I fixed the leaky pipe under the sink in the main bathroom for now, but you should get a plumber in to take a look. The number for the management company's on the fridge. If you call them in the morning, they'll make arrangements for someone to come out." In denim overalls, a long-sleeved white T-shirt and with her hair in a bouncy ponytail, she paused on the step above where Trevor stood. "What's wrong?"

"Nothing." Even to his best friend, Trevor couldn't admit how lost and uncertain he felt. While he'd thought starting his new job today would anchor him, three back-to-back emergencies had left him nearly as overwhelmed as he'd been as a teenager after his first day cleaning kennels at that same clinic.

"It'll be okay. Give everything time." Laura's voice was low, for Trevor's ears alone, and then she gave his shoulder a comforting squeeze. "Danny?" She set the toolbox on the floor by the door and continued into the living room. "If that box of yours holds anything important, you'd better move it. Otherwise, I'll take it out to the garage. Got it?"

"Yeah." Danny gave her an embarrassed smile and swung himself out of the chair. "Sorry."

Laura nodded. "I could use a cup of cocoa. Anyone else?" She glanced between Trevor and Danny.

"With marshmallows?" Danny gave her a hopeful look.

"Of course." She raised her hand for a high five, which Danny returned. "How's that homework coming along?"

"I don't get it." As Danny moved the box, his hair flopped across his face.

"What don't you get?" It was the first Trevor had heard Danny might be struggling at school. He'd always seemed like a smart kid, and Renée had never mentioned any academic issues. Trevor put a hand to his shoulder where Laura had squeezed it. He could almost feel the imprint of her fingers and warmth and comfort in her touch.

As a friend, he reminded himself. That unexpected reaction he'd had to her, the one that felt like attraction, hadn't dissipated. If anything, it grew stronger each time Trevor saw her. However, he had to dismiss it. His life was in turmoil so how could he be sure of anything, let alone those new and complicated feelings for a woman who'd been his closest friend?

"Math's different. Everything's different here." Danny straightened and, for a brief moment, his bottom lip trembled. "I miss Manchester."

"I know you do, buddy, but…" Danny had to be Trevor's focus. An orphaned teen who missed his mom and his life with her more than any actual place. As the three of them moved through the hall and into the kitchen at the rear of the house, Laura turned on lights and then pulled down the blinds to shut out the night. She was more familiar with this house than Trevor, and she also seemed surprisingly at home here with him and Danny. *Almost like she belonged.* Trevor made himself park yet another unexpected thought and once again return his attention to Danny. "Do you want me to talk to your teacher?"

"No way." Ambling to the breakfast nook, Danny tucked his chin into his chest but not before Trevor glimpsed the boy's horrified expression.

"I'm pretty good at math. If you want, I could take a look at that homework with you." Laura brought mugs out of a cupboard and a container of cocoa and marshmallows from a tote bag she'd left on the counter earlier.

"Okay, I guess." Danny took his backpack from where he'd left it under the table and pulled out a worn binder. Not one of the new school supplies Trevor had bought him.

"Why don't you handle cocoa making while Danny and I make a start on math?" From the other side of the large kitchen island, Laura's gaze caught Trevor's and held. *I've got your back*, her expression seemed to say.

"Sure." Trevor was "pretty good" at math, too. He'd had to be to get through vet school, but that didn't mean he'd be any good at teaching Danny. He turned away from the murmur of voices from the breakfast nook, then heated milk and tore open the package of marshmallows as if on autopilot.

Apart from his family, Laura knew him better than anyone. She'd found him the perfect temporary place to live. And somehow, she instinctively knew how and when to jump in to support Danny. Whenever Trevor stumbled in life, she'd been there for him and they could always talk about anything.

Except once. As he filled Miss Sarah's feminine, floral-patterned mugs with cocoa, Trevor let himself recall the time he'd kissed Laura almost as a joke at that party after their senior prom. Had he been attracted to her back then? He'd convinced himself he wasn't and they'd both moved on. Trevor to university on almost a full scholarship, and Laura to a local community college, which she'd commuted to from Strawberry Pond. However, neither of them had ever spoken about that kiss.

He put three mugs, spoons, paper napkins and a bowl of marshmallows on a tray and carried it to the breakfast nook, where Laura and Danny sat working on Danny's math problems. "Here you go." He slid into the curved bench seat on the other side of Danny from Laura.

"Great job, Danny. You did it." Laura beamed at the boy before taking one of the mugs and spooning marshmallows into it.

"I did." He smiled back at Laura, seemingly oblivious to Trevor. "You're great at explaining."

"Thanks." She ducked her head as if embarrassed by the praise. "When I was your age, I thought about maybe being a teacher."

Trevor took a sip from his own cocoa, without marshmallows. He didn't remember Laura ever wanting to go to teacher's college. As far as he knew, she'd always wanted to stay in Strawberry Pond and have a horse farm. Which she'd done. Had he ever truly known Laura or had she changed?

"So, about the pet-grooming and photo-shoot event." As if conscious of his scrutiny, Laura tucked a loose strand of hair from her ponytail behind one ear, stirred her cocoa and returned to a topic they'd spoken about earlier. "It's next weekend at the community center, and it's great you two are coming. What kind of volunteer role do you want, Danny? There's everything from chatting with people waiting with their pets for grooming or photo sessions, to serving refreshments or even working alongside the groomer or photographer. Take your pick. As for you, Trevor, what do you say about staffing a table answering animal-related questions?"

The subject was ordinary enough so why wouldn't Laura look at him? And why did Trevor all of a sudden feel so uncomfortable? "Sure, sounds good to me."

"I'd like to work with the groomer." For an instant, Danny's eyes sparkled.

Being part of the "Save the Animal Rescue" activities would be good for Danny. The teen's animated face as he talked with Laura about pet grooming told Trevor that, with his mom's encouragement, he'd admitted he'd been wrong and made the right choice this time around. As a veterinarian, his own input was certainly needed.

Perhaps talking to folks about something—anything—apart from his sister's death, would help him both fit in here again and make life feel more normal…whatever that meant.

"Pitching in and working together is the Strawberry Pond way, right, Trevor?"

"What? Oh, yes, of course. What's with you two?" He glanced between them, aware of their suppressed laughter.

"It's…you." Danny laughed and clutched his stomach. "You've got cocoa on your lip. Like a mustache."

"You look like you did when your facial hair was starting to come in, remember?" Laura pointed and laughed along with Danny. "No, don't rub it off. Here let me." She picked up one of the pink napkins and scooted out of her seat to come around to Trevor's side. "Now, you have a pink mustache like a flower."

Danny laughed harder, and Trevor played along, even making the napkin into other cartoonlike shapes.

It was for Danny. A moment of lightness at a tough time. Except, it all of a sudden seemed like more. As if he'd turned a corner with Danny and was also seeing Laura through new eyes and appreciating what she meant to him. Not the friend he remembered, although that would always be precious, but the woman she was now.

And that the "Strawberry Pond way" wasn't only about working together to support a community cause. Rather, it was also about roots, family, friendship and a woman he might have taken for granted, but who was more important to him than he'd ever considered.

Despite the unpacking they'd done, which Trevor had thought would make him feel more settled, instead he was even more off balance.

"WANT TO GO down a few more times, Danny?" On Sunday afternoon, Laura shaded her eyes with a mittened hand and gestured to the snow tubes they'd pulled up the hill at the public sledding and tubing area the town council had built a mile west of Strawberry Pond. "You aren't getting too cold, are you?" She took a closer look at his face, checking for signs of blue lips, white patches or anything else that could indicate frostbite.

"Nope. I could go five more times at least." Danny grinned and adjusted the helmet he wore over his winter hat, then got into the tube again and held the handles before bouncing and spinning down the gentle incline.

"He's sure having fun." At Laura's side, Trevor tucked his gloved hands into a parka Laura remembered his late dad wearing. "I'd thought we'd go sledding on that hill behind the high school, but this one's much better. You're great at knowing what Danny will like."

"Having so many nieces and nephews helps, but I'm also used to telling out-of-town clients who are looking for homes about fun things to do in this area." Laura waved at several people she knew, including her friend Alana Hansen, the local librarian, who also worked at her family's apple orchard, market garden and Christmas-tree farm. Although the temperature was well below freezing, it was sunny with a bright blue sky, so the townspeople were out in force enjoying what Laura considered to be a perfect day.

"I'd forgotten how beautiful New Hampshire is in winter." Trevor gestured at the expanse of sky and rugged, snow-covered mountains in front of them.

"It is and we're lucky places like this one are right on our doorstep." Laura drank in the view. Her real estate business was slower at this time of year so she had more free time. When Trevor and Danny had invited her to go sledding it had sounded fun. But now that she was here, she was reminded of how rarely she took time off for herself. Most days, she was either working at her real estate business or on the horse farm, doing something for or with family, or involved in one of her many community volunteer activities. Between all that, when was the last time she'd actually stopped for fun and leisure, like today? She couldn't remember, which was more than a little unsettling.

"I need to get more winter gear." Trevor gestured to his coat with a wry smile. "The one heavier coat I have is okay for when I'm only outside a few minutes, but not for much longer. Luckily, my mom still had this old parka of my dad's in the hall closet." His smile disappeared. "I always thought Dad was such a big man, but I guess not. It's snug on me."

"Your dad *was* a big man in the most important ways. Like his character, integrity and how he lived his life." Mr. Kaminski had reminded Laura of her own dad, and when Trevor's dad had passed almost ten years ago, it was like losing a parent all over again."

"He was a good man, for sure." Trevor gestured to Danny, who'd joined another boy who looked to be around his age. "I've got big shoes to fill being a father figure to Danny."

"You'll be great. It's not like Danny ever had a dad of his own to look up to, not really." Renée had only been married a few years, and was expecting Danny, when her husband had been killed in an accident at work. She'd been a single parent from the start.

"No, although Renée talked about Danny's dad a lot. She wanted Jeff to be part of Danny's life. Both their lives. Jeff was a great guy so that makes me stepping in with his son feel like an even bigger responsibility." Trevor was wearing sunglasses, so Laura couldn't see his eyes, but his voice was worried.

That responsibility was one of the reasons why Laura had never wanted to have children of her own. Having helped raise her younger siblings, she'd had enough responsibility for kids to last a lifetime. Although she loved spending time with her nieces and nephews, she also cherished her independent adult life and couldn't see that changing. "Don't forget you have your mom, me and, if you want it, most of the town. All you have to do is ask."

"My mom said something similar." His expression lightened.

"How's your new job going?" Trevor had enough family worries. Hopefully asking about his job would be a distraction.

"Okay, I think. It's busy with Dr. Berner transitioning to retirement and working part-time to be free to travel with his wife and visit their kids and grandkids, but that's good for him and me. It feels strange, though, to be back where I worked in high school and first got the idea of studying to be a vet." His chuckle was soft and warm, as always, so why did it sound different, more intimate? "As the clinic's owner,

Dr. Berner's still my boss but it's not the same. We're more like colleagues. There's a part of me that can't quite believe I'm not there in the back cleaning kennels."

"Believe it. You've been really successful. Own it. From everything I've heard, Dr. Berner's thrilled to have you on board. When I talked to him about volunteering for Save the Animal Rescue, he said he could only help out in an occasional advisory capacity if we need it. It's time for him to 'pass the baton,' as he put it, 'to us young ones.'" Laura tried to laugh but the sound stuck in her throat. She had to get a grip. What was she doing savoring Trevor's endearing chuckle? And why was she looking at him standing beside her, a few inches taller and, despite that old parka, seeing him as an attractive man?

"We've both been successful. Mom said you've been the top real estate agent in this area three years in a row. You've won awards, the last one before Christmas. Why didn't you tell me?"

"It never came up. Besides, before Christmas…" She stopped. Before Christmas was when Renée had died. There'd also been Josie and Heath's wedding, so Laura's professional-achievement award had gotten lost in everything else going on.

She tugged on her scarf so it covered her mouth and nose. Maybe because she hadn't gone to college like Trevor, she'd always felt more reticent in sharing her achievements with him. Or maybe it was because although her family loved her, they all had their own lives so anything Laura did wasn't as important. She'd celebrated her achievements with her friends Josie and Alana, and their pride in her had seemed to be enough. But was it?

"Well, that award came up now, so let me take you out for dinner." Trevor's voice was decisive. "What about after the pet-grooming and photo-shoot event next Saturday? Danny already planned to spend the evening with my mom so we wouldn't be leaving him on his own. Sure, he's old enough to stay by himself, but I don't want him to feel lonely or left out. Not that he couldn't come with us but… I'd like to take you to a nice restaurant. He still thinks a burger and fries are fine dining."

Was that redness on Trevor's cheeks only from the cold or was he embarrassed about asking her out? "Sure, that'd be fun, but you may have forgotten Strawberry Pond has pretty limited restaurant options." It wasn't a date. The two of them would be going out for dinner as friends, like they often did when Trevor was in town. Except, he hadn't been back here in a few years and now everything about him, her and "them" seemed different. And, inexplicably, she'd found herself remembering that kiss he'd planted on her after senior prom. One she'd never let herself think about and the two of them had never spoken of, either.

It'd been a joke, nothing more. He'd been teasing. That's what she'd convinced herself of, so why was she recalling it now? Any brief flash of romantic attraction had been over in an instant, and their friendship had been the same as before. So why did it now feel like that friendship was changing and the ground under her feet shifting?

"Then we'll go to dinner in Conway, or I'll make a reservation at a restaurant at one of what we used to think were those 'fancy' mountain hotels. My car's arriving tomorrow so I'll have my own wheels, not a rental." Trevor stared at Danny trudging back up the hill again.

"Okay." Laura often took clients out to dinner, and the most recent real estate awards banquet had been held in one of those hotels Trevor had mentioned. She hugged herself. Going there with him shouldn't be any different, yet somehow it was. "Your mom must be relieved you didn't drive here from California in the winter."

"That's why I had my car shipped." Trevor dug a small snow trench with one boot. "I get it. She was worried about an accident. I know why she's so sensitive to the idea of losing any more people close to her. But still, you have to make each day count. Not that I'm good at taking that advice."

Laura wasn't, either. Time to change the subject again. "Do you think your mom would like a dog for company? She must be lonely living alone, and there's a quiet and gentle senior toy poodle at the rescue. Smaller than the poodle your family had when we were growing up, but Mabel's a sweetheart."

"You know, you may be right." Finally, Trevor looked at her. "Mom's mentioned Benji a few times lately. She sure loved that dog. We all did. But a smaller poodle would be easier to manage as would a senior pet. Not as much work as a puppy. I'll ask her."

His smile was the easy, friendly one Laura remembered. "You must be freezing standing here all this time. Want to go down again?" She indicated the sleds Trevor had rented for them along with the snow tubes.

"Are you suggesting I've gotten California soft?" Trevor gave her a mock outraged expression. "Places like Tahoe get lots of snow."

"Except you didn't live anywhere near Tahoe, did you?" Laura teased him back. "Come on." She sat on the first sled and put on her helmet. "Let's see what you're made of, surfer dude."

"You're on, Sullivan. I was surfing the New Hampshire coast long before I ever surfed in

California." He sat on the other sled and eyed her from under his own helmet. "Ready?"

"You bet." Laura pushed off, and the sled picked up speed.

As she steered down the slope, aiming to beat Trevor, like she'd done as a kid, she almost felt like that child again with the cold wind whipping against her cheeks and pulling her hair free.

But she was a woman, and Trevor was a man. And everything was a whole lot more complicated than when they'd been kids together.

CHAPTER FOUR

"MOM, MEET MABEL." Trevor kneeled and patted the toy poodle's soft white head. Several days after going sledding and snow tubing, he'd arranged to meet his mom at Strawberry Pond's animal rescue and asked Laura to join them. It made sense. Laura was the one who'd thought his mom might like a dog for company and had suggested Mabel in the first place. Yet, Laura was running late, and if she didn't get here soon, his lunch break would be over and he'd have to return to the vet clinic. He'd counted on seeing her today and had looked forward to it the whole morning. As a friend, of course, he once again reminded himself. He couldn't have other feelings for Laura. It would complicate their long friendship, maybe even break it. He didn't want to consider what his life would be like without having her as a friend.

"Hi, girl." His mom reached out one hand to the dog, who sniffed it. "She's sure cute. And so tiny compared to Benji."

"Hey, sorry I'm late." Laura rushed into the rescue and greeted Trevor and his mom. "I had a meeting and it went longer than expected."

In a tailored black coat over black trousers, and with pearl stud earrings in her delicate lobes and straight blond hair in a simple knot, Laura looked more dressed up and elegant than Trevor had ever seen her. His breath caught and, in the sudden silence, he had to stop himself from staring. "Glad you made it. Watch your pants and coat. This little girl's stressed so she's shedding more than usual." Focus on the dog, not how gorgeous Laura looked.

"It's fine. What's a bit of dog hair? Anyway, I have a clothes brush in my bag." Laura kneeled to pat Mabel.

Of course, she had a brush. Laura was always prepared for every eventuality, even ones that would've never crossed Trevor's mind.

"If you want to hold her, go right ahead." The animal rescue volunteer, a brown-haired woman in her mid-twenties who'd introduced herself earlier as Kelsey, gestured to Trevor's mom. "Mabel loves snuggles."

"Sure, I guess." His mom looked uncharacteristically hesitant.

"Here you are." Trevor picked up Mabel and gave the dog to his mom, who now held her arms out.

"Hey, sweetheart." His mom cooed over the dog, and Mabel wagged her curly tail.

"Mabel's owner's living situation changed so she wasn't able to care for her any longer. That's why Mabel's here at the rescue." Laura glanced at Kelsey, who'd gone back to the reception desk. "They want to make sure Mabel finds the perfect home, so she'd need to be fostered first."

"That's sensible." His mom didn't look up from the dog, seemingly enchanted by her.

"We're nearly ready for the pet-grooming and photo-shoot event." Laura moved to speak to Trevor to let his mom continue getting to know Mabel. "It's been so last-minute but everyone's pulled together."

"There's a poster in the vet clinic. I saw one in the grocery store as well. They look good." At first, Trevor had been surprised that plans for the event had sprung up so fast, but then he'd remembered it was Strawberry Pond. When the whole town wanted something to happen, any bureaucratic red tape and other obstacles seemed to disappear like magic. "This animal rescue looks like a really professional and well-run organization."

New since he'd left town all those years ago, the rescue had been a surprise because he'd expected something smaller and more ad hoc. He knew it wasn't run out of someone's home, but the bright, clean and airy premises with big windows, separate areas for cats, dogs and other animals, as well as a secure outdoor play space, more than met the usual standard.

"It *is* professional and well-run. Why else would we want to save it? The building's perfect and fit for purpose." A small smile played around the corners of Laura's mouth. "It'd be a shame to have to start over and build a rescue from the ground up again. If we don't raise enough money and this rescue has to close, there's the immediate problem of what to do with all the animals it currently houses. The need also keeps growing. Only this week, they took in a puppy and two senior bonded cats."

"Of course." Laura's smile said Trevor needed to get with the program, and its sweetness mixed with compassion, like a burst of sunshine on an overcast day, inexplicably made his heart beat faster.

"Is there anything I can do for Renée's celebration of life?" Laura lowered her voice and darted a quick glance at Trevor's mom. "When I was in the bank earlier, a few people asked me about it. I mean, we know when and where it is, but do you need food or anything?"

Trevor shook his head, that brief sense of lightness evaporating. "The funeral home's handling all the arrangements. Hiring a caterer, ordering flowers and the rest. Along with the minister, they're making it easy." Which meant that

Trevor, his mom and Danny had the hard part. Saying a final goodbye to his sister, a woman they all loved who'd been taken much too soon.

"I'm here for you, Tuna. Everyone is." Laura's brown eyes were soft with compassion. "Danny, too."

"I know, but see, I don't really know what I—we—even need." In the past six weeks, Trevor's entire life had been upended. He felt like he'd been dropped from a height and was still dangling in the clouds while ordinary life went on below him. "Danny met a boy from his school snow tubing, though, so he might be making a friend. That'd be good. It's not like I can order one for him online." He grimaced. "Sorry, bad joke."

"No, it's honest and I—"

"Trevor, Laura?" His mom's voice interjected. "Mabel and I are getting along fine. I want to apply to foster her with a view to adoption. What do you think?"

"That's great, Mom." He swallowed the unexpected lump in his throat. Life went on, no matter what, and if his mom had Mabel, she'd have someone to care about at home, and that someone would care about her, too.

His gaze drifted to Laura, who was already walking with his mom and Mabel over to the reception desk. Danny was his priority, Trevor reminded himself, along with his mom and his new job. He'd had too much change and taken on so many new responsibilities in such a short time, he couldn't trust his feelings or think about a relationship with any woman, let alone Laura.

Even if he might want to.

ON SATURDAY AFTERNOON, Laura looked around Strawberry Pond's crowded community center, and some of the tightness in her chest eased. Somehow, this first "Save the Animal Rescue" event had been organized in record time and, despite a few last-minute hiccups behind the scenes, so far everything was going smoothly.

She gave a thumbs-up to Josie, who'd set up a basic dog-grooming station in a nearby corner and, with Danny, was giving the mayor's fluffy Bernese mountain dog a final brush before his photo session.

"We sold out of all the baking, for people *and* dogs." At Laura's side, her friend Alana gestured to the empty table and full cashbox. "It was a good idea to sell a few baked goods today before the big pet-themed one with the art show. There was lots of interest and folks have been so generous."

"That's fantastic, but I'd intended to buy a package of Mrs. Kaminski's peanut butter and pumpkin dog cookies for my two. It's been so busy I forgot." Laura had spotted the cellophane-wrapped parcels tied with green ribbon bows earlier. "I remember how Benji, their family dog, used to gobble those cookies up. Star and Cooper would've loved them." The two basset hounds were brother and sister and, after their previous owner died, she'd adopted them from the rescue three years before.

"You're in luck." Alana reached under the table and presented one of the packages with a flourish.

"Thanks. Here." Laura dug in the pocket of her jeans for money.

"No need. Trevor paid for it." Alana's slow, sideways glance was knowing. "He said you'd done so much work for this event it was the least he could do."

"Oh." Trevor had always been thoughtful, but he was already taking her out for dinner. However, maybe she was overthinking what he undoubtedly intended to be a kind, friendly gesture. "Don't run, kids. And watch where you're going." She stepped forward to divert a group of four excited girls, their faces painted to resemble different animals, from crashing into several members of the Strawberry Pond Knitters.

"Sorry." A white cat with a pink nose and black whiskers, who, upon closer inspection, was Laura's six-year-old niece, gave her an impish smile.

"It's fine." Laura patted Everly's head. "Having fun?"

"You bet." Everly was off again before the words were even out of her mouth.

"Group photo?" Fred Sinclair, the newspaper editor, had already nabbed Josie, Alana, Trevor and several others, and was now making a beeline for Laura.

"Where's Danny?" She glanced back at the throng of people.

"Right here." Danny's voice came from behind her.

Except when Josie had asked him to work with her on grooming, Danny had stuck close to Laura for most of the day. He'd run errands, taken care of several cleanup jobs and kept the line for pet photographs moving smoothly. Although he hadn't said much, he'd still been a big part of the event's success.

"You should be in any photo for the newspaper. It's been a team effort, and you're part of the team, Danny." She gestured to him to stand beside her.

"Smile, everyone." After making sure that the mayor and her dog were front and center, Fred raised his camera.

"Some things here never change, do they?" Trevor said into Laura's ear, his warm breath brushing her cheek. "The last time I was in one of Fred's photos must've been our senior prom. Remember?"

"Yes." Laura kept smiling, but her stomach quivered. Above dark jeans, Trevor wore a blue shirt the same color as his eyes. He'd pinned the personalized veterinarian badge Laura had given him on the upper left of his shirt, nestled against his clinic lanyard, which held his official name tag.

At senior prom, as now, she and Trevor had stood close together, but back then it had been in a group with the rest of their graduating class. They'd gone to prom together because Trevor's girlfriend had broken up with him a few weeks before, and Laura's date, a friend from math club, had come down with food poisoning. She and Trevor had spent the evening joking around like they usually did until, later that night, he'd kissed her.

The next day, he'd left for a summer job at a veterinary clinic in Boston, followed by college. As the months and years went by, they'd only seen each other infrequently. She'd sometimes wondered if she'd imagined that kiss, but she hadn't, and now, all those confusing feelings she'd thought she'd suppressed had returned.

"All done." After patting the mayor's dog, Fred turned to Trevor. "It's good to have you back. Thanks again for those tips about cleaning my boy's ears."

"You're welcome. Like I said, beagles are

prone to ear infections but regular cleaning mitigates the risk." Trevor nodded. "If you have any other questions, give me a call or drop in at the clinic. I look forward to meeting Duke when you bring him in for his next checkup."

"You bet." Fred bustled away to take more pictures.

Trevor exuded warmth, friendliness and professionalism, so it was no wonder people trusted him to care for their precious fur babies. Yet, while Laura wouldn't hesitate to bring Star and Cooper to him for their checkups, she was drawn to him in an entirely different way. One she shouldn't be because Trevor was her friend. He and Danny were also a family. She'd worked hard to build an independent life, and while she wanted to be there for the orphaned teen, Laura knew what family life entailed. Could she handle all that responsibility? She didn't know, and she worried about letting Danny down.

"Grandma said she'd take me home with her so you guys can leave to get ready for dinner whenever you want." As the crowd around them dispersed and the event started to break up, Danny glanced between Laura and Trevor. "Like you planned, right?"

"Yes, of course. I need to go home and change. I worked on the event setup so I don't have to pitch in with cleaning up." She'd already explained that when she'd texted Trevor earlier so she hadn't needed to repeat it. She always prided herself on clear, concise communications, so why was she all of a sudden almost babbling? Maybe to compensate for that flutter in her tummy?

"I'll go home and change, too, before coming by your farm to pick you up." Trevor fiddled with the veterinarian badge as if he felt as awkward as Laura. "Have fun, kid." He patted Danny's shoulder and then jerked his hand back as if he might have overstepped. "What Grandma says goes, remember? Same rules as at home. And don't choose a scary movie because Grandma gets nervous. I'll pick you up by ten at the latest."

"I know." Danny's voice held that familiar "grown-ups are weird" note Laura recognized from her own nephews his age.

"I guess I'll go." Laura hugged herself. "I'll see you in an hour or so?"

"Sure." Trevor cleared his throat.

Laura turned away to find her coat and boots where she'd left them in a designated area near the entryway. But before she did, she caught something in Trevor's face and eyes that made her heart flutter even more.

CHAPTER FIVE

"To you. Lulu Sullivan, real estate agent and friend extraordinaire." Trevor raised the plate that held his half of the piece of luscious-looking chocolate cake they'd agreed to share. Sitting across from him at a window table overlooking a mountain peak, in a simple black dress and in the soft candlelight shining on her blond hair that she'd left loose around her shoulders, Laura almost seemed to glow.

"How many toasts is that? You must have made three or more by now." Her rosy lips curved into a smile that was both sweet and much too appealing for a woman who was only supposed to be a friend. "You toasted me with our glasses of wine, the main course and now, dessert. Seriously, enough." She picked up her fork and ate a sliver of cake.

Trevor made himself look away as he'd done throughout not only the meal, but also in the car on their way to this hotel and conference center half an hour from Strawberry Pond. He had no reason to feel uncomfortable with Laura, yet somehow he did. “I don’t know how I’d be managing everything without you. Before I came back to town, and now I’m here, I appreciate it. With Renée’s memorial service in a few days, knowing you’ll be there…it means a lot.”

Since his sister’s passing, he’d relied on Laura more than usual. That’s what good friends did. They stepped up when needed, and he hadn’t expected Laura would be any different. Still, why hadn’t he ever noticed how well she got along with his mom? She had an instinctive ease and rapport with Danny as well.

She was also a beautiful woman. From the distinguished silver-haired man who’d checked their coats, to a nearby table of younger men who, judging from snippets of conversation he’d overheard, must be on a skiing weekend, Trevor hadn’t missed the admiring looks she’d attracted. However, even though she’d dated over the years, and even been almost engaged once, Laura had never wanted to get married or have children. Did she still feel that way? It shouldn’t matter to him whether she did or didn’t, but somehow it felt significant and he didn’t want to examine why.

“Of course I’ll be at Renée’s service. You’ve always been there for me.” Laura reached out as if to pat Trevor's arm but then drew her hand away and continued eating cake.

"We're friends, right? Like always?" Except, for the first time, those words seemed hollow. Maybe he wasn't the only one feeling this discomfort between them. He took a forkful of cake and then dropped part of it on his plate. "Oops."

"Friends. Yes, of course. Nothing's changed." Laura kept her eyes on her own plate, and her light laugh sounded strained. "Great choice of dessert, right? Such rich chocolate." Her tongue darted out to lick chocolate frosting from her bottom lip.

Trevor swallowed as he maneuvered the dropped cake back onto his fork. He had to talk to her about this awkwardness, and maybe even these new and unexpected feelings he had for her—feelings he still couldn't let himself trust—but one thing at a time. He needed to get through Renée's service first. For himself and to give his mom and Danny the support they'd surely need.

"Say, you look familiar." One of the group of skiers came over to their table, a guy around Trevor's age, but burlier and with sandy brown hair. "Are you that real estate agent whose picture's on a billboard outside Strawberry Pond?"

"That's me. Laura Sullivan." She held out a hand for the man to shake, and Trevor tensed, pushing away a both unreasonable and unexpected flash of something that felt a lot like jealousy. “Are you looking to buy a home in this area?”

“Thinking of it. My divorce came through a few months ago, and it would be good to have a weekend and vacation place for me and my kids. Skiing in the winter and lake life in the summer sounds ideal. I’m from Boston. Brent McCarthy.”

“Pleased to meet you.” Laura’s voice was cool and professional as she took a business card from her purse. “Give me a call if you’re interested in seeing properties. We can talk about what you’re looking for, and I’d be happy to line up some suitable places.”

There was no need for Trevor to feel jealous or excluded. This guy had approached Laura because of her job.

“Will do.” Brent glanced at Laura’s left hand as if checking for a wedding ring and then at Trevor. “I apologize for interrupting your evening.”

“No problem.” Trevor meant it. Although he hadn’t yet seen that billboard Brent had mentioned, as a Realtor, Laura must be kind of a public figure around here. The other man had been polite and respectful, and Trevor didn’t have a romantic claim on Laura. If she wanted to get to know Brent and date him, she was free to. So what was with that sour taste in Trevor's mouth?

"Sorry." Laura finished her cake and gave him a wry smile. "Comes with the 'real estate agent extraordinaire' job, I'm afraid. I guess I'm always what for you would be 'on call.'"

"No apology needed. I get you have a busy profession." Like he did. "Brent seems nice. If he calls you, maybe—"

"Oh, please." Laura rolled her eyes. "I'll do my best to find him a cottage or ski chalet, sure, but he's so not my type. Also…" She leaned across the table and lowered her voice. "Did you notice he mentioned his divorce came through a few months ago? Mega red flag. That tells me he needs to deal with the end of his marriage before rushing into a new relationship."

It made sense but still, Trevor's tension eased. "How come you're not dating anyone?"

Laura shrugged. "My farm and real estate business are enough." So there was Trevor's answer. "What about you?"

"My last serious relationship ended almost a year ago. It wasn't working so we both decided it was better to move on. I've never found the right woman to settle down with." Because no other woman "got him" like Laura did. He drew in a shaky breath. "Now, with Danny, my mom and my new job, I have enough going on."

That's what he kept telling himself but did it now sound as hollow as him and Laura being "only friends"? His phone buzzed with an incoming text. "I'm not on call at the clinic, but I should check this in case it's my mom or Danny."

"Go ahead." Laura shook her head at a passing server who held out a coffeepot to offer a refill.

"Oh, no." Trevor read the text with dismay.

"What is it?" Laura was already gathering up her purse and the evening shawl she'd left over the back of her chair.

"Mom and Danny are fine, but remember that leaky pipe in the upstairs bathroom? The one the plumber supposedly fixed? The management company texted me. The water sensor alarm went off so they sent someone to the Brennan house. They think the pipe might have burst."

A FEW DAYS after her dinner with Trevor was cut short, thankfully not due to a burst pipe, but rather another leaking one, which was a quick repair, Laura shifted in her seat at Strawberry Pond's oldest church. A simple white clapboard building with a square clock tower, it had sat on a corner lot near the town green since the early nineteenth century. Less than a month ago, she'd been here for Josie and Heath's wedding, but today's memorial service for Trevor's sister, Renée, was a much sadder occasion.

Beyond Trevor, who sat at Laura's right, Danny had his head bowed, and Trevor's mom, on Danny's other side, held one of her grandson's hands. As when Trevor's dad had passed, Laura had been invited to sit with the Kaminski family. When they'd entered as a group, after the rest of the congregation were seated, Laura's discreet glance around had shown her that the church was packed, with people standing three deep near the rear doors and in the small balcony.

As a community choir joined the regular church choir for a song after the eulogy, her thoughts drifted. Renée was only forty-four, a few years older than Laura, when her life had been snuffed out. She'd had so much left to do, with Danny especially. Now, Trevor and his mom had to somehow try to fill the huge gap Renée had left behind. It must feel like an impossible task. When Laura's dad had died, she'd still had her mom, but Danny had never known his father. In terms of a parent, his mom was his everything.

The choir's voices rose and fell as they sang Louis Armstrong's "What a Wonderful World," and the backs of Laura's eyes burned. Mrs. Kaminski had chosen that piece of music because she used to sing it to Renée, and then Trevor, at bedtime. As the poignant lyrics swirled around them, Trevor sniffed, and his mom and Danny held tissues to their faces.

Laura took Trevor's nearest hand and held it tight, and when he squeezed her hand in return, warmth slid through her. While it felt right to be here with his family, it also somehow felt more momentous than it had at Trevor's dad's funeral.

After the minister delivered a closing prayer and final blessing, the organist played "Sing with All the Saints in Glory." Laura recognized the hymn from childhood, but even as the rest of the congregation sang the familiar words, Trevor still sat with his head bowed as tears silently rolled down his face.

"Oh, Tuna." The last time she'd seen him cry was when his dad passed. Now, her arms went around him in a hug like others they'd exchanged countless times before. "I'm so sorry, but I'm here. Somehow we'll get through this, everything." She held him close and then his arms encircled her, and they sat together in the pew as he buried his face in her shoulder.

As they embraced, despite everyone around them, to Laura it was like they were in their own small world of two. She was hyperaware of Trevor's ragged breathing, the crisp citrus scent of his aftershave and the slight tremble of his shoulders beneath the soft wool of his suit jacket. Her palms tingled and she stilled, enveloped in his warmth and an intangible connection between them that went beyond what had started out as an ordinary, comforting hug.

She held back a gasp and then moved away as gently as she could. While she'd tried to deny it, she was attracted to him. Not as a friend. Oh, no. She'd moved far beyond friendship. She was attracted to him as a man. "I—I should see if I can help with the refreshments in the church hall." As the hymn ended, and ordinary conversation resumed around them, Laura stammered as she forced out the words.

"But the funeral home is—" Trevor raised his head and his expression was both grief-stricken and puzzled.

"I know they're handling the refreshments with the caterer, but it's important to oversee… to make sure everything runs smoothly." *Liar.* The local funeral home, established more than sixty years before, was professional and experienced, and there was no need for Laura or anyone else to check up on them. The caterer, a company she often hired for business events, was similarly proficient. However, she had to find some excuse to detach herself from this situation. *From Trevor.* Her stomach lurched. What if Trevor had sensed her reaction to him? It would've been bad enough for her feelings to run away with her under any circumstances, but at his sister's memorial service? It almost felt like taking advantage of his grief.

"Okay, thanks." Trevor nodded. "I can always count on you, Lulu. We all can." He gestured to his mom and Danny, who now held each other and cried softly, with other more distant family members milling around them.

"No problem." Her face burned at her dishonesty. As she backed out of the pew, dodging some of her own relatives, and moved to the rear of the church and stairs that led to the hall, her chest was like lead. Her grief for Renée was mixed up with what had just happened… and what it might mean for her friendship with Trevor.

She couldn't lose his friendship so she'd have to keep pretending nothing had changed between them, but how could she make herself believe it? And he knew her so well, would he guess something was different? She had to focus on Danny, that was the only solution. The teen needed her, and he'd also be a distraction from his all of a sudden much too appealing uncle. Besides, given time, these unexpected feelings for Trevor would pass. Laura's emotions were heightened because of Renée. Trevor's were, too. She was getting herself worked up unnecessarily.

"Beautiful service, wasn't it, Laura? So touching." Laura was near the top of the stairs, intending to dart into a nearby ladies' restroom, but she halted at the sound of a woman's voice.

"Oh, yes. Very touching." Laura tried to focus on Mrs. Boudreau, who'd taught her high school civics and had also been her homeroom teacher junior year.

"Such a dreadful loss." Behind her glasses, Mrs. Boudreau's eyes shimmered with tears. "I'm glad Trevor has you for support. I always knew the two of you would get together one day. Your closeness in your school days was so special. Mark my words, I used to say in the staffroom, Trevor Kaminski and Laura Sullivan will make a match of it one day. Now, well, I'm delighted for you both."

"Oh, no. We're still just friends." When Laura finally managed to stop Mrs. Boudreau's flow of words, her face felt like it must be on fire. "Of course, I'll support Trevor. And Danny and Mrs. Kaminski, but there's nothing more between us. I mean… I'd… We'd never think such a thing and… I—" Her skin prickled and she stopped like a windup toy with a broken spring. She was making this situation worse, not better. "I'm sorry. I have to—"

"Laura?" Danny's voice came from behind her along with a gentle tug on the sleeve of her black jacket. "Grandma and Uncle Trevor are talking to people I don't know. Can I hang out with you?"

"I… Yes, of course." As Mrs. Boudreau muttered an apology and left, Laura tried to rearrange her features into what she hoped was a neutral expression. "Do you want to get something to drink or eat?"

Danny shrugged. "Not really." What he wanted, his face said, was not to be here at all.

Laura could relate. In an instant, she was only a year or so younger than he was, and at her dad's funeral. The cloying scent of the flowers in the stale air of a crowded church. The murmured condolences from friends and family, both familiar and those she hardly knew. How her dress had scratched the back of her neck, and she'd rubbed at the spot until her skin was raw. And how it had felt like she was somehow outside her body, separate from everyone else, alone on one side of a thick pane of glass with no way of breaking through to the rest of the world.

"Sure, you can hang out with me." Her surprising, confusing feelings for Trevor had nothing to do with Danny. And having just resolved to focus on the boy, here he was coming to her. Although, from the cute way Danny wrinkled his nose when trying to figure out a tricky homework question, to the shock of hair that fell over his forehead and his love of animals, he was a lot like Trevor had been as a young teen. "Here." She guided him to the stairs. "We can find a quiet corner."

"Okay, but, Laura?" Danny tucked a hand into one of Laura's, for a moment looking and seeming like a much younger child. "Would you… could I maybe help you at your farm on Saturday afternoons? When I worked with her at the pet-grooming event, Josie told me about your horses. She said you need another Saturday stable hand. I could learn. I know I could." Danny's eyes and expression were earnest. "Before she… well, I talked to my mom about volunteering at a therapeutic riding stable for school community service, but now…" Danny's voice hitched and, as they reached the bottom of the stairs, he dipped his head, drawing into himself and the grief that seemed to envelop him like a thick fog.

Laura studied his tousled hair. Her first instinct was to say no. Trevor and Danny were already taking part in several "Save the Animal Rescue" activities. The more she saw Danny, the more she'd also see of Trevor, since it wasn't as if Danny could get to her farm and back to town by himself. And the more she saw Trevor, the harder it would be for her to hide her feelings for him. But, as Laura also knew from her own experience, being around horses was healing.

"I guess so, but only if your uncle agrees. He

might not want you doing barn work. It wouldn't qualify for community service hours and I'd pay you but—"

"Uncle Trevor will say yes. I know he will." Where they stood off to the side of the main traffic area in front of the Sunday school classroom, Danny gave her an exuberant hug. "You're the best, Laura."

"So are you, kiddo." As Laura returned his hug, her heart ached for this orphaned boy. Whatever it took, she'd do her best for Danny.

No matter all those emotional knots his uncle had her tied up in.

CHAPTER SIX

TREVOR SLOWED HIS SUV and turned left at the wooden sign with Sugarbush Knoll Stables in bold, black letters beneath a horse silhouette. While he didn't remember seeing the sign, he recognized the gate to Laura's property from when she'd driven him and Danny along this narrow, snow-covered country road on Trevor's second day back in town.

Now near the end of January, Danny was at school and Trevor was on his own. As he drove along the freshly plowed lane lined with tall, leafless trees, he drew in a deep, steadying breath. He'd come here for work to check on one of Laura's horses. However, he'd volunteered to make on-site farm calls this afternoon knowing Laura's place was on the list. He'd also left Sugarbush Knoll Stables for last because he needed to talk to her. This awkwardness and distance between them couldn't continue.

After that hug at Renée's memorial service, an embrace that had turned everything Trevor thought he knew about Laura and his feelings for her inside out and upside down, Laura had avoided him at the reception after the service. While he appreciated she'd looked out for Danny, Trevor hadn't had a chance to talk to her alone. Maybe that had been for the best because he wouldn't have known what to say. Now, though, he had a plan.

He parked the SUV in the empty space next to Laura's vehicle, clambered out and retrieved his medical bag from the back. Facing him was a traditional, rectangular New Hampshire farmhouse with a gable roof and side porch. The clapboard exterior was painted a soft gray. Lights glinted from the windows downstairs, and a wisp of smoke curled upward from a stone chimney. It was rustic, cozy, and from the simple green-and-white wreath on the front door, to the vintage snowshoes hanging on the porch wall, the place had a welcoming feel even before he'd stepped inside.

"Trevor." The front door opened, and Laura stood in the entryway wearing jeans and a sweatshirt, and pulling on a parka and pair of barn boots. "I didn't hear you drive in." Her face was pinker than leaning over to put on those boots warranted. "My office is at the back of the house. One of my sisters is here using my washing machine, and she spotted you driving in. Hers broke. Her washing machine, I mean."

"No problem." He gestured to what must be the stables, a peak-roofed red barn near a grove of trees at the end of a snow-cleared path a short distance from the house. "Want to show me to the barn?"

"Absolutely." Laura zipped up her parka and then donned a fuzzy green hat and mittens and joined him. "I wasn't expecting you'd be the one dropping by to check on Tootsie." She fiddled with her mittens, which matched the hat that covered most of her hair. "Not that you aren't qualified, obviously."

Trevor patted his medical bag, although he'd never felt less like a qualified veterinarian in his life. "I'm doing today's farm visits."

"You're sure you should be back at work?" Beneath her hat, Laura's brown eyes softened with concern. "So soon after the memorial service?"

"It's good for me to keep busy." Laura had pretty eyes. They were warm and had a hint of gold that echoed her blond hair. Trevor mentally shook himself. After all these years of never truly noticing what Laura looked like, now he was hyperaware of every detail. And while he still valued their friendship, all of a sudden he was more attracted to her as a woman. "It's also good for Danny to have a routine." That's what Trevor's mom had said, so in the absence of any child-rearing experience of his own, he'd followed her advice.

"That makes sense." Laura stuck her hands in her parka pockets as she walked at Trevor's side along the path to the barn. However, she stayed the width of the path away from him and her voice was cool, almost as if they were acquaintances instead of so-called best friends. "Everyone I've talked to said the service for Renée was a nice tribute."

"Yeah." Folks had said the same thing to Trevor but that whole day had been pretty much a blur. Only Laura's hug stood out, and then he'd been overcome with guilt. What was he doing admitting he was attracted to his best friend on the day they were honoring his sister's life? At first he'd tried to convince himself it was because he was already feeling vulnerable, but he'd felt that same attraction when he and Laura had dinner together. And when they'd shared that chocolate cake at the mountain inn restaurant, despite sharing desserts countless times before, it had seemed intimate.

Wordlessly, and still avoiding Trevor's gaze, Laura opened the barn door and they went inside.

"Which horse is Tootsie?" Wood, hay, shavings and the warm, musky scent of horses mixed together in a familiar aroma that Trevor, a town kid, had loved from his first visit to Laura's family farm.

"The Morgan on the far end. We've kept her on stall rest like Dr. Berner advised. Tootsie's not my horse, she belongs to one of my boarders, but I keep a close watch on all the animals here." As they reached Tootsie's stall, Laura took off her mittens and rubbed the horse's ears. The animal greeted them with a soft nicker.

"Hey, girl." Keeping his voice gentle, Trevor removed his own gloves, dug in his jacket pocket for a treat and then held out his hand, palm up, for Tootsie to investigate. "So, Lulu. I think we need to talk."

She stopped, about to pick up a flake of hay. "If it's about Danny wanting to work here on Saturday afternoons, I already said you'd have to be okay with the idea first."

"It's not about that. I already told Danny if he wants to muck out stables for you, it's fine." Trevor studied Laura's face.

"Then about what?" Under his scrutiny, Laura dropped her gaze to her boots.

"You know what." As Tootsie munched another treat, Trevor set his bag aside. "Come on, we've been friends too long to pretend with each other."

"I'm not pretending." Laura pulled off her hat and loose hair swung forward to almost hide her face. "Tootsie's doing fine. Her owner's away for work this week, but I've cared for her like she's my own horse and—"

"I'm sure you have, and I'll check Tootsie in a few minutes. It's you—us—I want to talk about."

"Us?" Laura's voice wobbled.

"Yes, us. We've always been honest with each other and now things feel…weird. Awkward and uncomfortable. And you've been, I don't know what else to call it except prickly. You've hardly looked at me since I got here."

"It's a professional visit. Time's money, right?"

"Only for accountants and attorneys. And plumbers. I'm glad I didn't have to pay the repair bills for fixing those leaky pipes at the Brennan house." Trevor tried to joke, but Laura remained stone-faced. "What is it? You're scaring me." When it came to talking about feelings, his own especially, he was in new and unfamiliar territory.

"You and me, we haven't always been honest with each other. We never talked about that kiss back in high school." Laura put a hand to her face as her skin bloomed bright red across her cheeks to her hairline. "I didn't mean…" She stuttered to a stop and turned away.

"No, we didn't talk about that kiss." Trevor followed her along the barn's middle aisle. "But that doesn't mean it wasn't important. At least to me." His own face heated.

"It was important to me, too." Still with her back to him, she hugged herself. "I never mentioned it because you didn't and I was scared."

"We're friends. We should be able to talk about anything. It's okay, truly." Even as Laura shook her head, Trevor's breath caught. When, if ever, had Laura been afraid of anything? Maybe she was as vulnerable as him. "I'm Tuna, remember?" When he was small, he hadn't been able to pronounce his given name and had insisted on being called "Tuna" instead. In the family, the nickname had stuck, as Laura's own childhood nickname, "Lulu," had.

"Yeah, you *are* Tuna, but all of a sudden it's like I don't know you. Not really, anyway." When Laura finally turned around to face him, she clasped her hands together, and her lower lip trembled.

"Hey, it'll be okay." Laura rarely cried. The last time Trevor remembered her shedding tears was when he'd left for college more than twenty years before. He covered her hands with his. "I don't feel like I know you, either, but what's becoming clear to me is you're not only my best friend, but I have other feelings for you. New feelings. Romantic ones." There, he'd laid it all out—heart, soul, everything. Whatever happened next was up to her.

"You do?" She raised her head and her gaze met his and held.

"Yep." He reached for her hands, squeezed them and hoped he wasn't making a fool of himself. "It's confusing, but something's changed. I kept trying to dismiss those feelings, but they're still there and only getting stronger.

"I have other feelings, romantic ones, for you as well and yes, it's confusing." Her voice quavered. "I don't want to lose you as a friend but now everything's different."

"It is, but that doesn't mean we can't figure it out." He exhaled. While it was a relief she felt the same way he did, what would the shift from a platonic to a romantic relationship mean? "We can take it slow." Usually, he jumped into life and relationships head first without thinking of the consequences but this time was different. If he didn't tread carefully, he could lose everything.

"You know me, slow and steady." Laura's laugh was strained. "But despite those new feelings, I still don't think we can be anything more than friends. It's too risky. There's Danny to consider as well. I care about him and starting something would be a slippery slope. You and Danny are a family. If things don't work out between us it'd be hard, but we're adults. Danny's a kid who just lost his mom. I don't want to hurt him or make him feel left out. Also, although I love Strawberry Pond, people talk. I don't want to be the subject of town gossip." She took her hands away from his.

"Me, neither." With moving back to town, his new job, Renée's passing and becoming Danny's guardian, Trevor already felt like he was in the glare of the local spotlight. He didn't want to attract any more attention. "And, yeah, it's risky moving beyond friendship, but I think the risk is worth it. For all of us. You, me and Danny. Of course, he's my priority, but we'd never exclude him." He already missed the warmth of Laura's hands in his and comfort of her touch.

"You've always been a risk-taker. I'm not." She paced in a small circle. "I need some time to think about what all this means for me, let alone us. If there can be a new kind of 'us.' I'm not ready for us to date, even if we kept it secret. When there's a kid involved, a relationship brings lots of other responsibilities and issues to work through. Ones I'm not sure I'm ready for or could handle, either. You've also had so many changes in such a short time, how can you be sure your feelings about anything, me included, are real?"

"That's fair." At first, he'd doubted his new

feelings for Laura for that same reason. His sister's death, moving back from California, starting a new job and becoming an instant dad to Danny was a lot. In fact, it was more change in a shorter time than Trevor had ever had before, but his sister's death had also shown him that you never knew what the future might bring. You had to seize life and not sit around on the sidelines. He tamped down his natural impatience. When it came to Danny and those responsibilities, what was Laura so worried about? She was fantastic with him.

Slow and steady. That's who she was, so that's how it should be. However, even if they weren't dating, they couldn't go on as they were. Not having both acknowledged those new feelings between them.

"To be honest, all I want is to kiss you again. That kiss at senior prom was amazing, but I told myself I couldn't be attracted to you. However, I'm not eighteen anymore, and now I know what I feel for you is real." It had to be because he'd never felt this way before.

Laura's mouth curved into a sweet smile. "That kiss *was* amazing. Over the years, I sometimes thought I must've imagined it." She hesitated. "While I still think we should stay friends, I've often wondered if…well, that kiss was a one-off. So, yeah, you can kiss me again." She tilted her face toward him.

For a second, Trevor stilled. He couldn't mess this up, and Laura was so beautiful inside and out. She always had been, except he'd been too blinkered to see it. He took a shaky breath, then leaned in and covered her soft lips with his in a kiss that was everything he'd hoped for and more. "Okay?" He murmured the word against her mouth.

"More than okay." Her warm breath brushed his cheek.

Then she kissed him back, and Trevor's heart pounded.

As he wrapped his arms around Laura, and she returned his embrace, the world seemed to stop. She wanted time, and that made sense, but the hard truth was Trevor never wanted what he had here, now and with her, to end.

A PLATE OF strawberry pancakes drizzled with local maple syrup, the Strawberry Spot Diner's "bottomless" cups of coffee and uninterrupted time with her close friends on a Saturday morning. For Laura, life didn't get much better than what she had right here with Josie and Alana.

Except, maybe it did. Kissing Trevor had been fantastic. And while at first it had felt awkward, then it had only felt right. Which now left her even more confused. She wasn't ready for an official relationship, but could they keep things casual without either of them getting hurt? If she left her heart out of it, maybe, but judging from those kisses, that'd be harder than she'd first thought.

However, she'd also been honest with Trevor. He was still new to day-to-day family responsibilities, but she wasn't. Could she take on all those obligations again, having organized her adult life to be on her own? She wasn't sure and, as she'd also told Trevor, she needed time to think.

In a cozy booth overlooking Strawberry Pond's Main Street, Laura tucked into her pancakes and made herself pay attention as Josie told them about the new store she and her family had recently opened on their farm.

"I'll be sure to send folks your way once we start up our roadside produce stand again in the spring," Alana said from behind a bowl of hearty oatmeal.

"I'm already suggesting my real estate clients and people who board their horses at my stables drop by your place." Laura paused with her coffee cup partway to her mouth. "It'll take time to build your customer base, but once people visit your farm store, they'll come back. Between locals and tourists, you'll soon be doing great."

"I sure hope so." Josie frowned. "It's scary is all. Between getting married and new ventures on the farm, my life has changed so much in less than a year."

"All those changes are for the better." Alana looked at Laura and then back to Josie. "You had the courage to tackle changes that already have or will make your life better. Josie's an inspiration, isn't she, Laura?"

"Yes, you are, Josie. And no matter what, Alana and me are behind you, always." Laura took another bite of pancake.

Her own big life change was buying her horse farm, and now, everything was great. At least it had been before those new feelings for Trevor had gotten her all churned up. Not that those feelings were bad, and friendship was part of any romantic relationship, but with romance mixed in, their friendship would be different than it had been. While it could be a good change, what if it wasn't?

Those kisses in the barn were even better than the one at senior prom, so they confirmed that she was attracted to Trevor as much more than a friend. But what if she took that next step and things didn't work out between them? She risked losing Trevor's friendship, and it had always been a huge part of her life. How would she fill that big, Trevor-shaped hole?

It'd also be awkward and uncomfortable seeing him around town. Her life was here, and now his was, too. While he could move on, taking his mom and Danny with him, it'd be another big upheaval for all of them. Yet he was only renting out his house in California, and most of his possessions were in storage there. Round and round, Laura's thoughts circled, fueling her uncertainty and fears.

"I know you two have my back." Josie gave them a dimpled smile as she finished her breakfast plate of eggs, hash browns and ham. "Speaking of being there for each other, Alana and me are there for you, too." She rested her elbows on the table and leaned across it. "So we've noticed you're different and we're wondering..." She darted a quick glance at Alana. "Is something going on with you and Trevor?"

"We're friends, like always." Laura made her expression neutral. Josie and Alana were younger so they hadn't been in the same class at school as Laura and Trevor. However, in a small town like Strawberry Pond, pretty much everyone knew of Laura and Trevor's close friendship. "Now Trevor's back in town, we're spending more time together. He needs my help with Danny and... everything." Wanting a distraction, she drained the glass of orange juice she'd ordered along with the coffee.

"Do you believe her?" Josie's eyes twinkled as she nudged Alana in the ribs.

"Nope." Alana shook her head. "I set up the Valentine's display at the library last week and have been rereading some of my favorite romances. I know a 'friends to lovers' trope when I see one." She laughed and exchanged a nod with Josie.

"There's nothing to tell. Besides..." She pointed an index finger at Alana and wagged it teasingly. "Real life's not the same as a romance novel." Laura gave an elaborate shrug and hoped she sounded—and looked—convincing. "You know me. I never wanted to get married or have a family. I'm also not into romance, in fiction or life. All those hearts, flowers and chocolates. Ugh." She made a face. "Give me a good mystery or thriller any day."

Still, hearts, flowers and the rest were only the outward expressions of romance. True romance was the feelings you had for someone. The kindness, caring, friendship and wanting to spend time together. Everything she already had with Trevor. She tried to dismiss the handsome image of him lingering in her thoughts.

"We do know you, but people can change. Look at me?" Josie chuckled. "Who'd have guessed I'd end up with a guy like Heath. Not me. We're an opposites-attract romance for sure." She sobered. "I always thought you and Trevor would make a good match. Somehow it's like you both fit together. As my grams would say 'just like a lid on a pot.' You sure looked comfortable with each other at Renée's memorial service."

"I heard some of the ladies at the library's knitting group talking yesterday," Alana added. "They said you and Trevor would make such a sweet couple. In fact, they expected the two of you would've been paired up long ago. Then there's Danny. You seem to be enjoying spending time with him."

"Danny's a great kid, but as for lids and pots and knitting group gossip, you're imagining things."

"If you say so." Josie's voice was amused.

"I do." Laura's feelings for Trevor were too new, unexpected and bewildering for her to share them with anyone, even her closest friends. The same went for Danny. While she enjoyed spending time with her nieces and nephews, after helping raise her younger siblings, she liked her own space and hadn't wanted the responsibility of children.

She'd never even dated a man with kids because she couldn't see herself taking on a "mom" role. However, in ways she hadn't let herself examine, with Danny it was different. She'd love Danny, anyway, because he was Trevor's nephew, but she'd begun to love him for himself.

Her mind went to the molasses cookies she'd gotten up early to make to give Danny for a snack when he came to the stables later. She hadn't made cookies in years. With her busy life, when she wanted cookies, she bought them at the local bakery. But at Renée's memorial service, Danny had said molasses cookies were his favorite, so she'd found her mom's recipe and several dozen cookies were now stored in tins in her pantry. It was a loving gesture as a friend. Not because of trying to be a mom.

"Laura?"

Josie's voice yanked her back to the present. "Yes? Sorry, did you ask me a question?"

"I asked how the fundraising's going for Save the Animal Rescue." Josie waved down a server for a coffee refill. "The thermometer outside the town hall looks good. I saw it on my way in today."

"Oh, yes, it's going okay." At Laura's suggestion, the mayor had set up a giant thermometer sign to track the town's progress in reaching their fundraising goal. It was even lit up at night so no matter the time of day, people would be reminded of the campaign and be encouraged to donate. "So far, so good, but we still have a long way to go in a short time. I keep worrying about what'll happen if we can't keep the rescue open. When I dropped in last week, one of the volunteers told me that a litter of kittens, nine of them, had been left in a cardboard box outside the front door that morning. They took them in, but since resources were already strained, they're now almost at the breaking point."

Perhaps sensing Laura's discomfort in talking about Trevor and Danny, Josie had moved the conversation on. Which was exactly what Laura wanted, but if it had continued, maybe she would've asked her friends for advice, at least in general terms.

She'd also never dated a single dad because his kids would, naturally, be his priority. Where would that leave the woman in his life? Laura had already felt overlooked growing up in her own family. She didn't want to fall into the same pattern in a romantic relationship. Yet, she also felt like a part of Trevor and Danny's lives and an important person to them in her own right.

"If anyone can hit the fundraising goal, you can. Along with the rest of Strawberry Pond, of course," Alana said with a reassuring smile. "What's the latest on the pet-themed bake sale and art festival? The posters and banners look great. From what I hear from library patrons, there's lots of interest."

"The whole town's really fired up about the

event. The art club's taking the lead, but it wouldn't happen without many other volunteers." Yet, as they talked about the bake sale and art festival, the next big "Save the Animal Rescue" event, which had been planned for the following weekend, Laura's thoughts wandered. She'd tried to joke and brush off what Josie and Alana had said about her and Trevor. But maybe she needed to think about what she really wanted. Josie was right. People did change.

And with Trevor, could Laura still be independent, but also part of a family?

CHAPTER SEVEN

"OKAY, DANNY." LAURA LED Tootsie from her stall and secured her in one that had already been cleaned. "You've got all your supplies?"

"Right here, like you showed me." Wearing old clothes and the work gloves and boots Laura had provided, Danny beamed and gestured to the wheelbarrow, pitchfork, broom and clean bedding they'd set out earlier. "And if I have any questions, I should ask you or Mason." He inclined his head to the high school student who was one of Laura's part-time stable hands.

"Good." Laura smiled back and gave him a thumbs-up. "Go for it." Would Danny's enthusiasm for mucking out stables last? When he was Danny's age, Trevor had begun working Saturdays at Laura's family's farm. Soon, they'd relied on him, and after Laura's dad's passed, Trevor had been a big help in keeping their farm going.

"Sorry about that." Trevor came back into the barn and tucked his phone into his jacket pocket. "My mom asked me to pick up a few groceries for her. She also needed to…" He rubbed a hand against the sandy stubble on his jaw. "Talk, I guess." He glanced at Danny, absorbed in cleaning Tootsie's stall. "Do you have a minute?"

"For you? I'll always have much more than a minute." Especially now. However, since they'd kissed, while she didn't feel as awkward around him as when they hadn't shared their feelings for each other, she had a whole different kind of uncertainty. They weren't dating, but, despite her insistence on friendship, there was a new awareness between them. Laura felt drawn to Trevor like a magnetic pull, and when they made eye contact, their gazes lingered and seemed somehow charged. Albeit exciting—she got butterflies in her stomach whenever he was near—it was also new and strange. "If you're sticking around, you can work with me on reorganizing the tack room. Starting in the spring, I've hired someone to offer riding lessons here so I need to get the tack sorted."

"You're always busy, aren't you?" Trevor walked with Laura along the barn's aisle to the tack room. It was a compact room near the rear with two doors, one from the main part of the barn and the other that opened out into a riding arena. "Don't you ever stop and do nothing?"

"Why would I?" Laura's chest tightened. Although she'd never told Trevor or anyone else, keeping busy made her feel safe. It also meant she didn't have time to think. "Can you see me lazing around on a beach or sitting with my hands folded?" Even when she watched TV, she usually worked on a craft, puzzle or other small task.

"No, but that doesn't mean you couldn't. You might surprise yourself and even enjoy it." As they went into the tack room, toasty warm thanks to a portable space heater, Trevor touched Laura's arm. "If you don't have a to-do list, the sky won't fall."

"I know." She forced a laugh and then trembled as he linked his fingers with hers and leaned closer as if to give her a kiss. "We can't. Danny's out there. Mason, too." Although if they hadn't been, she'd have wanted him to kiss her. And she'd kiss him back.

With her feelings for Trevor out in the open, at least between the two of them, she'd expected to feel more settled. Less off balance in herself. Instead, those feelings grew, like a plant flourishing in a sunny window.

Trevor nodded, took his hand away and, with a rueful smile, blew Laura a kiss instead.

Trevor wasn't pushing her for anything more, but now, even his once-familiar teasing seemed laden with unspoken meaning. Laura retrieved one of the clear plastic storage bins she'd bought at the same time as a package of adhesive labels. She planned to organize equipment both by season and purpose, but first she needed to take an inventory of what was already there.

"So how's your mom doing?"

"Not great, although I shudder to think what she'd be like without Mabel. That dog's fantastic for her. Companionship, caring and unconditional love all in one cuddly package." Trevor gathered up scattered horse blankets and saddle pads. "For now, Danny goes there after school and we eat most of our evening meals at her place. It's nice for Mom because she needs human interaction. It's also helpful for me because I don't have to plan meals or cook them or worry about what Danny's doing after school at home alone, but it still feels weird."

"It must." Laura couldn't imagine dropping by her mom's place so often. While they saw each other most Sunday afternoons, they both had their own lives. Laura liked it that way, and she assumed her mom did as well. "It'll take time to find a 'new normal,' I guess."

"It will, but I also feel guilty because I want the 'old normal.' Ski trips to Tahoe, a few days in Mexico, booked last-minute when I got some unexpected time off. Now, I have to get supplies for Danny's science fair project, make healthy packed lunches he'll actually eat and remember to sign what feels like a never-ending stream of school permission slips." Trevor shrugged as if it didn't matter, but in the bleakness of his blue eyes, Laura saw the truth. He was struggling, maybe even as much as his mom. And while they were all dealing with Renée's death, for Trevor especially the realities of family life, with its logistics, challenges and managing a myriad of details, were also setting in. Everything Laura had helped her mom with and, as soon as she'd been old enough, wanted to escape.

"Why not get Danny to pitch in with making his lunch and buying supplies for his project?" Laura folded horse blankets and put them in the storage bin. "I had to do things like that at his age. You did as well."

"You're right, but I suppose I'm afraid of asking too much of him, too soon."

Was that what he also feared with her? With them? Laura's stomach knotted. "Like any teenager, if you don't set clear boundaries and expectations, Danny will take advantage." *Focus.* They were talking about Danny, not their own relationship. Which wasn't truly a relationship. Not yet, anyway. Laura put a lid on the bin and then found a label to list the container's contents. "I bet Danny's on his phone or playing games on his computer while you're running around catering to him. Complaining about his lunch like you're a short-order cook."

"That's about right." Trevor shook his head. "How'd you get so smart?"

"I was a teenager. I also remember you at Danny's age." And she'd had a bunch of siblings who'd tested limits every chance they got.

Trevor laughed. "Remember when we left school without permission, and my mom caught us ordering milkshakes at the diner?"

"I sure do. She marched us right back and into the principal's office." Laura joined in his laughter. "It was all your doing as well. I'd never have skipped school without your encouragement."

She'd been a serious kid who'd grown up to be a serious woman, but maybe that's because she'd had to. Trevor was the kind of guy who'd go skiing or to Mexico on a whim. Now, he had responsibilities, but he'd always wanted adventure. Could he ever truly settle in Strawberry Pond? He used to say life here was boring, but Laura liked its uneventfulness. It was home and she'd never needed excitement or been compelled to put down roots anywhere else. That was a big difference between them, but as their friendship changed and if they became a real couple, would it be too big to overcome?

"We had lots of fun back in the day." Trevor's voice softened. "And now—"

"Laura, Uncle Trevor?" Danny bounded through the half-open tack room door. "I cleaned Tootsie's stall and gave her fresh bedding like you asked. Mason said I did great, so now what?" He glanced between them, his eyes bright, and looked happier than Laura had seen him since he'd arrived in Strawberry Pond.

"You can help me bring Tootsie back to her stall and groom her so she looks nice and pretty for when her owner comes to see her later. Then, I've made molasses cookies for us to have before we make more posters for the art show and bake sale." Along with the art club members, Laura's aunt, Anne Sullivan, and several others had done most of the actual event organizing, but Laura had volunteered to handle advertising and signage, and recruited Trevor and Danny for her team. "We need signs to show visitors where to park, directions to the restrooms and to identify the different bake sale tables. We don't want pet treats getting mixed up with people treats, do we?" Laura resisted an unexpected urge to brush a piece of Danny's hair away from his eyes.

"Nope." Danny pushed the hair away himself and laughed. "Molasses cookies are awesome. Grandma's making dog biscuits *and* people cookies. She said I could be her assistant."

As Danny chattered about cookies, and then Tootsie and the other horses, Laura swallowed a lump of emotion. Like Danny, Trevor had that same energy and enthusiasm for life. A kid who'd always been eager for more, while Laura, more hesitant, had held back.

Would adult Trevor always want more, too? Maybe more than Laura could ever give him?

"HANG ON, DANNY, and don't run, okay? Be careful not to drop those boxes with Grandma's baking." Holding the large painting, which Sarah Fournier, whom Trevor still thought of as "Miss Sarah," had asked him to find in the Brennan house's attic and bring to display at the art festival and bake sale, Trevor let the door of the community center swing shut behind him.

"That picture's sure ugly." As Danny slowed to a walk, he studied the lurid-colored oil of a herd of sheep grazing in a field under a stormy sky, with what appeared to be a growling black-and-white sheepdog in one corner.

"It's different, that's all. We don't all like the same things, remember?" Privately, Trevor agreed with Danny that the painting was nightmare-inducing, but as the adult he had to be polite. Did Miss Sarah also dislike it and was that why she'd stored it in her attic behind a bunch of old furniture and boxes? "Leave the baking with Laura and then come help me hang up the picture."

"Do I have to?" Danny made a face. "Art's boring."

"Yes, you do." Since Trevor had talked with Laura, he'd set more boundaries with Danny, and although his nephew had complained, he'd mostly fallen into line. Trevor was the grown-up and setting rules was his job, even though it was hard. "This pet-themed bake sale and art festival is to try to save the animal rescue, but even if it wasn't, it's still good to volunteer." During his years away, Trevor had almost forgotten about small-town community service, but now at the beginning of February, after almost a month in Strawberry Pond, he once again recognized its importance. "Like Grandma says, making the world a better place begins with you."

"Yeah, yeah." Danny rolled his eyes, but he still did what Trevor asked, and followed him to the art display area.

Although the event had only opened ten minutes earlier, it was already busy. Trevor dodged townspeople and out-of-towners as he made his way through the throng surrounding the bake sale tables to where the art show and sale had been set up near the community center's small stage.

"Oh, thank goodness you're here." Anne Sullivan greeted him with a harried expression. "With his bad back, Tom Ryan shouldn't be climbing ladders but nothing Martha nor I have said will dissuade him." She gestured to the woman at her side, and then, the white-haired man who stood atop a stepladder with a hammer in one hand and strand of decorative lights in the other. "Can you try?"

"Sure." Trevor tried not to laugh. Josie's gramps, Tom Ryan, was one of Strawberry Pond's old-timers, but as active as he'd ever been. "Mr. Ryan, let Danny and me give you a hand." He set Miss Sarah's painting against the wall and stopped by the ladder. "I think your wife and Mrs. Sullivan need you to do something else."

Tom made a harrumphing sound as he climbed down the ladder, as nimble as someone half his age. "They're fussing about me, aren't they?" He shook his head. "It's always the way. Now, there's Josie comin' to join them. You, you're single and can do what you want." With more grumbling, Tom joined his wife, granddaughter and Anne.

Trevor mounted the ladder and, as Danny held one end of the long strand steady, he hung the lights on hooks that had long ago been placed there for such a purpose. He also kept glancing over his shoulder. Despite his bluster, Tom and Martha were as happy together as Trevor's mom and dad had been. With one arm looped around Martha's shoulders, Tom's face, as he looked at his wife of over half a century, was filled with love, respect and devotion.

It was the kind of relationship Trevor wanted for himself but had never found. Could he find it with Laura? He wanted to see, but he understood her need for caution. Everything was changing, including their friendship, and it had all happened fast. Could he trust that in only a few weeks, he'd truly found a lifetime love, and she'd been right in front of him for almost his entire life?

He hooked the last light into place and then scanned the crowd, his gaze drawn to where Laura stood behind a table selling homemade pet treats. Was she still as opposed to marriage and family as she used to be? It wasn't a topic they'd talked about lately, but they needed to. Yet Trevor held back, fearing what she might say. Instead, rather than talking, he wanted to kiss her. Kisses that made him think about having a home and family of his own…with her.

"Uncle Trevor?" From where he stood at the bottom of the ladder, Danny broke into Trevor's thoughts. "After we hang the picture, can I go outside with Landon and Isaac? Remember, Landon's the one I met snow tubing, and he's in my homeroom? Isaac's in my gym class." He gestured to two boys who stood near the community center's door, looking as bored and uncomfortable as Danny did.

"What would you do outside?" Trevor tried to give himself time to consider Danny's request. "I thought you wanted to join that painting workshop with me." Led by a local artist, Trevor had hoped it would be something he and his nephew could do together. Perhaps it might offer a chance for them to bond more.

"You wanted us to do that workshop. *I* didn't. But all Landon, Isaac and me would be doing is watching the pick-up hockey game. It'd only be for a short while and the rink's right behind the community center. I could come back for the art." Danny's face and voice were pleading.

"Okay, but don't forget we're working a volunteer shift later as well." The two of them had been assigned to help the Strawberry Pond Painting Pals package up sold art pieces and, if needed, assist in carrying them to their new owner's vehicles. "If you hand me Mrs. Fournier's painting, it can go on this shelf right here." A narrow rail, rather like the plate rail in the dining room at the Brennan house, ran around the wall on this side of the room. It was wide enough to hold the painting, and also high enough to keep it out of harm's way. "Great, thanks." Trevor carefully took the framed picture from Danny. "Off you go. Be back in half an hour."

"Sure." Before the word was out of his mouth, Danny was already partway to the door.

Trevor adjusted the painting, propped the small card he'd made that said Not for Sale, and Displayed with Thanks to Sarah Fournier (Brennan) beside it, and then dismounted the ladder. It was natural that Danny wanted to have fun with kids his own age. When he'd met him, Landon seemed like a good kid, and although today was the first he'd heard of Isaac, the boys would be nearby and it was the middle of the day. He and Laura had run around Strawberry Pond by themselves when they were much younger than Danny. Trevor had nothing to worry about.

CHAPTER EIGHT

AN HOUR LATER, in the community center's activity room, Laura swirled green paint on the white canvas propped on an easel in front of her. Along with the bake sale and art show, these informal, drop-in art workshops were also raising money for Save the Animal Rescue. While Laura hadn't taken art beyond middle school, it was surprisingly freeing to create something without any specific plan. On impulse, she added a blue swirl above the green and then a yellow circle.

"What're you making?" Next to her, Trevor glanced at Laura's canvas.

"I don't know. It's an abstract. Like Mr. Bouchard said, I'm letting my imagination guide me." She inclined her head toward their instructor. Now retired, he'd taught art at the high school for years. "Hey, that's good." She leaned forward to take a closer look at Trevor's sketch pad. "You've really captured Tootsie." The deceptively simple pencil sketch showed the horse looking over her stall door. With her ears pricked forward, which was how Tootsie showed she was alert and interested, and with gentle dark eyes, in only a few strokes Trevor had brought the horse to life.

"It *is* good." Mr. Bouchard, who was circulating around the room speaking with participants in turn, nodded his approval. "You should join one of my weekly art classes. I offer several, both day and evening sessions, for all ages. It might be worthwhile for Danny as well. Such a pity about Renée. I taught her all the way through high school. She was a lovely girl and so creative. Perhaps Danny has inherited her talent?"

"I… I'll think about it." Trevor's voice hitched as he took the class brochure Mr. Bouchard held out.

As the art teacher moved away, Laura touched Trevor's arm. "That might be fun. It'd also be something the two of you could do together. Another way of bonding." Family wasn't only about managing chores and responsibilities. It should be about sharing activities and making memories, too.

Laura's breath caught as some of her own memories assailed her along with fresh realization. Before her dad died, she'd had chores and responsibilities, sure, but they'd been part of family life, not the burden they'd later become. After her family had changed so drastically, had she lost sight of what one could be? A unit linked by fun, sharing and inside jokes, and family members supporting each other and working together rather than in isolation.

Trevor studied the sketch he'd made of Tootsie. "When I met with Danny's guidance counselor, she suggested art therapy might be beneficial for him to express and process his grief. That's why I thought this session today might— Hey, where *is* Danny?" He looked around the room.

"He was here a few minutes ago." Pushing those surprising thoughts about family to the periphery for the moment, Laura scanned the room as well. "With Landon and Isaac at the back." But now, there was no sign of the teens. Mr. Bouchard's daughter, Marie, and her two young daughters sat at the table where the boys had been.

Trevor pushed back his chair and, ignoring the scattered art supplies, got to his feet.

"Danny can't have gone far. Maybe the kids went to get a snack. The canteen's open." Laura stood, too. "Why don't you call or text him?"

"Good idea." Trevor already had his phone out. "No answer. Straight to voice mail." He typed a text, his thumbs flying over the phone's screen. "Tracking also hasn't updated on his phone, and it's almost time for our volunteer shift."

"Come on. I'll help you look for him. Maybe

Danny's phone's run out of battery." After speaking to Mr. Bouchard and asking him to set their artwork aside, Laura hurried after Trevor. "Could Danny be with your mom?" In the main part of the community center, less crowded now, because the event was winding down, there was still no sign of the boy.

"No." Trevor headed toward the entrance, where visitors had left their coats and boots. "Because of Mabel, Mom went home early. She didn't want to leave her alone too long."

"Makes sense." The poodle and Mrs. Kaminski had settled so well together that Trevor's mom had now adopted the dog. "Maybe Danny went back to the outdoor rink."

"He said the game ended." Trevor grabbed his coat from a hanger, and Laura did the same.

"Look." Laura pointed out the entryway's window as she put on her parka. "There he is."

"Okay, I overreacted." Trevor shook his head and gave a shaky laugh. "I know Danny's not a little kid, but after losing Renée and this instant dad thing, I guess I'm more prone to worry." Together, they took in the sight of Danny gliding around the ice, seemingly oblivious to the other skaters. "But where did he get skates? As far as I know, he doesn't have a pair of his own."

"He must've rented them." Laura gestured to the skate shack that was new since Trevor's last visit here. "It's obvious it's not his first time skating. Did he play hockey?"

"Not that I know of. He only played soccer and baseball in community leagues." Trevor studied Danny as if he almost couldn't believe his nephew was right there, safe and sound. "As a single mom, Renée couldn't afford to enroll him in expensive sports. Whenever I asked if I could help her out with anything financially, she always said no, she was managing. When Danny first got here, I asked him if he wanted to play sports or take any kind of lessons but… wow. How'd he learn to spin like that?"

"Maybe he taught himself. He seems like a resourceful, independent kid." As Danny skated near the window, still oblivious to them or anyone else watching, Laura followed his smooth, practiced movements. "He's having fun."

"He sure is, although he still should've texted or told me he was leaving." Trevor let out a breath of what sounded like frustration.

"Remember the teenage brain? Danny likely forgot to let you know and wouldn't realize you'd worry. Don't give him too much of a talking-to, okay?" Laura gentled her voice. She understood where Trevor was coming from, but it was great to see Danny enjoying himself like an ordinary teen.

"I won't. At his age, I also had more freedom,

but it was a different time." Trevor opened the community center door. "What do you say about joining Danny on the ice later? After we finish our volunteer shift."

"I haven't gone skating in years." Laura's first instinct was to say no. What if she fell and broke a bone? Or even if she didn't, she might look ridiculous. "After the event closes, I'm in charge of counting the money we raised today."

"I haven't skated in ages, either, but maybe it'll be like riding a bike and we'll soon get the hang of it again." As always, Trevor's half grin was way too appealing, and those ever-present butterflies took flight in Laura's stomach. "Come on, Lulu. It won't take too long to count money. I'm sure I heard Anne Sullivan say there's a group doing it."

"There is, so okay." Agreement popped out before she'd had a chance to think about it. "I don't have any other plans." It almost, but not quite, felt like a date, albeit with a thirteen-year-old tagging along.

"You don't have any plans on a Saturday night?" Trevor stopped with one hand on the community center's outside door.

"Nope." She wasn't about to tell him that her typical Saturday night consisted of doing whatever barn work might be needed followed by taking a relaxing bath. Then, if she didn't have to catch up on real estate work, she watched a movie or read in her PJs with Star and Cooper snuggled at her side.

"I'd like it if you let me change that." Trevor's voice was low, almost intimate. He touched her hand and, for several endless seconds, their gazes locked.

Then Trevor was gone to find Danny, leaving Laura alone.

But not truly by herself.

TREVOR SLID TO a stop and bent to tighten the laces on the pair of hockey skates he'd rented half an hour earlier. After only a few minutes of unsteadiness, wobbling along and gripping the boards, he'd gotten the hang of skating again. From the soft brush of the wind against his face, to the rhythmic push of his legs across the ice, long-forgotten childhood memories rushed back. How had he let himself get so far away from such simple joys?

As he straightened, he glanced around. Pop music came from the rink's speaker system, and beyond the floodlit ice surface, the dark shapes of mountains rose above to encircle the town. Voices and laughter from other skaters rang out in the cold, crisp air and the first stars twinkled overhead. His gaze settled on Laura, who still skated near the boards, as if ready to reach out and grab hold of them at any moment. "Want to take my arm again, Lulu? I won't let you fall."

Except, with each moment they spent together, he was surely falling for her even harder. He'd wanted to kiss her in the community center's entrance after they'd found Danny, and he wanted to kiss her again now. With her rosy face beneath her white stocking hat and matching scarf, pieces of blond hair sticking out, she looked like an angel atop a Christmas tree. He smiled to himself. Maybe it sounded sappy but it was the truth. She'd admitted she had feelings for him like he did for her, so why was she holding back?

"You aren't laughing at me, are you?" Laura stopped as Trevor skated over.

"Of course not." He cupped her chin in one of his gloved hands. "It's okay not to feel confident about something and take your time." Although Trevor now didn't doubt the romantic feelings he had for her, there was also a part of him that feared taking the next step.

Here it was only skating, but maybe the innate cautiousness in Laura's character had rubbed off on him. She was wary of risking their friendship, and if he was honest with himself, he was, too. He also worried about Danny. Trevor sure wasn't confident in parenting him. How would he focus on Danny if he spent even more time with Laura? Would Danny feel neglected? So many questions, and Trevor didn't have any answers.

"I never skated much even when I was a kid. I was usually looking after the little ones." Regret clouded Laura's expression. "Maybe I should get one of those penguin things." As she took Trevor's arm, she jerked her chin toward a small girl in a pink parka who was pushing a penguin-shaped safety aid, her mom and dad on either side cheering her on.

"You don't need a penguin. You've got me." Trevor tried to joke as he held out his arm and she took it, but then he stilled. "Hey, Lulu. What's up?" He'd always been attuned to her moods and feelings, and now, that awareness had kicked up several notches. Despite his fears and uncertainty, it was like she was another part of himself. A piece he hadn't known was missing. "You look sad." While he'd always wanted to make her happy, now more than ever he wanted to be the one who put a smile on her face.

"It's not important, not really, but I guess I'm remembering all the things I missed out on when I was younger. Not only skating but playing soccer, taking dance or gymnastics classes, going on that school trip to New York City our senior year." She focused on her feet, putting one skate in front of the other in small, determined steps as if she was marching. "Between school, chores and being responsible for my younger brothers and sisters, I didn't have much time for fun, especially after my dad passed. As a farming family, there were some tough years, and there also wasn't enough money for extras for so many kids."

"It *is* important." Trevor wanted to give Laura everything she'd missed, along with the sun, the moon and the stars. "But it's not too late for fun and to do things you missed out on before. Like travel."

He'd never really thought about what Laura's life had been like back then. He'd just enjoyed spending time with her. Working on her family's farm was a novelty and, unlike her, he'd been able to leave and go back to his own home in town. One with two parents, where, although his folks weren't wealthy, unlike farming, his dad's job as a police officer and his mom's part-time office work meant a predictable, steady income.

"No, it isn't too late, but why am I thinking about all this stuff now?" Her expression was troubled. "I've got a great career, and I love real estate. It's so satisfying working with people to find them their perfect home. Or selling a house for someone who needs to move on. I also have my horse farm, which is my childhood dream come true. I have a wonderful, close family and lots of fantastic friends." She continued skating, picking up speed. "And I live here in this beautiful place. Tourists often say it's one of the most stunning places they've ever visited."

"It is but..." Trevor hesitated, afraid of saying something that would either hurt Laura's feelings or make her defensive. "Maybe you're wondering if there's something more?" Like he was. "You hit your forties and boom, it's midlife, isn't it? And with Renée's passing, I have a whole new understanding of my own mortality."

"That must be it." Laura's clasp on Trevor's arm tightened, and he trembled. "Sorry. I didn't mean to get so serious." Her smile was forced. "We should be celebrating. Between the entrance fee, sales of baking and art and what people donated to take those art workshops with Mr. Bouchard, we raised several thousand dollars today."

"Wow. That'll make the fundraising thermometer shoot up." Like everyone else in town, Trevor checked the thermometer regularly, and was invested in its upward progress almost as much as Laura.

"It will, but we're counting down until the mid-March deadline when the building's lease is up." She frowned. "After two events in such quick succession, have we exhausted the town's goodwill?"

"Never. It's Strawberry Pond, remember?

We'll all pull together for as long as it takes." He made his voice encouraging, although privately he still wondered if the fundraising target and timeline were too optimistic. "I heard ticket sales for the car dealership's vehicle raffle are going great and lots of other businesses are donating, too."

"They are, but there's only so many local businesses. There's also lots of other charities and people in need, not only animals." She brushed her free hand across her face. "I'm doing the best I can—we all are—but will it be enough? If the fundraising falls short, what're we going to do? I keep imagining abandoned pets and no facility to take them in. No place to house the animals currently being cared for, even temporarily."

"Sometimes your best is all you can do, but like you, I care about saving the animal rescue." Although he cared about her more. "Try not to consider worst-case scenarios just yet. What about contacting pet-food companies? Some of them must have charitable-donation programs."

"I hadn't thought of that, but, yes, you're right." She gave a shaky laugh. "Good idea. Tom Ryan, Josie's gramps, has also started making social media videos inspired by farming and small-town life. Maybe he could give Save the Animal Rescue a mention. That could attract interest and donations from a bigger area."

"See? There's lots of options. I'll talk to Dr. Berner. Remember he offered to get involved in an advisory way if we need him? He's back from a cruise with his wife, and he'll likely have other ideas. We could put a 'Save the Animal Rescue' donation collection box in the clinic." Something Trevor should have thought of before. "The clinic has clients from all over the White Mountains and beyond, not only Strawberry Pond."

"Thanks, Tuna. I knew I could count on you. Whenever I'm down, you know what to say to encourage me and I…" As Laura looked at him, her lips parted and she held his gaze.

"Hey, guys." Danny skated up to them and stopped in a spray of ice. "I'm starving. The canteen's closed but the outdoor snack bar's still open. Can we get burgers?"

"Didn't I give you money for food an hour or so ago?" Trevor made his voice joking and tried to focus on his nephew, not how he'd wanted to kiss Laura in view of Danny and a bunch of other skaters, most of whom they knew.

"Grandma says I'm a growing boy." Danny rubbed his stomach over the front of his parka. "Besides, unlike you two, I've actually been skating. Have you even made it around the rink once?"

"Of course, we have." Laura's cheeks were pink, and she avoided looking at Trevor. "I have another idea. It's getting colder. Why don't we go to the diner and eat inside, where it's warm? My treat. You two were such a big help with the event today, consider it a thank-you."

"Can we?" Danny looked at Trevor. "Please?"

"Sure." What else could he say? Trevor was selfish in wanting to keep Laura to himself.

"Great. Why don't I call your mom and ask if she'd like to join us." Laura's voice was almost too bright. "We could pick her up on our way to the diner. The more, the merrier, right?" She already had her phone out, assuming Trevor would agree.

"That's really thoughtful. Mom will appreciate the invitation." It *was* thoughtful, and Trevor had always appreciated Laura's kind and caring nature. Except now, he wanted much more.

CHAPTER NINE

"I CAN'T REMEMBER the last time I went out on a Saturday night in winter. Nowadays, I don't like driving in the dark when there's snow and ice." Sitting beside Danny in one of the booths at the Strawberry Spot Diner, Cheryl beamed at Trevor and Laura across the table from her. "It's so nice of you to include me." While being away from home and with other people didn't take away the ache of grief, it eased it somewhat. "Mabel's settling right in with me and taken to crate training with no fuss at all. She's such good company." It had only been a few weeks, but the poodle already felt like Cheryl's family.

"That's wonderful, Mrs. Kaminski." From behind her milkshake glass, Laura's brown eyes shone.

Cheryl glanced between her son and Laura. There was more than friendship between those two, she was certain of it. There was something new, almost an awkwardness between them, and Trevor was unexpectedly reticent whenever Cheryl asked about Laura. She suppressed a sigh. Why had both her children been unlucky in love? Renée losing her husband so young and never giving her heart to another man. And Trevor, although he'd dated some fine women over the years, never finding the right one to make a life with. Or had the right woman been there the whole time?

"Oh, hi." At a touch on her shoulder, she looked up to see her friend Martha Ryan standing next to their booth. "Laura told me how much money we raised today for the animal rescue. Isn't it amazing?"

"It surely is." Martha's face creased into a warm smile. "It's good to see you out and about."

"That's thanks to Laura, although it seems like half the town's here." The Strawberry Spot was always busy, but except for church, her knitting group and grocery shopping, Cheryl had kept mostly to herself since Renée passed. Looking back, she'd retreated into her grief, which wasn't healthy but it had been the only way she'd known to cope. Now, while all the people and voices were somewhat overwhelming, it was part of rejoining the world again and being supported in her loss. It was also what she needed to heal. Something Cheryl had to do for Renée, as well as herself and Danny. She'd do everything she could to help her beloved grandson. "You're with your family?" She turned her attention back to Martha.

"Tom, Josie, Heath and the girls." Martha gestured to a booth on the other side of the diner, where her tween great-granddaughters sat between their great-grandfather and new stepdad. "What about getting together for lunch this week before knitting club? I could show you Josie and Heath's wedding pictures. The photographer took some wonderful shots."

"Okay." Cheryl nodded her agreement. "That'd be real nice." Although, after losing Renée, life would never be the same, with Martha's gentle kindness and support maybe Cheryl could build a new life. She still had Trevor and Danny.

And if Trevor and Laura got together, she'd have a daughter-in-law to love and cherish. No, she was getting ahead of herself. Wishful thinking was just that—wishful. It was no good hoping for something that could end in disappointment, for Trevor most of all. She knew her son, and although he might think he was keeping it hidden, he was what in Cheryl's day would've been called smitten.

"Fred Sinclair also took lots of candid photos at the wedding and reception," Martha continued. "We never know when and where Fred will pop up." She chuckled and focused on Trevor, Danny and Laura. "That was a wonderful picture of you three in the group on the front page of the local paper. From the pet-grooming and photo-shoot day, wasn't it? As I used to say to Tom, you hardly ever saw Trevor without Laura and vice versa. Now, Trevor's back in town it's like old times. Well, there's Tom waving at me. He'll be wanting to be off home. No lingering for him after eating. Enjoy your evening."

After Martha bustled off, Trevor stared out the window at the darkened main street, and Laura twirled her straw, looking into the depths of the milkshake glass as if it held a key to the meaning of life. Only Danny continued to eat his burger, oblivious to any undercurrents.

As the silence lengthened, Cheryl knew she had to break it, but how? She took a sip of her tea. Sometimes being quiet was good, but now, it wasn't. More than anything else, this heavy pause told Cheryl she wasn't mistaken about how that old friendship between Trevor and Laura had changed.

"Can I have money for the jukebox? Please?" Danny wiped his mouth with a napkin and gestured to his now empty plate. "And go look in the display case at the pies?"

"You may." Cheryl found her wallet and handed him several coins. "Don't tell me you're still hungry?"

"No." Danny gave her Renée's smile, and

Cheryl caught her breath. "But we could get a pie to take home. Right, Uncle Trevor?"

"There's no need to buy a pie when I can make you as many as you'd like." Trevor seemed unaware Danny had spoken. "What kind of pie do you want?" It would be good for her to get back to baking. With a concrete task to focus on, maybe she'd feel like she was accomplishing something instead of drifting through the days as if disconnected from reality.

"I dunno. Maybe a dirt pie with worms?" Halfway out of the booth, Danny paused. "Mom used to make it. She said you taught her."

"Yes, I did. And now, I can teach you." Although Cheryl hadn't made her "dirt pie" in years, with chocolate cookies, gummy worm candy, chocolate pudding and marshmallows, it was a favorite with kids *and* adults.

"I remember you making that pie for a few of Trevor's birthday parties." Laura's smile was bittersweet. "You had great parties for him. I kept the necklace I got in my loot bag one year. It's a silver-colored heart with a pink stone in the middle. I loved it. Still do, actually."

"If you want, I can teach you to make my dirt pie along with Danny." Laura's mom had done her best, but after losing her dad and with so many younger children to care for, Cheryl often wondered if Laura had to grow up too fast.

Whenever Laura spent time with Trevor, Cheryl had tried to do a bit extra for her, things she'd have done for Renée. Like that heart necklace, which had only been in Laura's loot bag, in addition to the candy and small toys the other kids had been given.

"That'd be great. What do you say to a baking date with your grandma and me, Danny?" Laura touched the boy's arm, the gesture almost maternal.

"Sure. Can I go now?" Danny gave her a lopsided grin. He was still a kid always rushing forward to the next thing.

"You certainly can. Choose an oldies song for me." Cheryl laughed. "Maybe 'Cherish' by David Cassidy? My mom used to say she'd lose her mind if I played it one more time on my record player. Your grandpa and I danced to it right here in this diner, too." When they were teenagers and thought life was an adventure. Which it was, but only in some of the ways they'd thought.

As Danny went over to the jukebox at the front of the diner, Cheryl turned to her son. "Trevor? Is something bothering you?"

"No, everything's great, Mom." Trevor's smile was forced. "Tired, that's all. It's been a long day, and I was on call at the clinic last night."

Yet, as the familiar music and lyrics of "Cherish" swirled around the diner, and Trevor talked about Danny's science fair project, Cheryl couldn't shake the sense that something was going on with her son.

Something that went beyond whatever new feelings he might have for Laura.

"Come on, you two." Laura gripped the handle of Star and Cooper's double leash and tried to direct the two basset hounds around a snowbank while also managing the laptop bag and purse slung over her other arm. "Here we are." She reached for the front door of Strawberry Pond's veterinary clinic— located on the ground floor of a nineteenth-century brick building that had once been a hotel—and banged her elbow on the frame. "Ouch." She'd been running late all day, and she had to meet a client for a house showing outside town in less than an hour, followed by a "Save the Animal Rescue" planning meeting after work. "Hey, Julie," she greeted the receptionist, a second cousin on her dad's side. "Thanks for helping me out with these guys today, especially at such short notice." She stamped snow off her boots, unzipped her parka, pulled off her knit hat and stuck it in a pocket.

"No problem." Julie, a petite brunette in her early fifties, came around the reception desk to take the leash from Laura. "Your precious fur babies will be fine with me, won't you?" She crouched beside Star and Cooper and made kissing noises.

While the veterinary clinic offered pet boarding, Laura rarely used it. Her stable hands checked on Star and Cooper when she was out, but today all of them had called in sick. "You're a lifesaver. Wow. It looks like you're really busy." She glanced around the crowded waiting room filled with people and their pets, both furry and feathered.

"We're always steady, but since Dr. Trevor joined, business has really picked up. We're even getting clients coming all the way from Vermont." Julie gave Laura sideways smile and lowered her voice. "Dr. Berner says word's gotten out that Dr. Trevor's single and, well, you know…" She chuckled.

Laura *did* know. Her face heated, and she bent to pat both dogs. "Have fun with Julie. Oh, I almost forgot. I need to pick up more of that ear wash Dr. Berner recommended for Star."

"Sure. I'll set aside a bottle and add it to your bill. Come on, guys." As Julie disappeared with Star and Cooper walking nicely at her side, Laura stood.

"Oops. What's…?" She blinked and looked up. Heart doilies in red, pink and white hanging from strings crisscrossed the waiting room, and one was now tangled in her hair.

"Hold on." Trevor's deep voice came from behind her.

"It's okay, I can manage."

"How can you manage if you can't see where your hair's actually caught?"

"I guess." She shrugged, even though his gentle touch on her head made her nerve endings tingle.

"There you go." With a final pat, Trevor extricated her, and a smattering of applause broke out from the "audience" in the waiting room.

Laura cringed slightly. "Thanks. I have to get going. I have a house showing soon and…" Her shoulders slumped. All of a sudden, everything seemed too much.

"Hey, Lulu. What's wrong?" Trevor drew her into an empty office off the waiting room and closed the door.

"It's fine. You're busy." She sniffed.

"I'm never too busy for you." He smoothed her static hair away from her face. "Talk to me."

"It's been one of those days." One of those weeks, and if life had a rewind function, she was more than ready to either start over or fast forward it to the weekend. "I have lots going on with work, and my stable hands are all sick. My mom's upset I couldn't get out to see her last Sunday afternoon, so I need to visit, and I'm worried about how we're going to raise more money for the animal rescue. We started strong, but what if we can't keep up the pace? I also don't know what I'm going to do about you, us. I'm all mixed up. Maybe it's the winter blahs, I don't know." She tried to smile but there was no hiding that wobble in her voice.

"Hey." Trevor wrapped her in a hug that was warm, comforting and exciting all at once. "You're always there for everyone who needs you, but when *you* need help why didn't you call someone? Like me. Or did you call Josie, Alana or anyone in your family?"

Laura shook her head. "Everyone's busy."

"So?" Trevor squeezed her shoulders. "That doesn't mean we can't lend a hand. I passed Julie in the hallway and she had two basset hounds with her. Yours?"

"Yeah, I'm boarding Star and Cooper here overnight. I'll be out late for a meeting, and I don't have anybody to check on them."

"Because your stable hands are sick, likely with that virus going around." He put a hand to Laura's forehead. "Hey, you're burning up. Are you getting sick as well?"

"Maybe." She'd felt off since last night but had tried to push through the discomfort. "But I have to show a house. The guy who approached me in the hotel restaurant—you remember Brent Mc-

Carthy? It's him and he's keen to buy so I don't want to lose a sale."

"I understand, but I'm sure Brent doesn't want to get whatever virus is currently flattening half the town." Trevor shook his head and gently pushed Laura into the desk chair. "One thing at a time. Why can't someone else in the family visit your mom? Like your sister who was using your washing machine? She must owe you. I bet the others do as well."

In more ways than Laura wanted to admit, but having gotten used to being the family linchpin who kept everyone together, it was hard to say no or give up any of what she'd always thought of as her responsibilities. "I'll ask in our sibling group chat. Mom's also capable of coming into town if she wants company. Maybe I don't always need to go out to the farm. Mom could come to my place sometimes."

"There you go." Trevor nodded. "As for your stable hands being sick, Danny and I'll come to muck out stables for you. I bet if Danny put out a call at school, you could get some temporary help. Or what about if Josie or Alana could loan you a few workers? This time of year isn't likely as busy for them. Want me to ask?"

"Yes, please." Laura rested her all-of-a-sudden-too-heavy head in her hands. If she hadn't been so overwhelmed, she could've figured all these things out for herself, but it was surprisingly nice to have Trevor take charge.

"Okay, so that leaves your real estate business. You've never mentioned an assistant. Do you have one?" Trevor's voice was gentle. He wasn't judging, only trying to make useful suggestions.

"No. Business is up and down so I don't need an assistant all the time. I have a bookkeeper and a person who does website support, but the other stuff I do myself." Laura had never wanted to admit how overloaded she often became, but also how scared she was of giving up any control of her business to someone else.

"I bet my mom would love to help you out." Trevor kneeled at Laura's side. "Mom worked in an office, remember? She also took interior-decorating classes at the community college. At one point, she even thought about getting her real estate license. If you were okay with it, Mom could show Brent that house."

"That'd be great." As he seemed to solve each of her problems in quick succession, all Laura wanted to do was go home, get into bed and pull the covers over her head. "There's still my meeting. It's planning for the animal rescue fundraising."

"You don't have to be at every meeting, do you?" He rubbed her back in a circular motion that even through her parka was so soothing

Laura never wanted him to stop. "There's lots of people involved, including your aunt Anne. She's sure a dynamo."

"You're right." *If you don't have a to-do list, the sky won't fall.* The words Trevor had said to her that day he'd worked with her organizing the tack room reverberated in Laura's head. At the time, she'd tried to laugh the idea off, but now it pricked at her.

What would happen if she didn't always take responsibility for everything? Others would have to step up, wouldn't they? Maybe being busy didn't actually keep her safe, but only exhausted. And if she let herself stop and think, maybe she'd figure out what she truly wanted to do about Trevor, instead of going round in perpetual circles. Although he hadn't mentioned the "us" that had popped out when she'd spoken before thinking, he'd have noticed it. They weren't an "us," but letting herself think about it was half wonderful, half scary.

"I'm..." She rocked back and forth. "I'm not feeling good at all. Oh, no." She pressed one hand to her stomach and the other to her mouth and glanced wildly around.

"There's a restroom over here." Trevor took her arm and hustled her through another door, which was thankfully propped open.

"You can't... I... Go away." She glanced at the

sink and two toilet stalls. She'd been sick in front of Trevor before, in first grade when they'd both had stomach flu. But this, now, was different. It wasn't only embarrassing, but also awkward, humiliating and the worst ever.

"It's okay, Lulu." He opened the nearest stall door, pulled off her parka and held her hair back from her face. "I'm here for you."

CHAPTER TEN

"HOW'S THE PATIENT?" A few days later, Trevor glanced around Laura's light-filled front hall as Alana let him in. As befitting an old, but restored, New Hampshire farmhouse, Laura had decorated the place with antiques and other vintage pieces. From rag rugs on the gleaming knotted pine floors, to the wooden blanket box that served as seating inside the front door, the place was homey, welcoming and down-to-earth. Much like Laura herself.

"She's getting cranky from being cooped up, so she'll live." Alana grinned as she took a wrapped bouquet of tulips from Trevor before he removed his winter gear. "Laura's out of bed and resting on the sofa in the living room, so go see for yourself. I'll find a vase and put these flowers in water before I leave."

"Thanks." Trevor smiled back at Laura's friend. Since Alana was younger, he hadn't known her at school, but now as adults, a five- or six-year difference in age didn't seem so big. "I'll stay until Josie gets here."

Once Trevor had sent out what he'd called a "group chat all-points bulletin," Laura's family and friends had rallied around and set up a visiting schedule to make sure that while she was sick she'd never be on her own. Along with Trevor, his mom and Danny, another group had pitched in to handle Laura's farm and real estate business work.

"Hey, Laura." In his socks, Trevor crossed the hall and went into the living room. "Star, Cooper," he greeted the dogs, who left Laura's side to come and say hello. "Your mom didn't let me see you yesterday because you were sleeping. I popped in early before work."

"Mom told me." In the bright February sunshine flooding through the living room windows, Laura looked paler than usual, but she was sitting up, wearing a raspberry-pink sweatshirt, wrapped in a cozy red-and-white blanket. "Don't come any closer in case I'm still infectious." Avoiding his gaze, she gestured to an armchair across the coffee table from the sofa. "I'm sorry about…everything." She frowned.

"It's fine. You couldn't help being sick." While she'd obviously been embarrassed, Trevor had been matter-of-fact. After all, he was a doctor of veterinary medicine and in no way squeamish.

Like he said, he wanted to be there for her. Yet, what he hadn't counted on was how seeing Laura so vulnerable would make him feel.

He'd known he was attracted to her but was this more, maybe even love? Not so much a sudden rush of overwhelming emotion, but feelings that had grown slowly and steadily until, for an instant, he was filled with a sense of rightness and purpose, and a conviction that with Laura he was exactly where he was supposed to be. No, it couldn't be love. If so, he'd have recognized it years ago. Besides, he'd been in love before, and these feelings were so different. And with everything else going on in his life, he felt pulled in many directions. Yet as he sat in the comfy chair and patted the basset hounds, his thoughts whirled.

"Still, it was pretty humiliating throwing up in front of you." She forced a laugh. "I owe you big-time."

"You don't owe me anything, ever." If anything, he owed her for how she'd stepped up for him and Danny since Renée's passing. "What's between us isn't some kind of business deal."

"It isn't but..." She stopped as Alana came in with the flowers.

"See what Trevor brought you?" Alana set a glass vase on the coffee table. "Do you need anything else before I head in for my library shift?"

"No, I'm okay. Well, as okay as I can be right now. That clear soup was exactly what the doctor ordered, and my throat's not as sore."

"I'll be back tomorrow and don't even think of arguing." Alana waved an index finger at Laura. "Your visitor schedule's on the fridge, and we're not leaving you on your own for a while yet. Right, Trevor?"

"Right." He gave Alana a fist bump. "You scared all of us, Lulu." He leaned back in his chair as she admired the tulips. "You got sick so fast." The outside door closed with a soft click behind Alana and then a car engine started up. "I can't believe you were sick and tried to keep going."

"You sound like my mother." Laura made a face. "Who, I have to say, has been really great. You have been, too. And Danny and your mom. Thanks to your mom, Brent's made an offer on that house and the seller accepted it. The paperwork's waiting until I'm better."

"As it should, but congratulations. Mom will be thrilled." After showing Brent around the chalet vacation property, Trevor's mom had seemed more like herself than since Renée's death.

"Brent also mentioned he'd like to hire your mom to advise him on redecorating, and then coordinate with local tradespeople to do the work since he won't be here a lot or have time." Laura chuckled. "Your mom made quite an impression on him. Do you think she'd be interested in helping Brent, but also staying on to work with me more officially?"

"You'd have to talk to her, but I'm sure she'd love it. She's never really enjoyed being fully retired." Working with Laura would also give his mom a new interest, which was even more important than any extra money she'd earn.

"Okay." Laura nodded. "I've wanted to grow my business for ages, but I have this thing about control."

"Gee, I hadn't noticed." Trevor tried to keep his expression deadpan but failed and laughed. "Seriously, I'm proud of you. It's not easy for someone like you to sit back and loosen the reins."

"Okay, enough with the teasing." Laura's brown eyes twinkled. "I'm only letting go a bit, and your mom's different. I trust her, and she's like family, but not *my* family if you know what I mean."

"No expectations?" Coming from a much smaller family, as a kid Trevor had sometimes envied Laura all her relatives and their close bond.

"In part, but it's more than that." Laura paused. "Growing up, your mom always made me feel special. She really listened to me, and she still does. I know she'll work with me and not try to take over. You're like her that way. Maybe that's one of the reasons why we've always been such good friends. With you, I can be myself."

"Maybe, but..." Trevor took a deep breath as everything still left unsaid reverberated between them. "The other day you said you were mixed up, and you didn't know what you were going to do about me, us."

"You mean before I was sick in the vet clinic's staff restroom?" Laura rubbed Cooper's ears when the dog returned to relax next to the sofa. "I guess it was too much to hope you'd have missed that part of me having an emotional meltdown. Can we forget it? All of it?"

"Nope." Trevor shook his head. "Well, I'm happy to forget about the being-sick part, but as for what you called 'an emotional meltdown,' you're human. That's good." His heartbeat sped up and, while he tried to crack a smile, his palms got damp and his jaw tightened. "We can't go on as we are. This weird 'friends but more than friends' limbo. As a start, if you're feeling up to it, we could go to the Valentine's Day costume party fundraiser for the animal rescue. What do you say?"

"You mean like a date?"

"Exactly." While it was a risk, Trevor was all in with taking that next step and seeing where things might go between them, but he needed to know Laura was as well. "Although Danny will likely be there."

"Okay, a date." She clutched the blanket as if he'd suggested they go skydiving, which he wouldn't because although it was fun, Laura was scared of heights.

"Great." His rapid breathing steadied. He and Laura were going on a date. It'd be fine.

But even though *he* wasn't afraid of heights, he still felt like he'd jumped out of a plane and was in free fall, without the security of a parachute.

"SEE? MAKING COSTUMES is more fun than buying or renting them." Two days before the Saturday night Valentine's "Save the Animal Rescue" fundraiser party, Laura stood in the family room at the Brennan house and studied Danny. He wore the oversize brown hooded sweatshirt and sweatpants she'd borrowed from one of her nephews. "Now, I need to add the mane, ears and a tail. Turn around in a circle for me so I can check the placement." She retrieved the dark brown ribbon and a multicolored ball of brown yarn from the craft bag she'd brought with her.

"Looking good, Danny." From where he was sprawled on the sectional sofa, eating popcorn and half watching a hockey game on the big-screen TV, Trevor nodded his approval. "Great idea to dress up as a horse." His gaze slid from his nephew to Laura. "Is there anything else we need for our cowboy and cowgirl costumes?"

"Nope. You got everything on the list I gave you." Laura measured a piece of ribbon against Danny's hoodie-covered head. "I still think I could've put everything together myself. I'm fine. I'm back at work. I even went to a meditation workshop last night." Yet, she tired more quickly than she had before she'd gotten sick and wasn't up to much beyond office work and house showings, not even mucking out stalls.

"You been working in the barn yet?" Trevor put on one of the two white cowboy hats he'd found in a box of party supplies and costume accessories in his mom's basement, tilted it at a rakish angle and gave her a teasing smile.

Had he read her mind? "No, because my stable hands are back. However, I'm keeping an eye on them and the horses." But the animals were fine, and the hands knew how to do their jobs and did them well. Maybe she didn't need to hover over them as much.

"Of course, you are." Trevor tried to hide a smile by yawning.

"Are you implying I'm a control freak again? Hang on." Laura grabbed her phone from a nearby table and snapped a quick picture. "I'll print this one out and put it in a frame." She gave him a teasing smile. He looked younger in that hat, like the boy she remembered. Trevor's folks had worn those hats to a party years before, and his mom had been happy for them to be reused. "Or maybe the vet clinic would like it for their website. You know, a photo that shows you looking more casual and approachable. The picture they've got up could be a police mug shot."

"You, a control freak? Never!" Trevor raised his eyebrows and his look turned flirtatious as he stood and stretched. "You checked me out on the clinic's website, did you?"

"Only for work." Her face warmed. After setting her phone aside, she took more measurements for Danny's tail. "I sold a house to a family moving here from Maine who has dogs. Since they're looking for a new veterinarian, I recommended you." Except, she'd also looked at the clinic's website previously and then she *had* been checking Trevor out.

"Hello. I'm still here." Danny waved one hand covered with a brown mitten from a pair Laura's mom had made. "What's with you guys, anyway?"

Laura glanced at Trevor. Danny was Trevor's nephew. If anyone was going to say something about the change in their relationship, it should be Trevor.

As the silence lengthened, Laura looked out one of the family room's windows. The days were getting longer, and the curtains had been left open to catch the last of the sunshine. Now the sky was tinged rosy pink above the snow-laden pine trees that ringed the backyard. With the two red Adirondack chairs outside the patio door, and a red-painted bird feeder on a stake nearby, the scene was like one of the watercolors she'd spotted for sale at the Save the Animal Rescue's art festival fundraiser.

"Well?" Danny put his hands on his hips. "You're dating, aren't you?"

"Yes. No. Well, sort of. We're planning on going on a date." Trevor came over to Laura and Danny. "I was trying to think of the best way to tell you. I didn't want you to be upset or—"

"Why'd I be upset? It's not like you're my dad." Although there was no malice in Danny's voice, Laura didn't miss Trevor's slight flinch. "It's about time you two got together. That's what everybody says, anyway. Even Grandma. I heard her and Mrs. Ryan talking when they were looking at Josie and Heath's wedding pictures. That day I went to Grandma's for lunch because I forgot mine."

"Oh." Trevor took a step back. "Well, it's early days." He rubbed the back of his neck and looked around as if trying to figure out how he could escape.

"It is." Laura took pity on Trevor's obvious discomfort. "It's not like we're going to make a big announcement or anything." That's why going to the Valentine's costume party was a perfect "official" first date. It would be low-key, easy, and with Danny there and part of their costume theme, it wasn't too big a step into coupledom.

While Laura still had doubts, she'd also decided she couldn't pretend those sparks between her and Trevor didn't mean anything. They'd just have to set new boundaries and expectations as they went along. Easy. Not.

"You won't, like… kiss in front of me? That'd be…eww." Danny made a pained face.

"No kissing in front of you." Laura laughed. That would be boundary number one, she supposed. "You can go get changed. You don't need to wear your costume while I sew these wool bits and felt on it so you look like a real horse."

"Okay." Danny paused partway to the family room door. "You and Uncle Trevor, that's okay, too. Really. It's kinda nice having you around. I miss my mom and, well, you're not her but you do mom stuff. Like how you made me cookies and this outfit." He ambled across the carpet and into the hall toward the stairs leading up to his bedroom.

Mom stuff? Laura's legs trembled and she sat on the couch. Whoa. She'd never wanted to be a mother. Hadn't even thought of filling a maternal role for Danny. She was the boy's friend, that's all. When it came to Danny, her biggest concern had been he'd feel left out. Not that he'd see her as a maternal figure. That role was another huge leap.

"I guess I was worrying about nothing." Trevor sat beside Laura and looped an arm around her shoulders. "It's only because Danny's had lots of changes in a short time. I didn't want him thinking he'd have less of my attention now you and I will be seeing more of each other, romantically, I mean."

"No, it's okay. Danny's your priority." Laura's thoughts spun and, unable to sit still, she got up again to gather her scattered sewing and craft supplies. "Once Danny brings his costume back, I should head home. I have a farm showing at eight tomorrow morning, and then a meeting with the president of the chamber of commerce. It's part of planning for the annual Strawberry Festival, although we'll also be talking about 'Save the Animal Rescue' activities."

Laura stuffed wool, felt, her scissors and measuring tape into the colorful quilted patchwork bag Josie's mom had made for her birthday several years ago. Tonight was the nicest Thursday evening she'd spent in ages. And as she got ready to leave, a big part of her wished she could stay. Not to do anything special. Finishing Danny's costume while the three of them watched the hockey game. Helping Danny if he got stuck on a homework assignment. Talking together. Not about anything important, but ordinary aspects of their lives. Laughing and joking and maybe playing a board game or cards.

"Sure. I understand." Trevor got up as well and went to close the curtains.

Much like how she had never thought she wanted to be a mom, she hadn't seen herself as a wife, but had the perfect husband for her been right under her nose?

And since Trevor came with Danny, could the three of them make a family together? Her hand closed on the top of her bag and the colored patches danced in front of her eyes. It would be a patchwork family, one they made by choice, but perhaps also offering new and unexpected possibilities. Ones she'd never even considered.

CHAPTER ELEVEN

"WHENEVER YOU WANT a hand with anything, give me a call." The next day, a Friday Trevor had off work owing to several weeks of Saturday shifts at the vet clinic, he maneuvered his mom's new armchair beside the living room window. "Is here okay?"

"Maybe, but you know me. I'll have to try it for a few days to be sure." His mom surveyed the room. "If I keep the chair there, I should move in that end table from the den." She cocked her head to one side as if mentally visualizing the arrangement. "But then I'd need to move pictures, which could mean having to repaint."

Trevor hid a smile. While the armchair was new, his mom wanting to move furniture around wasn't. It was one of her hobbies, but maybe it also made her feel better and gave her a fresh perspective. "When Danny and I get our own permanent place, you'll have to help us decide where to put stuff."

Apart from Danny's bedroom, the Brennan

house was almost exactly as Sarah Fournier had left it since Trevor was only renting until June. She and her new husband would be back then, so he had to find somewhere else to live. So far, though, he hadn't looked at any places. He'd been too busy with his new job, Renée's estate and getting Danny settled, but he'd have to start getting his act together soon. But whenever he thought about house hunting, it seemed like too big a job on top of everything else.

If he asked, Laura would offer to organize viewings, but now that felt different, awkward even. And when Danny had mentioned Laura doing "mom stuff," Trevor's heart had skipped a beat. Having Laura in his life was already good for Danny. How much better might it be if Laura was there for always?

"Trevor?" His mom's voice pulled him out of his ramblings.

"What?" He took his hand away from the armchair, which was still covered in plastic sheeting from the furniture store.

"I said I'd be happy to give you input on furniture arranging." His mom sat on the sofa and patted the spot beside her. "However, I'll have to fit you in between redecorating Brent's house and the work I'll be doing for Laura. I expect it'll be pretty hectic."

"Sure." Trevor settled on the sofa and rubbed

Mabel's ears when the dog came to nose his hand. "It's great you have new things in your life."

"It is. While lots of folks enjoy retirement, I've found I'm not one of them. Even before Renée, well… I was on my own too much. Working part-time will suit me." His mom picked up her teacup and eyed Trevor over the top of the rim.

"I'm sorry. I should've moved back home sooner." It hadn't been fair for his sister to shoulder most of the responsibility of looking out for their mom. While it was too late for Trevor to apologize to Renée, now that he was back in Strawberry Pond he was determined to do better.

"No, you needed to build your own life." His mom drank some tea and then set her cup back on its saucer. "Get away from here for a while. If you hadn't, well, you'd have always been champing at the bit." Her smile was both loving and knowing. "So how are you feeling about everything?"

"Okay, I guess." Although less impatient than he once was, Trevor was still restless, but he'd learned to hide it better. "Laura's great. She's really been there for me and Danny." She also made Trevor laugh, and they already knew each other so well that apart from kissing her goodnight and in greeting, while their relationship felt new, it was also steady and familiar. However, he didn't want to get into everything that had changed between him and Laura with his mom; at least, not yet.

"Laura's *always* been great." His mom studied Trevor's face and he tried to keep his expression neutral. "However, it's not Laura I want to talk to you about."

"It's not?" Given what Danny had said about Trevor's mom and Martha Ryan talking about Trevor and Laura getting together, from the moment Trevor had come through the front door he'd expected questions. Instead, this was the first time Laura had come up and it'd been Trevor who'd mentioned her.

"No. Something's bothering you and maybe it would help if you talked to me. Is it Danny?" In the light from the living room window, filtered even in winter by the branches of the big maple tree his mom and dad had planted when they'd moved into this house soon after they married, the lines on his mom's face looked deeper. Still, like always, she didn't miss much, and from the keen awareness in her eyes as her gaze met Trevor's, he expected she might've already put the pieces together.

"Although it's sort of to do with Danny, it's more me." Trevor let out a long breath. "You and dad were great parents, and Renée was a fantastic mom. I'm…me, an unmarried, until now childless, man. How can I be what Danny needs?"

"You can't but that doesn't mean you aren't doing your best." Trevor's mom covered one of his hands with hers. "I can't be what Danny needs, either. Nobody can because he needs his mom and, if not her, his dad. A dad he never had a chance to know. Losing both parents so young is a tragedy."

"True, but it's like I don't—or can't—measure up." Trevor's shoulders slumped. "Last night, Danny said I wasn't his dad. I know I'm not but it still kind of...hurt." He'd known it wouldn't be easy, but taking on guardianship of Danny was even harder than he'd expected. "Danny doesn't exactly talk a lot to me. I don't even know much about what he likes. He's good at skating, but when I asked if he wanted to play hockey, he rolled his eyes and walked away. I was only trying to think of something he might like. He talks more to Laura." Which also hurt more than Trevor wanted to admit. "Laura said I need to set boundaries with Danny, and I have, but it's like I never know what I'm doing."

"No parent or guardian does—not really, or not for long, anyway. As soon as you think you've got one part of raising a kid figured out, there's a new issue." His mother's laugh was wry. "In your case, it's even more challenging because you haven't 'parented,' if you can call it that, Danny until now. Any teenager can be challenging at times, even if you've raised them from the start, but in Danny's case, before now, you've only seen him for vacation visits."

Trevor glanced at the framed photo on the fireplace mantel of his sister embracing a younger Danny under a palm tree. Trevor had taken it in California when the two of them had visited him. "Danny seems to be doing okay at school. No bullying I've heard of, not like at his school in Manchester." Which, although Danny hadn't mentioned it, Trevor knew had been a big issue. "He's even made a few friends. From what I've seen, his grades are okay, although he hasn't had many tests or projects so far. So what *can* I do?"

"Give yourself time. Give Danny time as well. It's still early so don't rush. Let your relationship with him evolve." His mom gave Trevor a one-armed hug. "I appreciate it's hard, but really, beyond giving Danny a loving, supportive and safe home, one where he feels secure and that he belongs, right now, there's not much else you *can* do. One day, likely when you least expect, he'll open up."

"I hope you're right." He glanced at Mabel, curled up in her new bed and surrounded by toys. She'd settled well with Trevor's mom, but Mabel was a dog, and a confident one at that, so she'd adapted quickly to her new owner. People, especially kids who'd lost their only remaining parent, were different.

"Don't be so hard on yourself." His mom's expression was compassionate. "Also, remember that if you trust your instincts, you won't go far wrong."

Good advice, so should Trevor take the same approach with Laura?

IN THE PARTY room at Strawberry Pond's town hall, Laura adjusted the pink bandana she'd paired with a checked, Western-style pink-and-white shirt, jeans and a pair of cream, fringed cowgirl boots she'd borrowed from one of her sisters. The boots coordinated with her hat, which matched Trevor's. "How's it going, pardner?" She eyed him from under the hat as they stood near a table where several high school students sold sodas, fruit juice and bottled water.

"Never better." Trevor tipped his own hat and, when he moved in time to the dance music played by a local DJ, the fake spurs on his boots jingled. "Where did Danny get to?"

"He's near the door." Laura pointed to where Danny sat in his horse costume at a table with a zombie, a banana and two girls dressed as cheerleaders. "No, don't go over there. You don't want to embarrass him." As Trevor stepped forward,

Laura grabbed his arm to hold him back. "He's with his friends. It's not like it's a school dance because half the town's here, but I bet Danny would still rather we keep our distance."

At around Danny's age, despite having lost her dad, when she was with friends, Laura hadn't wanted anything to do with her mom. Although she knew her mom loved her and was there for her, she had to become her own, independent person. Yet, that independence had stuck with her, and somehow, in spite of weekly visits, she and her mom had never regained the closeness they'd shared when Laura was small. Caught up in her busy life, Laura had always thought it was too late for them to move beyond chatting about superficial things, but maybe it wasn't. And maybe since she'd been the one to break away, she needed to be the one to take the first step and try to get to know and understand who her mom was now.

"Oh, right." Trevor's smile was forced. "I forgot about kids being 'allergic' to parents at that age. Not that we're Danny's parents but I guess it's similar. I keep thinking like an adult, not a kid." Trevor shrugged in what seemed like an almost helpless gesture. "Even though I was close with my folks, I didn't like being seen with them for a few years as a tween and early teen. Do you remember how we used to try to hide in the back seat of the car going through town when my mom was driving us somewhere?"

"I do." Laura laughed. "We must have been so obvious—cringeworthy, actually—but your mom never said a word." That was one of the many things she liked about Mrs. Kaminski. Trevor's mom had given her kids and their friends space when they wanted it, but she'd also always been supportive when any of them needed her.

Laura glanced around the room. Red, white and silver hearts hung on strings from the ceiling, and white lights were looped along the walls. An artificial fir tree decorated for Valentine's Day took pride of place by one of the windows. A small display held framed pictures of various animals the rescue had saved and rehomed, including Laura's dogs, Star and Cooper, as well as Buttons, Sarah Fournier's basenji. As befitting the dog of Save the Animal Rescue's biggest donor, the picture of Buttons was larger and occupied the center of the display.

"Hi, Aunt Anne. Mrs. Ryan." She greeted the two women as they passed, both carrying sparkly wands and wearing princess crowns. If Josie's grams was here, Josie mustn't be far away, but Laura hadn't seen her or Alana yet. Laura turned back to Trevor. "Although it's tough being in this situation of having to raise money to save the animal rescue, especially so quickly, all these events have sure livened up winter." She waved at several of her siblings and their spouses and kids. "After Christmas and New Year's, except for work, my fitness class and getting together with family and Josie and Alana, I usually pretty much hibernate at home between January and March."

"Like a bear, are you?" He playfully rubbed his nose against hers, knocking her hat off and onto the refreshment table. "Oops."

"Tuna." Laura shook her head at him as she retrieved the hat from a teen who'd scooped it up from atop a box of juice cartons. Trevor had always been more demonstrative than her, and she hadn't missed the looks from family and friends when they'd arrived together with Danny. Looks that had intensified after Trevor had put an arm around Laura's shoulders, and his mom had given them a broad smile.

"What? You don't like me being affectionate?" His blue eyes teased her.

"I do, but it still feels kind of weird." In ways she couldn't explain to herself, let alone Trevor.

"For me, too." His expression sobered. "It'll get easier in time." He gave her a quick hug and dropped a light kiss on her cheek.

"Laura." As Josie's gramps drew Trevor aside to talk about one of their cows who was losing weight, Josie, dressed as a butterfly, joined Laura. She was followed by Alana, who'd come as a bumblebee. "Having fun?"

"I am." She smiled at her friends. "Great costumes."

"Duct tape, cardboard and felt, mostly." Alana laughed and pointed to the black tape she'd fixed to a yellow dress to make bee stripes and then her felt-covered wings. "Can you tell I'm a librarian who does lots of children's programming?"

"Thank goodness." Josie laughed as well. "Alana also made my costume. Unlike you guys, I'm not crafty." She came closer to Laura. "So, you and Trevor?"

"Yes." Laura tried to tamp down her smile. "And I didn't tell you because it's really new." She'd also felt unexpectedly reticent. If everyone in town had expected them to get together years ago, she hadn't wanted to prove them right or be talked about even more.

"It's okay. Your business is your business." Josie gave a decisive nod. "But we're happy for you."

"We are," Alana said. "I bet Trevor's mom is as well." She inclined her chin to where Mrs. Kaminski sat at a table with several other women. "She thinks of you as another daughter. I've heard her say so."

Laura's stomach flip-flopped as if her friends' butterfly or bee wings had gotten stuck in her midsection. "Mrs. Kaminski's always been great to me. Nothing new there."

She'd long considered Mrs. Kaminski like a second mom. That was another reason this transition from being friends with Trevor to a couple scared her. If dating Trevor didn't work out, she didn't only risk losing his friendship, but also his mother's. *One step at a time.* As well as being cautious by nature, she tended to worry about things that might never happen. She needed to break that pattern, one she'd long ago recognized had been forged in childhood, and enjoy what she had here and now.

Easier said than done. The voice in her head seemed to mock her.

"With such a large crowd, the 'Save the Animal Rescue' fundraising thermometer should take a big jump up again," Josie said. "My girls love checking its progress when we come into town. They're also taking part in the school's read-a-thon and walk-a-thon to raise money."

Had Josie noticed Laura's discomfort? Even if she hadn't, Laura welcomed the change of subject. "We also got a nice donation from a pet food company through their corporate community partnerships program." That windfall was in part thanks to Trevor, since he'd suggested Laura contact such businesses and then reviewed and made suggestions to strengthen the request for funding letter she'd drafted.

"That's great." Alana beamed. "Our 'Friends of the Library' group is organizing a used book sale and silent auction, and I've got a donation box set up at the circulation desk."

"This Save the Animal Rescue has really taken off." But once again, the familiar worry bobbed around in Laura's head like a small boat on a choppy sea. Would all their efforts be enough? She'd stopped in at the rescue again this week to take more photos to use in advertising the fundraiser and chatted with several of the volunteers. From a seventeen-year-old chihuahua who'd arrived following his owner's death, to a stray orange tabby cat with a torn ear who needed sutures and antibiotics, the rescue was overflowing with animals in need. Seeing their little faces, Laura's heart hurt, and she was even more determined to save the place that was giving them care, shelter and love.

Trevor rejoined them and greeted Laura's friends. "If you'll excuse me, ladies, I'd like to have a dance with Laura. Shall we?" He held out a hand to her.

"I'd like that." She let him lead her into the area set aside for dancing. In all the years they'd known each other, except at senior prom they'd never danced together. Even then, it had been dancing in a group with friends and not to a slow song. Laura drew in a soft breath as the track changed to Ed Sheeran's "Perfect," and Trevor's arms went around her.

"Okay?" He held her close and then her hands were on his shoulders and their faces were only inches apart.

"Yes." Such a simple, ordinary word for everything Laura was feeling. Strawberry Pond had always been a strong and caring community as well as her home, with family, friends and roots she cherished. But now, tonight, it felt different, even better. Was that because, here in Trevor's embrace she had something she didn't even know she'd been missing?

CHAPTER TWELVE

AFTER THE VALENTINE'S costume party, Danny was having a sleepover at his grandmother's, so Trevor dropped the two of them off first before driving Laura on to Sugarbush Knoll Stables. As he glanced across at her in the passenger seat of his SUV, his heart skipped a beat. This new togetherness felt even better than he could've imagined. Tonight's date and kissing her in front of half of Strawberry Pond was something he'd never forget.

"What're you thinking about?" His vehicle's headlights cut across the narrow country road. A plow must have just gone through because, despite the snow falling steadily from the dark sky, the pavement was clear.

"Nothing much. Letting my mind drift like the snowflakes." Laura gestured to where the soft swishing of the windshield wipers caught them as they fell. "Tonight was good."

"It sure was." How good Trevor couldn't let her guess, in case he scared her and destroyed the new understanding between them, as fragile as the gossamer snowflakes. "You were great with my mom and Danny." Laura had always had a knack for making people feel included, and she'd done it with his family at this evening's party. From keeping an eye on Danny without hovering, to making sure Trevor's mom wasn't ever left on her own, she'd still had time for Trevor.

"Your mom and Danny *are* great." Laura's sweet smile was like a hug.

What would it be like if he was driving them to *their* home, together. Like Heath, whom they'd met in the town hall's parking lot, warming up his car for Josie and her daughters so they wouldn't be cold. New protectiveness surged through Trevor. He wanted to care and look out for Laura in all the ways he could. *For always.* The thought slid through him, and he caught his breath.

"I got lucky with my family." Before Renée's death, although Trevor hadn't intended to, he'd sometimes taken them for granted. No more. "You had lots of your own family there tonight. Everywhere I looked, I saw a Sullivan either by birth or marriage."

"Sounds like a Strawberry Pond party." Laura's laugh was light. "My family tree keeps growing. My youngest brother's wife just announced she's expecting her third child, and my sister, Courtney, and her husband are due with their fourth in early April. When my mom used to ask me about having kids, I'd tell her she had more than enough grandchildren to keep her busy. Besides, I never met the right man to have a family with."

"But you were almost engaged once." Trevor turned into the lane to Laura's property and slowed his vehicle as the tires slid on fresh snow.

The first and, as far as Trevor knew, only time Laura had dated anyone seriously was when she was in her early twenties. He was in veterinary school but that year he'd been volunteering and traveling in Asia with friends. Although he and Laura still kept in touch, their lives had already diverged, hers fixed in Strawberry Pond and his not. She'd never said much about that "almost engagement" and Trevor had never asked, but now he was curious.

"That marriage proposal was years ago." As he parked near her front door, where a lantern-style light cast a cozy golden glow into the swirling snow, Laura gave him a familiar side-eye and huffed out a breath. "Looking back, I was still almost a kid. I said 'thanks but no thanks' because Jonny wanted someone that even then, I knew I could never be. He went on with his life and so did I. Last I heard, he's married with a couple of kids and working as an electrician back in Vermont near where he grew up."

"Okay." Trevor kept the SUV running because with the temperature well below zero and dropping, they'd be freezing in only a few minutes without heat. "So...no regrets?"

"None. No big heartbreak, either. I have my independence, my farm, lots of family and friends. And you." Her voice hitched. "For now, anyway."

"What's that supposed to mean?" Sure, he'd never thought much about settling down, especially in Strawberry Pond, but that didn't mean he wouldn't. "I'm not going anywhere."

"Of course not." Laura gave him a too-bright smile.

He knew her so well, Trevor recognized when she was faking an emotion, but, unlike when they'd only been friends, he didn't know how to call her on it. "I mean it. I'm sticking around." And he'd do whatever it took to prove it to her. "Although actually, I *am* going somewhere but only for a few days. Las Vegas for a big veterinary conference in early March. Dr. Berner asked me to go and represent the clinic because it's also his niece's wedding." While Trevor's first instinct had been to say no to the trip, he appreciated the trust Dr. Berner had placed in him. "I also might take Danny and my mom on vacation somewhere this summer, but we haven't planned anything yet. Mom mentioned she'd like to go to Old Orchard Beach in Maine. You remember my family went there almost every August when I was a kid?"

"I do. It all sounds nice." Laura's tense expression eased. "You brought me back a fridge magnet with a picture of a lobster from one of your trips to Maine. It's still on my fridge." She reached for her purse on the console between them.

"You kept it all these years?" Trevor stared at her.

"Sure I did. At the time, except for a few trips to Boston to see my mom's sisters and their families, I'd never been out of New Hampshire. I'd also never stayed in a hotel. For me, Old Orchard Beach was exotic. I tried not to show it, but I envied you. Unlike me, you had something interesting to write about for those 'what I did on my summer vacation' assignments teachers gave us." She pulled her winter hat farther down over her ears. "It's late. I should go inside, and you should get back to the Brennan house before the snow becomes any heavier." She unbuckled her seat belt and avoided Trevor's gaze.

Like not appreciating his family as much as he should have, Trevor had never truly appreciated those family vacations. It was as if he'd been wearing a blindfold, and Renée's death, these new feelings for Laura and his return to Strawberry Pond had all shown him what really mattered. "I'll walk you to your front door, but what about a good-night kiss first?"

Before, as friends, he'd likely have gone into the house with her and watched a movie. Or, just sat and talked about anything and everything. Now, however, without either of them saying so, things were different. Tonight was a date and it ended here in the car.

"I'd never say no to a good-night kiss from you." Laura gave him a teasing smile and leaned toward him.

Trevor met her halfway, and as their lips joined in a kiss that was slow and sweet, his heartbeat sped up. Laura's lips were soft and warm, and he breathed in her light floral scent mixed with a hint of chocolate from the cupcakes they'd had at the party.

And when he drew back, and stared into the depths of Laura's eyes, as familiar to him as his own, this time he knew for sure. She was the woman for him and she always would be.

"DON'T WORRY, MOM." Laura held her cell phone to one ear while mixing pancake batter with her free hand. "I'll see you later in the week instead of today. Why don't you come to my house for lunch?" With Star and Cooper sitting by her feet, she looked out the window of her cozy country kitchen. Snow had drifted across her laneway almost to the top of an old barrel that, in summer, held a pot filled with geraniums. "Sounds good." She nodded as her mom agreed to come to lunch. Progress. For one of the few times in recent memory, her mom was coming to see her here rather than the other way around. "No, the snow hasn't let up. I won't be going anywhere except to the barn to do chores." She'd been out earlier, and in several places had waded through snowbanks to her knees to check and feed the horses. "Okay, call me if you want to chat more, but remember, use your cell phone to reach your neighbor if you lose power and can't get the generator started."

After saying goodbye to her mom, Laura let out a long sigh. Star, who was more empathetic and closely attuned to Laura's emotions than Cooper, nudged Laura's leg with her chin. "It's okay, girl."

But was it? Her mom was lonely as well as isolated out on the farm, but she also didn't want Laura's brothers to fully take on the responsibility for it. So whenever Laura tried to casually mention it might be a good idea for her to start thinking about moving into a smaller house or apartment in town, her mom always said it was too soon to even consider such an idea.

As Laura spooned pancake batter into a pan and adjusted the heat on the stove, she turned what she'd come to think of as "the problem" over in her mind. She understood where her mom was coming from, but moving into town didn't mean giving up her independence. Or would it? Apart from her jobs away from the farm, agricultural life was all her mom knew. When Laura herself got older, she wouldn't want anyone suggesting she sell this house and move somewhere else, so maybe she shouldn't try to convince her mom to do what was essentially the same thing.

She flipped the pancakes over and went to the fridge for a pitcher of orange juice, then took a glass from a cabinet. She loved this house and surrounding land and couldn't imagine living anywhere else. Yet, for the first time here, despite the dogs, she also inexplicably felt alone and restless.

As she poured orange juice into the glass, her gaze drifted back to the fridge and that lobster-themed Maine magnet. Why had she told Trevor she'd kept it? It made her seem sentimental, which she definitely wasn't. Or was she? And why was she missing Trevor after just seeing him the night before?

She slid the pancakes onto a waiting plate and carried it and the juice across to the white-painted breakfast nook tucked into what was usually a sunny corner of her kitchen. "You two have already had your breakfast." She shook her head at Star and Cooper, whose matching pairs of limpid, puppy dog eyes made it clear they'd be happy to have more food if Laura was inclined to share.

She couldn't stop thinking about kissing Trevor good-night after last night's party.

The kiss had been more natural, and that sense of "rightness" between them had intensified, but Laura still couldn't figure out why it was only now she felt so much more for him than friendship.

As she ate her meal, followed by an orange from the fruit bowl, she eyed her planner and laptop on the small desk adjacent to the breakfast nook. She prided herself on being organized, analytical and pragmatic. Her farm and real estate business ran like clockwork, and she'd organized her volunteer work and time with family and friends the same way. Always knowing where she stood in her personal and professional lives gave her a sense of comfort and control.

However, when it came to Trevor and what was between them, this new uncertainty was unsettling. They'd gone on a "date" but they weren't "dating," no matter what he might think.

She'd always loved Trevor as a friend, but now was she truly falling *in love* with him? Since Trevor had mentioned that long-ago almost engagement, Jonny was on her mind as well. Laura had never doubted she'd made the right choice in not accepting his marriage proposal. Back then, she'd known she didn't love Jonny in the way she should to make a lifelong commitment. But had she ever let herself be truly open to romantic love?

The thoughts spun around in her brain, moving faster and faster but without any resolution. That confusion was also new, almost as if her life was split into two parts. On one side, her work would go on as it always had. But her personal life couldn't be so easily or neatly organized. She got up from her chair to toss the orange peel into the kitchen compost bin, but was drawn back to the window, and now, the rumble of a vehicle outside.

The snow had lessened, and the wind had dropped, so it was likely the man from the snow removal company she'd hired to keep her lane, parking area and path to the barn cleared in the winter months. About to turn away, she took a closer look. It was a plow all right, hitched to the front of a pickup truck, but it wasn't the familiar red truck and orange plow combination. This truck was green and the plow yellow.

As she watched, a tall figure in a parka and snow pants with a scarf almost covering their face got out of the truck, followed by a smaller one wearing similar clothing. They both waved at the pickup truck's driver, who turned in a neat circle and drove back along the freshly plowed lane to the road.

New Hampshire people were hardy, but who on earth would come visiting in such a big snowstorm? Followed by both dogs, Laura hurried to her front door as the bell chimed.

Cooper let out his signature braying bark, and Star joined in.

As she opened the door, Danny launched himself toward her, bringing a blast of cold, crisp air and shower of snow into her front hall. "Hey, Laura. Surprise!"

"Hang on, kid. You'll knock Laura over." Trevor followed his nephew, spoke over the cacophony of barking, shut the door and, as he unwound the scarf from his face, gave Laura an apologetic smile. "Given this wild weather, we wanted to make sure you're okay. I called your cell but it was busy. It was a spur-of-the-moment trip out here. The dad of Danny's friend Landon has a snow-clearing service so we hitched a ride with them." He bent to greet the dogs, who wound themselves around his legs.

"I was talking to my mom but it's fine. Welcome." Warmth curled around Laura's heart. She was usually the one who checked on people, but within a short time Trevor had twice made sure she was taken care of. First, when she was sick and now, even though she didn't need it, today. "And thanks. Come in. Do you want cocoa or…?"

"Later, but first do you want to make a snow fort?" Under his parka hood and beneath the black beanie hat she'd given him, Danny's gaze swung from Laura to Trevor and back again. "That's what mom and I used to do when I was little, and well, it's still kind of fun…" His voice trailed away.

"I haven't made a snow fort in years." Not even with her nieces and nephews, because with them she usually planned an activity. Today, she'd expected to do her usual Saturday cleaning, catch up on work and finish the book she was reading, but plans could change. "Sure, why not? A snow fort sounds fun."

"Great." Danny's wide-eyed smile made her feel like she'd given him the best gift ever.

"Yeah, it is, Laura. Really great." Trevor's grin was full of mischief.

When he wrapped one arm around her and,

mindful that Danny had turned away, gave her a quick kiss on the cheek, she was sure of what she was feeling for her friend. Instead of trying to control the uncertainty, maybe Laura should embrace it. And let herself, and her heart, be fully open to Trevor and Danny.

Not only the chaos the two of them brought with them. Her gaze drifted to Danny chasing Cooper around the hall. And Trevor, maneuvering Star into her pink parka.

But also the love.

Although it was new, scary and risked turning her ordered world upside down, the bumpy, roller-coaster journey could also be worth it.

CHAPTER THIRTEEN

SEVERAL HOURS, AND SEVERAL warm-up breaks inside Laura's place later, Trevor crawled into the hollow he, Laura and Danny had dug at the base of one of the big fir trees not far from the house. With snow piled on either side, it was a simple but effective shelter, and the tree's lowest branches made a roof over the top. "What do you think?" He held out a gloved hand to Laura, who slid in on her tummy behind him.

"Great job." After giving him a high five, she dropped Trevor's hand and shaped more snow into a ball. "And not as complicated as that igloo your dad helped us build in your backyard the winter we were in fifth grade. Remember how he made drawings on graph paper? He went all out." She laughed, and between her hat, parka hood and scarf, all Trevor could see was her eyes. They sparkled as if she was having as much fun as him and Danny.

"I learned more about geometry that winter than I ever did in school." Trevor laughed as well. "My dad should've been an architect. The dollhouse he made for Renée was a masterpiece." For the first time, a memory of his sister held more happiness than pain.

"I loved that dollhouse." Laura sat back on her heels and added a snow brick to a wall. "It might've been all those hours arranging and rearranging furniture in it that made me want to do something with houses for a living. What happened to it?"

"My guess is it's in my mom's basement. Neither she nor my sister would've gotten rid of it. Why?"

"If your mom would let me borrow it, that dollhouse would be great to use in some of my advertising. I'm not the only one who grew up in Strawberry Pond who'll have fond memories of it. Long after Renée outgrew it, your mom still let every kid in the neighborhood come play with it." She looked at the greenery above them. "I already use technology to give clients a three-dimensional dollhouse view of properties online, so it'd be fun to have an actual dollhouse in my office here at home."

"I bet my mom would be fine with the idea. She loves working with you." Like he'd suspected, helping Laura a few hours a week *had* given his mom a new interest and focus, both of which she needed. "It would also be a nice way of remembering Renée." Although Laura had never directly mentioned Trevor's grief for his sister, the time they spent together was getting him through it.

"And your dad." Laura scooted closer and touched Trevor's hand. "I'll give your mom a call later. One day, I'd like to have a real estate office in town, not only in my house, and I can already imagine that dollhouse sitting in the front window. Your mom and me could give the house a fresh coat of paint and even add a brass plaque with your dad's and Renée's names."

Typical Laura. If she wasn't doing something, she was planning it, but this time Trevor wouldn't tease her. It was a good idea and would mean memories of his dad and sister would live on. "That'd be wonderful." His voice caught and he cleared his throat.

"What are you guys doing in there?" Danny stuck his head over one side of the snow wall. "I made a dog like Cooper and Star. Come see." He lobbed a snowball at them.

"Unlike you, we needed a rest from all the shoveling." Laura caught the snowball and tossed it back to Danny. She crawled out of the shelter and brushed snow off the knees of her waterproof, insulated pants. "Wow." She looked over her shoulder at Trevor. "We were just talking about your dad's talent for design. I think Danny's inherited it."

"He sure has." Trevor's eyes widened as he took in what Danny had called a "dog," but was in reality a finely crafted snow sculpture, part animal and part bench. "That's fantastic."

"Try it out." Danny gestured to Laura to take a seat on the dog's back. "I packed the snow real hard. Don't you think it looks like Cooper and Star?" He gestured to the dogs, who, after a brief playtime in the fresh snow, were now happy to be cozy indoors and look out at them through the glass patio door in Laura's family room.

"It's fantastic." Laura's wide smile and raised eyebrows told Trevor she was as amazed as him by what Danny had created, let alone in such a short time. "I thought you didn't like art."

Danny shrugged. "I don't, not really, but building stuff's different."

Although his nephew might disagree, designing things required artistic talent. How could Trevor help Danny nurture it? Mindful of what his mom had said about not pushing Danny, and giving him space and time to open up, Trevor tried to make his voice casual. "Have you built other things?"

"Lots. It's fun with online drawing tools. I also designed and made Mom a jewelry box for her last birthday. I used scrap wood a neighbor gave me." Danny turned away to smooth part of the snow dog's nose. "If you want, I can show it to you later. It's in my room. In my chest of drawers."

"I'd love to see it." Trevor glanced at Laura over Danny's bent head. His nephew had finally opened up about something important. He didn't want to say or do anything that might spoil this precious moment.

"That sounds really special, Danny." Laura's smile was warm. "Your mom must've been thrilled."

"I guess." Danny still ran his hand back and forth across the snow sculpture. "She showed it to all her friends, which was kinda embarrassing but also kinda nice." The strip of his face visible between his scarf and hat revealed eyes bright but teary. "That firepit you've got over there. Could we build a fire and maybe roast marshmallows? If you're not too cold. My mom used to get colder than me."

"I *am* getting cold so that's really thoughtful." Laura scooted closer to Danny. "The wind's also picking up again and it feels like it's coming right from the North Pole. So why don't we go back inside and roast marshmallows there instead? I've got a big fireplace and we can make popcorn and cocoa as well. It'll be like camping indoors. We'll also be with Star and Cooper, who look like they're missing us." She gestured to the dogs, who were still staring at them through the patio doors. "What do you say?"

Trevor held his breath. Although he hadn't spotted it until now, whenever Danny asked him for something, if he was rushed or the place or timing didn't work, he'd automatically say no. Unlike Laura, who'd given Danny an alternative and made it sound like it wasn't a big deal.

"Sure, that'd be okay." Danny nodded. "You go into the house and get warmed up, and I'll put the snow shovels and other stuff back in the shed."

Trevor didn't let his mouth drop open, even though he wanted to. Danny rarely offered to help, and Trevor usually had to remind him to do his assigned chores. Now, it was like his nephew was a different kid.

"Thanks, Danny." Laura patted the boy's arm. "I know you aren't scheduled to work today, but if it wouldn't be too much trouble, I'd also appreciate you pitching in with barn chores later. With all the snow, my hands aren't able to come in."

"Like you even have to ask." Despite the eye roll and sarcastic tone, Danny's grin told Trevor he was joking. "Taking care of Tootsie and the others isn't work. It's fun."

"It is, usually." Laura laughed and gave Danny's

arm a final squeeze. "But it sure goes faster with more people doing the job."

"That's what my mom used to say." Danny nodded. "You ever need help with anything else, ask me. You don't need to pay me, either. Looking out for others is the Strawberry Pond way." He picked up the nearest shovel.

"Did your mom used to say that as well?" Trevor asked around a lump in his throat as Laura went to the house, leaving him alone with Danny.

Along with Laura, Trevor needed that "Strawberry Pond way." He hadn't been in the right place or time in his life to recognize it before, but now, he did. What was the point in always seeking out new and different adventures and experiences if you didn't have people you loved to share them with?

True happiness also came from things that were stable and solid. Before Renée's passing, Trevor had never given much thought to his own mortality. But now, he was all too aware life was short, and he needed to make the most of each and every moment. His gaze drifted to Laura's house. The two of them made a good team. Together, could they make a real home for Danny?

"Earth to Uncle Trevor?"

Danny's voice yanked Trevor back to the present. "Sorry, what is it?"

"You asked me about Mom? The Strawberry Pond way?"

"I did. Sorry. I'll take the other shovels and that bucket. Share the load to go back to Laura's shed so you don't have to make two trips." He gathered them up, aware he was babbling. "What about your mom?"

"Mom didn't say it was the Strawberry Pond way. Not exactly. She used to say it was the 'life way.' Do unto others and be kind. Grandma's the same."

"She is, and your mom…" Trevor swallowed more emotion. "Renée was a great big sister. She always looked out for me, even when I didn't think I needed her to." Now, it was up to Trevor to do the same for her son, while still giving Danny his own space to grow and be independent.

"Yeah, Mom was a great mom." At Trevor's side, Danny's voice hitched.

"She was." Trevor took a deep breath and, as they neared the shed door, he put a tentative hand on his nephew's shoulder. "I know I'm not your mom, and there's nobody who'll ever take her place, or your dad's, either, but I want to make sure you know I'm here for you. Whatever, whenever you need."

Since his sister's death, Trevor had read a couple of books about teens and grief. He'd talked to a counselor as well. But now, everything he'd learned went out of his head and all he could do was speak from his heart.

"Okay." Danny's voice was thick with tears. "I miss Mom, you know? Dad as well, even though I never even got to meet him."

"I know." Although how much Danny missed his parents, Renée especially, Trevor couldn't begin to fathom. "I miss your mom, too. And your dad. He was a fantastic guy and he loved your mom and you so much."

Trevor had been so busy with all the administrative work that came with a death, he hadn't really stopped to fully comprehend what losing Renée meant personally. But without his big sister, even though they hadn't seen each other often, his life was emptier. All those shared childhood memories were now his alone. Looking out for their mom was also now only on him.

Danny turned away, and as he wrenched open the shed door, a muffled sob erupted.

"Hey." Trevor followed him into the shed and put his hand on Danny's shoulder again. "It's okay to let it out. Whatever you're feeling." That's what one of those grief books had said, but, at the time Trevor had almost skipped over it, his feelings so raw he'd instead needed to put them away somewhere deep. Somewhere he wouldn't have to face them.

Then, whether Danny moved first or Trevor did, he didn't know, but all of a sudden, he held his nephew in his arms. And as Danny buried his face in Trevor's parka and cried, Trevor shed some tears of his own.

He still didn't have much of an idea of how to parent or be a family with Danny. However, after today, and with Laura's help, he'd made a start.

And that was enough.

"YOUR POSTER'S LOOKING GOOD, Danny. The animal print molds as well." Laura nodded at the teen. In Mrs. Kaminski's kitchen, still almost as familiar to Laura as her own, she measured chocolate cookie crumbs at the counter near the window. Today, after Danny had returned from school, Trevor's mom was teaching them to make the dirt pie they'd talked about at the diner after the pet-themed art show and bake sale. When his grandma left to take a call, Danny continued assembling his science fair project on the kitchen island.

"My science teacher said I'm the only kid in school who's finding and collecting animal tracks." Danny glanced at Trevor, who sat on a stool on the far side of the island catching up on paperwork but ready to pitch in if Danny needed him. "That book's kinda interesting, too." Danny gestured to a novel about a boy lost in the mountains, having to learn to survive until rescued. The worn copy was half-buried among the middle of the construction paper, glue sticks, cardboard and other materials he was using to make his project display. "I don't like reading much but that story's different."

As Danny glued information about New Hampshire animals and their tracks that he'd researched, written about and then printed out onto one of the green panels he'd made for a display board, Laura exchanged a small smile with Trevor. In the past while, Trevor and his nephew had seemed to come to a new and better understanding. When Trevor had dug out the old paperback that had belonged to his dad and told Danny he might enjoy it, the teen had agreed to give the book a try.

"That was Martha Ryan on the phone." Mrs. Kaminski returned to the kitchen and washed her hands at the sink. "She was telling me about a special team-building event with folks Heath works with in Boston. As part of it, his company's made a five-hundred-dollar donation to Save the Animal Rescue."

"That's fantastic." What felt like the ever-present calculator app in Laura's head mentally totted up how much that donation would add to their existing funds and how much further they still had to go. March would be here before she knew it, and the rescue's building lease would be up in the middle of the month. Could they match the funds in time? Whenever Laura thought about it, she got a sick feeling in the pit of her stomach. "Heath's such a big help." On a voluntary basis, Josie's new husband had advised the rescue on their financial reporting, and was also overseeing the current fundraising project to make sure they did everything needed to meet regulatory and other requirements.

"He sure is." Mrs. Kaminski opened a bag of gummy worm candy. "Martha also said that like you asked, Tom's getting the word out about the rescue in those farming videos he's recording for social media. Every bit supports the cause."

"It does." Those videos which Josie's gramps had recently become involved with alongside two of Laura's cousins, reached a big audience far beyond Strawberry Pond.

"Some of my mom's friends in Manchester and the company she worked for are sponsoring me in the walk-a-thon." Danny looked up from gluing a picture of a snowshoe hare to the display board. "A bunch of Uncle Trevor's friends in California also signed up to support me. They've never even met me."

But they knew Trevor, and he'd always made friends easily. Laura's gaze drifted over to him again. While building that snow fort had been good for him and Danny, it'd been good for her as well. Since then, she'd continue to let herself imagine what it would be like if the three of them were a family. Her gaze caught Trevor's and held. That softness in his blue eyes, and the way his mouth tilted into a smile... For an instant, Danny, Mrs. Kaminski and the kitchen disappeared and it was as if the two of them were alone.

Laura drew in a shaky breath. She cared about Trevor. Of course, she did. And she'd always loved him as a friend, but once again she was reminded of how the feelings coursing through her were so much different. Was this really what true and lasting romantic love felt like? It wasn't as if she could ask anyone. Certainly not her mom or sisters. After years of insisting she didn't need a man in her life, they likely wouldn't believe her. Despite their close friendship, she couldn't even talk to Josie and Alana. She was the oldest of their trio and the one who always seemed to have her life together. At her age, it'd be embarrassing to admit she was struggling trying to figure out something so basic. Something most people experienced in high school or soon thereafter. She was on her own, like she always was, but now, that independence wasn't reassuring. No, it was, dare she even think it, uncomfortable.

"Laura, dear?" Mrs. Kaminski's voice interrupted her thoughts. "Put that base mixture in the fridge to chill. Then I'll show you and Danny how to make the filling."

"Sure." She picked up the pan and went across the kitchen to the fridge.

"Okay, Grandma." Danny joined his grandmother, chattering about his project and the various animal tracks he'd identified in both the snow and tracking boxes. He'd left the latter—trays with sand—in the backyard at the Brennan house as well as at Laura's place and Alana's and Josie's family farms.

While Mrs. Kaminski and Danny got more ingredients and baking materials organized, Laura pulled out another stool from the kitchen island and sat next to Trevor.

"Danny's having fun, isn't he?" In Laura's ear, Trevor's voice was low, and his warm breath feathered her cheek and hair.

"He is." Her voice caught. "It's good." Family, community and Danny's own inner resilience would help him heal from Renée's death. And while he'd never forget his mom, he'd find a way to move on in his life, like Laura had when she'd lost her dad.

"It's neat to see him reading that book of my dad's. I remember Dad sharing it with me when I was about Danny's age. Back then, I enjoyed it for the main character having adventures and surviving in the mountains. But now, I see it more as a story of personal growth and coming of age. It also nurtured my love of the outdoors and nature." Now Trevor's voice held a new, almost bittersweet note. "I always thought I'd pass it on to a kid of my own one day. A son or daughter. It wasn't Renée's cup of tea. She preferred historical romances and the classics. That's why I don't think she ever read it."

"Uncle Trevor. Laura. Come see." Danny waved them over.

Laura made herself get up from the stool to go and look at what Danny wanted to show them, forcing herself to smile as if nothing was wrong.

A kid of my own one day. A son or daughter. Trevor's words reverberated in her head. He'd never talked about having kids so she'd assumed he felt the same as her and was happily childless.

But what if he still wanted a child or children? She couldn't deprive him of having a family of his own. Not one cobbled together from awkward pieces like the two of them and Danny might make. What if Trevor found a woman who not only wanted children of her own, but could also take Danny under her maternal wing?

A woman who was everything Laura wasn't. Her stomach lurched. A woman who could likely give Danny *and* Trevor everything they both wanted and needed. Not just now, but always.

CHAPTER FOURTEEN

THE NEXT DAY, after his shift at the vet clinic, Trevor sat on the sofa in the family room at the Brennan house and scanned the email with the property listings Laura had sent him. He couldn't procrastinate any longer. His rental agreement only ran until early June so on the cusp of March he had to start looking for a more permanent place to live. While he and Danny could stay with Trevor's mom while waiting for a house sale to close, which might take several months, or Trevor could even look for another rental, this time longer-term, he wanted to minimize what would be another upheaval in Danny's life.

It had been Laura who'd pushed the house issue, drawing Trevor aside yesterday at his mom's to ask if he'd given any thought to buying a place in Strawberry Pond. If so, she'd be happy to show him listings. She'd sounded so matter-of-fact, and assured him she often assisted family and friends in buying and selling property. While any awkwardness Trevor had felt about working with her had become a non-issue, he now had a much bigger problem.

He scrubbed a hand through his hair as he clicked on the links in Laura's list. Knowing her as well as he did, it was too soon to tell her the only house he wanted was with her. One where they'd live as a married couple with Danny.

However, Laura loved her home and life at Sugarbush Knoll Stables. It was her childhood dream come true. Now, having visited the place, Trevor could see why it was so special. From the barn and paddocks for horses, surrounding woodland with old maple trees, to the traditional New Hampshire farmhouse, sensitively updated for the modern world, it was perfect. He couldn't ask her to uproot herself, but would she be comfortable with Trevor and Danny one day living there as well?

So what was he going to do? He couldn't waste Laura's time looking at what would likely be perfectly suitable houses if he wasn't serious about making an offer on one of them. He also had to figure out what to do with his house in California. Although he'd enough saved to make a down payment on a house here, if he sold his place in San Diego he might not even need a mortgage. It had gone up a lot in value since he'd bought it, and property in Strawberry Pond wasn't as expensive. But if things didn't work out with Laura, would he want to stay here? Would his mom want to move to California or somewhere else with him? Trevor wouldn't leave her alone. No matter what, she and Danny needed to be part of any such decision.

Round and round the thoughts went, and instead of getting any clarity, he was even more confused.

In the front hall, Miss Sarah's landline rang and, as Trevor got up to answer it, Danny's footsteps thundered down the main staircase.

"Uncle Trevor? The phone." Danny's voice came from the hall, followed by the sound of him going into the kitchen and opening the fridge and cupboard doors.

"Coming." Renée hadn't had a landline, so Danny wasn't used to answering one. He picked up the receiver. "Hello… Oh, Miss Sarah. Sorry, Mrs. Fournier." He corrected himself.

"It's fine. You can still call me Miss Sarah or even Sarah. You've long been grown up." In the background, Trevor heard barking. "Quiet, Buttons. That cat's a friend. I'm so glad I caught you, Trevor."

"I'm always available if you need me. Like I said, feel free to call my cell." Although Miss Sarah had a cell phone and often texted Trevor, for long-distance calls she seemed to prefer using a landline. "What's up? How's Florida?"

He looked around the hall. Danny's parka was on the floor outside the closet, and his winter boots and several pairs of sneakers were scattered between the front door and the stairs rather than on the boot tray or shoe rack.

The disarray was yet another reminder that Miss Sarah's house, usually in what Trevor's mom and other women of Strawberry Pond called "apple pie order," was now what might politely be described as "lived in."

"Florida's lovely and warm. A balmy seventy-five degrees today. Jack and I just came back from golfing and are going out for dinner at a place with a patio overlooking the ocean. It's a wonderful extended honeymoon. No, Buttons. That cheese isn't for you, sweetie." Miss Sarah laughed and there was a rustling noise as if she was moving a plate.

Although Trevor had never met Buttons, everything he'd heard around town about the dog being a lovable mischief maker was evidently correct.

"You probably don't want to know how much colder it is here." Trevor nodded at Danny, who poked his head around the kitchen door, waved a loaf of bread and mouthed he wanted a snack. "There's also lots of snow." Miss Sarah undoubtedly hadn't called to chat about the weather, but in New Hampshire, like other places, people sure liked to talk about it.

"I miss home, but it's important to Jack and me to visit his extended family in Michigan before we come to Strawberry Pond for the summer. In any case… Buttons, come here, precious. Sit here on my lap." Trevor smiled into the phone. Miss Sarah's love for her pet was sweet. "Sorry, Trevor. If it isn't too much trouble, could you arrange to ship that painting you got out of the attic for the art show to me? And is everything still okay in the house?"

"Everything's fine." At least in terms of the house's structure. For the rest, he could hire a cleaner so it would be spick-and-span when Miss Sarah returned. "Sure, I can ship you the painting no problem. The one with the sheep and sheepdog, right?" He'd put it back in the attic with the other things Miss Sarah had stored there before shutting up the house. Although neither he nor Danny wanted to look at it, if it was special to Miss Sarah he'd make sure the artwork got to her safely.

"Yes, that one. I'll reimburse you for the shipping cost, of course, but it's such a comfort having you living in the house to keep an eye on things. Now that I think of it, perhaps you could ship my extra pair of golf shoes along with the painting? They're in a box on the shelf in the front hall closet."

"That's fine." Having left his cell in the family room, Trevor made a note of both items using the pen and paper on Miss Sarah's vintage telephone table.

"You always were such a dear boy, and it's wonderful you're back in Strawberry Pond. Like me and so many of us, your mother isn't getting any younger." Miss Sarah paused, although this time it wasn't to say anything to Buttons. "I hear Laura and the team are pulling out all the stops for 'Save the Animal Rescue' fundraising. Not long to go, is there? I've been reading all about it in *The Strawberry Pond Gazette*'s online edition." Her voice brightened.

"No, not long." Trevor already knew he needed to be there for his mom. He should have been there for her before now. The familiar guilt knotted his stomach. "Pretty much everyone in town's involved in fundraising activities of one kind or another."

From the kitchen, the refrigerator's door opened and closed once more, and Trevor added grocery shopping to his mental to-do list. Was Danny unique, or had he forgotten how much teenage boys ate?

"That's wonderful." Miss Sarah paused again. "Laura's a marvel. Right from a little thing she had such drive and determination, although sometimes I wonder…well, it's good to be busy, isn't it?"

"It can be." What had Miss Sarah wondered? Was Laura *too* busy? If so, why? And what might her full schedule mean for their possible relationship in the long term?

"I mustn't keep you. Like Laura, you have a busy life." Buttons barked again and Miss Sarah made soothing noises. "Do give my best to everyone, and tell Danny he can count on me to sponsor him in the walk-a-thon."

"That's really nice, but how did you know he was taking part?" As far as Trevor knew, a list of walk-a-thon participants hadn't been published in *The Strawberry Pond Gazette* or anywhere else online.

"Oh, Anne Sullivan, Fred Sinclair and others keep me updated on all the local news. Anne said Danny's settling in well." Miss Sarah's chuckle was almost girlish. "Small-town life, you know."

"Right." If Trevor didn't have so many other things on his mind, Laura especially, he'd have realized the town was interested in everything to do with his life, Danny included.

And as he said goodbye to Miss Sarah, he couldn't shake a persistent niggle of unease. Despite his new feelings for Laura, could he really live the rest of his life in a place where everyone knew everyone else's business? Miss Sarah knowing Danny was taking part in a walk-a-thon wasn't a big deal, but it nevertheless reminded Trevor of what he'd almost forgotten.

People here talked about their neighbors. While it was good to live in a close-knit and caring community, it could also be like living under a microscope. That was one of the reasons he'd left Strawberry Pond all those years ago and, until Renée's death, hadn't wanted to come back for anything except brief vacations.

"THE HEATING AND cooling systems were only replaced last year so they're still under warranty." Laura led the prospective buyers back through the family room into the spacious kitchen. She'd had a lunch get-together with Josie and Alana, replacing their usual Saturday breakfast, and now in the early afternoon she was back at work. "The owner also redid this kitchen eighteen months ago. As you can see, it offers ample space and convenience for both family meals and casual entertaining." She paused to let the couple admire the state-of-the-art appliances, counter space and large kitchen island with storage and a breakfast bar.

On paper, this house, a generous two-story on a large lot in Strawberry Haven, a newer subdivision on the outskirts of Strawberry Pond, was everything her clients, Becca and Evan, had told her they were looking for. However, Laura was an experienced enough Realtor to know that it wasn't only the amenities a property offered, but also how it felt. Did a house convey a sense of warmth, and could the buyer imagine themselves not just living there but, more importantly, did they feel like they belonged?

That feeling of belonging couldn't be measured in dollars and cents, but in all Laura's years of showing houses, it often helped close a sale.

With family roots going back generations, Laura had always belonged in Strawberry Pond and buying her farm had only strengthened her ties to the place. Although Trevor had a similar history here, even as a kid he'd dreamed of traveling the world. He'd borrowed travel books and magazines from the library and researched places he wanted to visit. He was also the first person Laura knew to get a passport, saying he had to be prepared. Prepared for what, she'd wondered? It wasn't as if at twelve either of them would be hopping on a plane to India, Paris or any of the other places he talked about. However, he'd saved his money, applied and the day that passport had arrived, Trevor's excitement rivalled Christmas or his birthday.

He still likely wanted to travel, but she was a homebody. Would that be another obstacle to any long-term relationship between them?

"So what do you think?" She made herself focus and turned back to Becca, a nurse at the local hospital who'd been several years ahead of Laura in school. Her curly brown hair was pulled up with a clip, and behind square-framed glasses, she squinted while fidgeting with her phone.

"It's a nice house, but..." Becca paused. "We'll have to think about it." As her husband took another look at the utility room, she rubbed one hand along the elegant white granite kitchen countertop. "Our kids are used to walking to school. Out here, they'd have to take a bus. Since it's on this side of Strawberry Pond, Evan would have a longer commute to the office. Only by about twenty minutes, but still..." Her voice trailed off.

Laura made her expression neutral. "But what about *you*?" The Becca she remembered from high school was popular and an honor student who served as president of both the student council and debating club. A natural leader, she was someone whom Laura had once wanted to emulate. "A house has to suit you as much as anyone else."

"Yes, but I also want my family to be happy."

Becca smiled and patted the gleaming countertop. “If it was only up to me, I’d move in here tomorrow for that dreamy spa-inspired bathroom in the primary suite alone, but family’s about compromise. I’m still my own person and so’s Evan, but it’s not only about me or him. It’s also us. Equal partners. Our children are part of that ‘us’ as well.”

“Of course.” Laura nodded. Becca was happy, and Evan, whom Laura also knew from school, was a great guy with a good job as an accountant in a town half an hour away. She shouldn’t be projecting her own fears and life experience onto someone else. However, as a child and teen, she’d always had to put her family first, usually at the expense of her own needs.

“How old are your kids now?” She often saw Becca and her family around town, but except in passing, Laura hadn’t said more than a few words to her since school.

“Seven, eight and ten.” Becca’s smile widened. “Two boys and a girl. They sure keep us busy, but we wouldn’t have it any other way. Each one’s a blessing. Sometimes, I wish I could keep them small for longer, but they’re growing up. That’s the main reason we need a bigger house. We outgrew our current home a few years ago, but it’s hard to think about living anywhere else. We have so many memories there, and it's where I brought my babies home from the hospital."

"Well, if this house doesn't work, I have several more for you to see." Laura's stomach knotted. Had she been so focused on one way of thinking, that having a family would mean losing her freedom, she'd never considered balancing independence with togetherness?

"Take some time to think about this property and, if you'd like to look at it again, let me know." She took her tote bag from the kitchen island and gave Becca the full property-information package she'd prepared earlier. "In the meantime, we're looking at those other houses tomorrow, aren't we?" She checked her phone and swiped to the calendar.

"Yes. You can't know how much I appreciate having you steering us through this whole process." Becca raised her hands and dropped them by her side again. "Looking at houses is already overwhelming, and we haven't even made an offer yet."

"That's what I'm here for. A guide and, I hope, a friend." She'd likely still get to know her real estate clients in a city, but here in Strawberry Pond she valued the close personal relationships she had with them. Relationships that, in some cases, spanned multiple homes across several generations.

"Hey, Becca." Evan returned from the utility room. "There's a bunch of teens playing road hockey out there. Can't you see our kids doing the same in a few years? And basketball in the summer. The driveway's sure wide enough to shoot some hoops."

Laura turned to look out the kitchen window where Evan had gestured. "Strawberry Haven's a great neighborhood. Family-friendly, but there's also people of different ages and life stages with lots of community connection and neighborliness. They even have block parties, like for the Fourth of July and—"

She stopped and moved closer to the window. Was that Danny out there? If so, shouldn't he be at school? It was only one-thirty on a Tuesday afternoon, and she'd fit this house showing around Becca's and Evan's work schedules.

"Laura?" Becca touched her arm.

"Sorry." She never got distracted during a showing, but that was Danny's parka, she was almost sure of it. "As I was saying, there's a really strong neighborhood feel here. People look out for each other." In that sense, despite having newer homes, this subdivision wasn't any different from the rest of Strawberry Pond. Laura turned back to her clients. "Unless you have any other questions, I'll see you again tomorrow." After locking up, she'd also wander over to that road hockey game. If it was indeed Danny, did Trevor know his nephew was here?

After saying goodbye to Becca and Evan at the front door, Laura did a final check of the house and then grabbed her tote bag, purse and coat before slipping into her boots. Would this house suit Trevor and Danny? It would likely be too big for only the two of them and, unlike the Brennan house, which was also too big, it was farther from the center of Strawberry Pond.

She eyed her phone. If she called Trevor's mom to check in, she could ask about Danny's whereabouts. Trevor had texted this morning to say he was working at Dr. Berner's clinic in Conway and wouldn't be back until early evening. On days they couldn't see each other, they'd gotten into a habit of morning and evening texts, followed by a good-night phone call. Almost without Laura noticing, she'd begun to count on those small connections and the closeness and caring they brought.

Still in the front hall, she scrolled to Mrs. Kaminski's number. Although Trevor's mom was only working for her half days, three days a week, Laura already wondered what she'd ever done without her. From organizing paperwork to arranging appointments and aiding Laura with market research, Mrs. Kaminski was much more than another pair of hands. She was becoming a trusted and reliable partner.

"Hi, Mrs. Kaminski," she greeted the other woman. "I've finished with Becca and Evan here in Strawberry Haven. Has anything else come up?"

"No, but I'd have messaged you if it had." Her voice was both warm and chiding. "How many times have I asked you to call me Cheryl?"

Too many for Laura to count. "Sorry. Old habit. Cheryl." It would likely get easier to use Trevor's mom's first name as time went on. However, from when she'd first met her as a kindergarten snack volunteer to a few weeks ago, Cheryl, like the other parents of Laura's childhood friends, had always been an adult authority figure, not a peer.

"Good. You're my boss now." Cheryl's laugh felt like a hug.

"Never. We're colleagues and I appreciate everything you're doing." Laura peered out the glass on one side of the door. Yes, it was definitely Danny out there. "I'm calling because I wondered if you knew where Danny is."

"He's at school. Why wouldn't he be there?" Cheryl's tone was puzzled. "He's coming to me after school for dinner and homework since Trevor's in Conway. Is there a problem?"

"I'm sure everything's fine. I must be confused. I thought today might be a professional development day for the teachers." Laura didn't want to worry Cheryl for no reason. Trevor's mom had a heart problem, and although it was well-managed with medication, she was supposed to avoid stress.

"No, the kids are in school today. Trevor also would've said if Danny was coming home early."

"Okay, no problem." Laura exited, locked up and returned the key to the lockbox. "I'll be on my cell if you need anything."

"Sure, honey. Drive safe. I heard the roads outside town are slippery."

As Laura ended the call, she tucked her phone into her coat pocket and made her way toward the hockey game. "Danny?"

"Laura?" He swiveled. "What're you doing here?"

"I could ask you the same question." She crossed her arms in front of her chest.

"Hey, DJ. You still playing?" One of the boys gestured to Danny.

Was that Isaac? He was the other kid Danny had been with the day of the art fair. It wasn't Landon. Laura would've recognized him because he'd been at the Brennan house with Danny one day when she'd dropped by.

"I can explain." Danny, or maybe he preferred DJ, shifted from one foot to the other.

"Why don't you explain in my car while I either take you back to school or to your grandma's?" Laura held the boy's gaze, willing him to do the right thing.

"I guess." He scuffed his boots in the snow. "I gotta go, guys." He waved to his friends, who'd already resumed their game. He dropped what must be a borrowed hockey stick by the side of the road and followed Laura to her SUV.

"Right, why don't you start at the beginning and tell me what happened." Laura got into the vehicle as Danny joined her in the passenger seat.

"It's not what you think. I wasn't skipping school, honest." Despite his flushed face and ears, Danny met her gaze.

"How do you know what I'm thinking?" Laura started the car. Danny was safe, which was the most important thing. Laura was thinking less about him, and more how she'd been here too many times with her brothers and sisters. She wasn't responsible for Danny, not really. In this situation, any caring adult would've done the same as her. It was part of looking out for others, that Strawberry Pond "way" again.

"I don't but you're probably mad." Danny tucked his head into his chest. "I don't even like hockey. Not really, but it sounded fun, and well…we were let out of school early because the heating stopped working. I know I should've called or texted Grandma to tell her where I was going, but Isaac and the rest of the guys… I didn't want to look like a little kid."

"I'm not mad. I was looking out for you because you weren't where I thought you should be." Laura's heart squeezed. How she felt about Danny was different than what she'd felt for her siblings as a kid. Then, she'd resented the responsibility, but Danny had worked his way into her heart. In some ways, he was also caught up in her new feelings for Trevor.

Independence and togetherness.

Becca's words now took on new meaning. Laura's house was her home, but that day Trevor and Danny had been there, it was like they belonged. On the one hand, maybe she was getting too involved in their lives. But it also felt right and not the burden she'd expected.

Family's a compromise. Us.

Becca had made it sound easy, but it wasn't. Now, Laura was on her way to maybe becoming an "us" with Trevor, but it was only the start of what, looking at Becca and Evan, could be a happy forever. Was she brave enough to take that risk? And what would she also risk losing if she didn't?

CHAPTER FIFTEEN

"GO, DANNY." A FEW days later, at the edge of the walking track in Strawberry Pond's arena complex, Trevor clapped as his nephew rounded the corner with Landon and several other kids. They were all taking part in the combined elementary and middle school's walk-a-thon to support the animal rescue.

"Did you get the mix-up with contact emails and phone numbers sorted out with the school?" At Trevor's side, Laura clapped and cheered with the rest of the crowd. Wearing leggings, a long-sleeved green T-shirt and a ball cap, with her hair in a ponytail, she looked happy, and a lot like the teenage girl he remembered.

"I did, so next time there's any unexpected early dismissal both Mom and me will get text messages, calls and emails." Trevor shook his head. "But why, since Danny knew I'd be in surgery, didn't he call my mom? And why did he think it was okay to go home with Isaac without telling anyone?"

"The still undeveloped teenage brain. All he could think of was not wanting to look bad in front of his friends." Laura touched Trevor's arm, the brief gesture of consolation reminding Trevor that she had his back. "We didn't always make the right choices when we were his age. The most important thing is he learned from the experience." She chuckled. "If he forgets, those extra chores you gave him will be a good incentive to think things through next time."

"But still, if you hadn't been there, how would Danny have gotten home? Isaac's parents were at work and those other kids all live in Strawberry Haven, too." Trevor fiddled with his key fob. He'd always been a spur-of-the-moment kind of guy so, at Danny's age, he'd have rejoiced in an afternoon off school and, like Danny, might even have hopped onto a friend's bus without a second thought. But as an adult, he had to be the responsible one.

"It all turned out okay." Laura leaned into Trevor's side. "If it'd been Isaac's usual bus driver, Danny would've been caught and questions asked much earlier, but since it was a new, temporary driver, Danny had some unexpected fun. He sure looked guilty when he saw me."

"I bet he did." Trevor had to laugh. He'd known it would be a big challenge taking on guardianship of his nephew, but it was the smaller, day-to-day things that caught him off guard and made him doubt himself. "This… everything…" He gestured to the group of parents cheering for their kids, many, like Trevor, having taken time off work to be there. "It's all new to me."

"You're doing great." Laura's voice was reassuring. "I've heard my mom say it takes a lifetime to learn how to be a parent. You hardly had time to get used to the idea before being thrown in at the deep end. As long as Danny's fed, clothed and makes it to school most days, I'd count that as a win."

Some of the habitual tightness in Trevor's shoulders eased. "He is and does, if you count several bowls of cereal with toast and honey for supper last night as being fed."

"Danny doesn't look as if he's malnourished." Laura pointed to the boy as he rounded the curve of the track again.

"No. He eats all the time. He'd had a snack earlier and emptied the fridge without telling me in time to go grocery shopping."

"So? Eating cereal and toast was a consequence." Laura's laugh rang out. "Not many laps left to go, DJ!"

"I can't get my head around calling him DJ." After so many changes in quick succession, Trevor needed at least one thing in his life, in this case his nephew's name, to stay the same. And while dating Laura was great, it was something else that meant in the past few months it felt like the entire world had shifted beneath his feet.

"I bet he'd be okay with you still calling him Danny at home." Laura squeezed Trevor's hand. "He's growing up, though, and maybe choosing to go by his initials is a way for him to express who he is."

"But *Danny's* what Renée called him." For Trevor, Danny going by "DJ" felt like another break with his sister.

"I know but it doesn't mean Danny's forgotten his mom. Besides, having a *J* in his nickname honors your dad."

"I never thought of it that way." Trevor's dad's name was James, and Renée had given it to Danny for his middle name. "I guess it's kind of nice." He looped an arm around Laura's shoulders. "How come you're so wise?"

"Lots of experience with my siblings." Laura's happy expression dimmed. "But I'm also not responsible for Danny." Her smile was forced. "He doesn't need me like he needs you."

Trevor would never see his responsibility for Danny as a burden. It was more of a sacred trust, and he'd vowed to do his best for his sister's son. Still, nothing had prepared him for becoming a de facto parent to a thirteen-year-old, and he'd be lying if he said he didn't often miss the freedom of his old life.

"I'm not going back to the clinic after the walk-a-thon so I thought I'd take Danny out for a meal. You want to join us?"

"Sure, but I have a house showing later at six thirty." Laura picked up her coat and shrugged into it. "Which reminds me, I need to get back to my office. Spring's coming, and the real estate market's picking up. I have to convince a woman whose house I'm about to list that while she treasures her porcelain bell collection, she needs to pack them away so potential buyers can actually see her living and dining room walls." She waved at several people Trevor didn't recognize. "Shall I meet you at the diner at five? Why don't you invite your mom to come along?" Laura dug in her bag for her hat and mittens and collected her coat from a nearby chair.

"I guess." With Danny also there, it wasn't like this meal would be a date, and Trevor's mom would welcome the company. Still, although he couldn't put his finger on it, Laura was all of a sudden more distant than usual. "I'll see you later then." As she moved into the crowd, Trevor turned away to watch the walk-a-thon participants again. Oh, hey, Alana." Laura's friend appeared at his elbow. She'd set up a table at the event to promote the library's programs for kids and families. "How's it going?"

"Fine, but I need a hand." She glanced around. "Would you mind sitting behind the library table while I run out to my car and get more rhyme time leaflets? It'll only take me five minutes, maximum. I'm parked right near the door. I don't want to leave the table because I've got a 'Save the Animal Rescue' donation box." She indicated one of the red, white and blue boxes covered in animal paw prints that were a familiar sight around town. "I don't think anybody'd take it but better safe than sorry."

"Sure." Trevor could still see Danny from the library table, and the walk-a-thon was almost over, anyway.

"You're a lifesaver." Alana let out a relieved sigh and smiled. "We're short-staffed so I'm running around everywhere today."

"No problem." He returned her smile. "Are the leaflets in a box? If so, I can go out to your car and get it so you can stay here."

"That'd be great." Alana's eyes twinkled. "I'm stronger than I look, but you're a good guy, Trevor. Laura's lucky." She patted his arm, then dug in her jacket pocket for her key fob.

"Thanks, but I'm the lucky one." And he continued to regret not realizing how right Laura was for him years ago.

He grabbed his parka and, after Alana described the color, make and model of her car and which side of the arena's entrance she'd parked on, Trevor scanned the crowd. If Laura hadn't left yet, he could walk outside with her. There she was, by the door, talking to one of his mom's neighbors.

As he made his way toward the exit, he waved to get her attention. Her gaze caught his for a second and then, with a brief wave in return, she was gone.

What was that about? Had she misunderstood and thought he was waving goodbye instead of asking her to wait? He reached the door and stepped out. Although Alana's car was right where she'd said it would be, Laura was nowhere in sight.

Despite the warmth of his insulated coat, Trevor shivered. Although it was almost March, that wind was an arctic blast. Yet, as he reached Alana's car and opened it to retrieve the box of leaflets, the chill was more inside him and went beyond the wintry weather.

Before Laura turned away, her face had crumpled and her chin jutted out in the way it did when she was upset. He'd assumed everything was good between them, but maybe he was wrong. And maybe he didn't know her as well as he thought he did.

LAURA REATTACHED ONE end of the pink-and-white It's a Girl banner over the fireplace in her mom's living room and took a step back to make sure it hung straight. The baby shower she'd organized for her sister, Courtney, was in full swing. And with pretty much every female member of her family who lived in a twenty-mile radius of Strawberry Pond here to celebrate, the noise level was deafening.

"Thanks again for a great party." Courtney looped one arm around Laura's shoulders. "I don't say it enough, but you're the best. After we lost Dad, you sure stepped up for Mom and all of us. You've always been like a second mother. We all, even the boys, say the same."

"Sure." Laura manufactured a smile. She loved her sisters and brothers, and growing up, she'd felt responsible for them. She'd also wanted to help her mom but that meant she'd sacrificed herself.

"I mean it." Courtney held Laura close, and her golden-brown eyes were serious. "It's only when I became a mom myself that I realized how much you gave up for us. There'll be an age gap between this new baby and my other three and it's gotten me thinking about you even more."

"How so?" As the party continued on around them, Laura stiffened.

"You went through a lot and you were only a

kid yourself. I look at my oldest and there's no way I can imagine him taking on what you did at about the same age." Courtney twirled a loose strand of light-brown hair around one finger. "Maybe…well, I guess we took you for granted."

They had, but they were just kids back then. And she'd felt such a keen sense of duty and loyalty. Except for waiting to be old enough to leave home and live her own life, Laura hadn't seen any way out. She'd lost sight of her own needs in order to support her mom and try to keep their family stable, but the cost had been high. In retrospect, she'd been exhausted, emotionally and practically, and hadn't really grieved her dad's death until years later.

"I'm sorry." Courtney continued. "I know it's too little, too late but I mean it, Lulu."

"Thanks, but it was a long time ago. You were four when Dad passed. Still almost a baby." Laura pushed away the wave of emotion that threatened to engulf her. "Now go sit down. You're the guest of honor."

"I will, but you can take a break from being a mother hen. I'm all grown up and a mom myself." With a warm smile, Courtney rejoined the others, one of Laura's sisters-in-law making a space for her on the sectional sofa at the far end of the room.

"I knew your family was big, but seeing so

many of them together in one place is something else." Josie picked up several scattered pink gift bags. "Put these with the rest in the den?"

"Yes, please." Laura pressed a hand to her head. In a big group her family could be overpowering, and what Courtney had said pricked at her. "I'll come with you." She collected several stray boxes from an end table. After three boys, her sister was having a girl, so this baby, due in a month, was being celebrated with even more exuberance than usual. "Alana's in her element, isn't she?" Laura nodded to their friend, who was leading a "change the baby's diaper blindfolded" game involving much laughter and dropping of dolls and diapers.

"She is. Alana loves kids." Josie's smile was fond. "It's a shame she doesn't have any of her own yet, but it's not too late. She only has to meet the right man."

Laura suppressed a sigh. Josie's newlywed bliss was wonderful, even more so because her friend's life hadn't been without hardship. However, Josie was optimistic by nature whereas Laura had always considered herself more of a realist.

"I heard that huff." Josie followed Laura into the small den, used as a farm office with a desk, filing cabinet, several chairs and small sofa, and closed the door behind them. "What's wrong?"

"Nothing." Laura set the boxes aside and restacked a set of pink-and-white blankets on a beribboned bassinet topped with one of Josie's grandmother's beautiful handmade baby quilts. "Courtney's gotten some lovely gifts. I suppose after three children, even if they'd been girls, lots of things would've been worn-out."

"Yes, but this baby's also somewhat of an afterthought, isn't it?" Josie patted the quilt embroidered with a bedtime prayer Laura remembered from her own childhood. "As Courtney said earlier, after almost five years, she and Josh thought they were done having kids, but oopsie." Josie's ready laugh rang out. "Don't try to change the subject. Something's bothering you. Is it this party and all the talk about babies?"

"I never wanted kids so it's not the shower. Honest. I'm happy being an aunt and dog mom and having my horse farm." Which was true, but now when she thought about the rest of her life, Laura wanted something else as well.

"But?" Josie sat on the sofa and patted the space beside her.

"But nothing. It's middle age creeping up on me, I guess." She forced a smile. Even if she could talk to Josie about Trevor, it wasn't the right time or place.

However, since seeing Trevor and Alana talking at the walk-a-thon, another worry had sprung up, as persistent as dandelions in springtime. Alana *would* make a great mom, and if Trevor got together with someone like her, he could have kids of his own while also making a family for Danny. As Laura sat on the sofa, her knees cracked. They'd cracked like that since her twenties, but now, it somehow sounded more ominous.

"Middle age?" Josie shook her head and scoffed. "Forty's the new thirty, don't you know? That's the attitude I'm taking."

"Sure, but unlike me, you're not actually forty."

"I expect that bad flu set you back and you're more tired than usual." Josie clicked her tongue against her teeth. "It sure did my girls when they had it. What do you think about taking a day off and pampering yourself. You could go to—"

The den door swung open and Alana stuck her head in. "There you two are. Oh…" She faltered. "I didn't mean to interrupt."

"You aren't." Laura stood. "I should gather up the remaining punch glasses and run the dishwasher. I meant to do that before we started serving tea, coffee and cake."

"No, what you should do is join the actual party." Alana came into the den and glanced between Laura and Josie, and then back to Laura.

"We're playing Pin the Pacifier on the Baby. You know, replacing the donkey and tail with a baby and pacifier. You've been so busy behind the scenes, I've hardly seen you."

"You know me." Laura smiled harder. "I want everyone to have fun, but I don't want my mom to overdo things." She was also used to taking charge—she couldn't sit idle at a family event.

"Your mom has other daughters and daughters-in-law, as well as sisters, cousins and friends." Alana stood with her hands on her hips. "Most of whom are here. Let them handle cleaning up."

"Alana's right." Josie nodded. "I also know what it's like to be too independent." Her smile was rueful. "Thanks to Heath, I've learned there's no shame in asking for help when you need it, or even letting others take charge in the first place. My grandparents are basically running our new store, and although it felt strange at first, life's easier now I don't think I have to oversee everything on the farm."

"It's not the same." Laura stared at her friends. Trevor had teased her about being a "control freak," and she'd been working on becoming less fixed in her thinking. But with her friends telling her the same thing, maybe she had to make bigger changes in herself than she'd thought.

What Courtney had said echoed in Laura's mind. Was all that sacrifice and being a "mother hen" why she still felt she had to control everything? Was that also why in her adult life she set such rigid boundaries around her independence, seeing it as all or nothing with no middle ground?

"The circumstances are different, but the issue isn't." A small smile played around Alana's mouth. "Besides, you're getting all domesticated with Trevor and Danny, and have other priorities. You're not indispensable to your family or anywhere else. Surely you saw that with everyone stepping up when you were sick?"

Laura considered that experience a one-off but perhaps it wasn't. "It'd be fun to join the game."

Domesticated. She'd always loved making a home and fixing things in her house, but she wasn't "domesticated" with Trevor and Danny. She wanted to be there for Danny's school events. She'd wanted to make his costume for the Valentine's party. She'd seen it as being helpful, but now Alana had pointed it out, Laura must be changing. Although she didn't like putting a label on it, she wouldn't be "dating" Trevor otherwise.

"Great." Alana clapped her hands. "Trevor's so kind and considerate, and he clearly adores you." As they made their way back to the living room, Alana kept talking. "When I told him you were lucky to have him in your life, he said *he's* the lucky one. Isn't that the sweetest? Danny thinks the world of you, too. He came to the library yesterday looking for books about horses. He wants to learn as much as he can, he said, so this summer he can apply to work for you full-time."

Laura's heart swelled with warmth, affection and a love that was wonderful yet still so new and unexpected. She'd be happy to have Danny work at the stables when he was off school for the summer. He didn't even need to apply. Like Trevor, he was family. When Danny had asked, she'd already offered to teach him to ride as long as Trevor agreed. There was no need to pay for formal lessons.

And now, there was no doubt. As Laura joined the circle of women playing Pin the Pacifier on the Baby, the thought of them becoming a family for real settled and rooted itself around her heart.

"Over here, Auntie Laura." Everly, her six-year-old niece, pointed to the poster with a drawing of a baby stuck to a wall. "Ms. Alana says it's your turn. You're last."

"Sure thing, sweetie." Laura kneeled as Everly, along with Martha Ryan, put the mask over her eyes.

"I'll hold your hand so you don't fall," Everly said. "Here." She put a sticker in Laura's palm. "You hafta put it on the baby."

"That's right, dear." Laura's mom's voice sounded close to her ear. "You tell your Auntie Laura what she needs to do. You're so much like she was as a child. A real blessing to your mommy, like Laura is to me."

"Aren't blessings only at church?" Everly's high voice rose above the multiple conversations going on around them.

"No, not at all. There's many different kinds of blessings throughout our lives." That was Laura's mom speaking again.

"Okay, go now," Everly said, still holding Laura's hand.

Laura leaned forward and, taking a wild guess, put her sticker on the poster.

Clapping and exclamations broke out, and Everly squealed, "You did it, Auntie Laura. You won."

As Laura took off her mask, Everly wrapped her arms around Laura's waist and squeezed. "I did?" Laura stared at the multicolored stickers on the poster and hugged Everly close.

"Of course, you did. You're excellent at games. Grandma's got your fuzzy socks for the prize." Everly held out her arms for Laura to pick her up and when Laura did, her niece pointed at the poster. "That's your sticker, the orange one, right there. It's the closest. And you don't even have any babies."

"It doesn't have anything to do with having babies." Laura glanced around the circle, feeling slightly embarrassed. "I was lucky, and you did a great job guiding me." She hugged Everly again before setting the girl down.

Laura's mom moved closer to hand her the pair of pink socks, part of a set Laura had bought to give as shower prizes. "Not giving birth doesn't mean a woman doesn't have a maternal instinct. There are all kinds of ways to have children in your life to love and guide. Family's what you make it. I never wanted you to be like me, your sisters or anyone else. All I ever want is for you to be happy with whatever path you choose." Behind her glasses, her brown eyes, almost a mirror image of Laura's own, were soft and loving.

"Sure, but…" As Laura's hand closed around the socks, she stopped. She'd always thought she'd let her mom down by not wanting to have kids, but she hadn't.

Her gaze drifted from her mom to Alana, now leading Everly and several other girls in a game to collect discarded ribbon and bows.

Maybe she was also imagining an issue where one didn't exist. Trevor had never mentioned wanting kids, and surely, at his age, he'd have had them by now if he did. It wasn't as if he was interested in Alana. From Laura's perspective, it was merely what she represented. Younger, for a start, and more obviously maternal.

If having children was important to Trevor, it was something they had to talk about. *Compromise. Us.* As had happened so often in the past few days, Becca's words at the house showing reverberated in Laura's head.

And they felt right and good. Two words on which to build a lifetime of love.

CHAPTER SIXTEEN

TREVOR NEEDED A sounding board and, except for Laura, there was nobody better than his mom. While they'd always been close, sharing weekly phone calls, frequent emails and annual visits, since he'd been back living in Strawberry Pond their mother-son relationship had grown and deepened.

He used his key to open the front door of his childhood home and called out to his mom. He'd texted her earlier so she'd be expecting him. "You in the kitchen?" As he took off his coat and boots, he sniffed the air, catching a faint scent of baking. "Hey, Mabel." He bent to rub the poodle's ears.

"I'm in your bedroom planting my seedlings." His mom's voice echoed from the second floor. "Come on up."

Trevor padded up the carpeted stairs in his sock feet with Mabel at his side. The dog was so good for his mom, giving her a new interest, a reason to get out for walks and, most importantly, unconditional love.

At the top of the stairs, he turned right toward his bedroom on one side of the hall across from Renée's on the other. Although his mom had long ago converted Trevor's sister's room into a sewing and craft space with only a single daybed, Renée's name was still on a plaque fixed to the door, like a similar one was on Trevor's. His grandparents had given them those personalized name signs one Christmas in elementary school. And, like many other things in this house, from the paint color in the hall, to the oak dining-room suite his parents had bought soon after they married, they were fixed and unchanging. Almost a time capsule of his early life.

"Mom?" He went into his old bedroom, now the guestroom, but which still held his pine bookcase with a cluster of framed photos on top, including his senior year picture.

She turned from the sunny window and a table of seedling trays with newspapers spread out to catch soil. "Here you are." In a few steps, she reached him and, after planting a kiss on his cheek, cupped his chin in her hands. "How's my boy doing?"

"I'm fine." Although Trevor was almost forty-one, his mom still considered him "her boy" and he'd made peace with the endearment. It was her way of showing love, and he was fortunate to have it and her in his life. After kissing her back, he sat on the edge of the bed, now covered in a blue-and-white floral comforter that gave the room a more feminine feel than when Trevor had lived here. "What are you planting?" He needed to ease into this conversation, especially because he was still trying to figure out what he wanted to say.

"Tomatoes, cauliflower, lettuce. The usual, although I'm trying eggplant again this year. Hopefully it'll be more of a success than it was last time. Your dad used to tease me about what he called that 'experiment.' I had blossoms but not one single fruit." She made a face and filled another small pot with soil. "However, he also reminded me that eggplant experiment was like life. You don't always reap what you sow, good or bad."

"True enough." Trevor's dad had been wise, and there wasn't a day he didn't miss him. "I was wondering…can I talk to you about something?" Mabel hopped onto Trevor's lap and nosed his hand to pat her.

"Sure." His mom was focused on her plants, but maybe it was easier that way than him having to look at her full-on. "Like I always said to you kids, I'm here if you need me, but now you're grown it's up to you to ask."

"It's about Laura and me." He stroked Mabel under her chin. "I love her. As a friend, of course, but now, it's more. Maybe I've always loved her that way, but I didn't see it before. I don't want to push her, but I also want to tell her how I feel."

"I see." There was a pause as his mom tucked seeds into soil. "Even back when the two of you were in high school, I often wondered if you had more than platonic feelings for her. And since you came back to town, well, it's plain as day to anyone who takes more than a second look that what's between the two of you isn't only friendship or casual."

"No, it's not. I… We…we're sort of seeing each other. I didn't want to make some big announcement and neither did Laura but…" Trevor took a deep breath. "I think I want to marry her."

"You think?" His mom chuckled.

"No, I know I do." Trevor laughed. "Marry Laura, I mean. I never thought I'd meet the right woman but she's been in front of me for almost my whole life. I need her, Mom, like I need Strawberry Pond. We make a good team, and I want us to make a life together here."

"That's wonderful, dear." His mom turned to face him and, standing in a beam of sunshine, she seemed to radiate love and kindness. "Your dad and I never wanted anything more for you, or Renée, than to find the kind of lasting happiness with someone the two of us had. And having you living so close is something I'm grateful for. I love Laura like another daughter. Have done since she was a child. She fits you and our family, and Danny loves her, too. She's a wonderful influence on him." His mom paused and brushed soil from her hands onto the newspaper.

"But?" Her voice held a hesitation Trevor hadn't expected.

"You're my son. My own flesh and blood, and I want you to be happy. I do, truly." She crossed the room to sit at Trevor's side, seedlings forgotten. "But it wouldn't be right or fair if I didn't also say you need to be careful."

"Careful how?" He tensed, and Mabel, now sleeping cuddled on his lap, puffed out a soft breath.

"Right from when she was tiny, Laura's always been set on independence. Many girls imagine their wedding day, and the children they want to have, but she never did. She didn't even like playing with dolls much."

"Laura was a kid. Lots of girls don't like playing with dolls. It doesn't mean anything important." Trevor tugged on one of his shirtsleeves.

"Maybe not, but I've never seen or heard anything to suggest Laura isn't happy with her life as a single woman. And with you, she wouldn't only be getting a husband, but also a family with Danny. That's a big responsibility." His mom's eyebrows drew together in what Trevor recognized as her "thinking expression."

"But you said it yourself, Danny loves Laura. She seems to love him as well." Trevor was more certain of Laura's feelings for his nephew than for him. "She's fantastic with him."

"She is but..."

"Say it, Mom. I need to know, don't I?" Despite his happy-go-lucky, often impulsive demeanor, Trevor also prided himself on facing reality, no matter how hard.

"I've often wondered if Laura's so set on independence because of coming from such a large family." His mom pleated the edge of the bib apron she wore for gardening. "Losing her dad so young was awful, anyway, but it also meant she had to shoulder more responsibility for her younger brothers and sisters as well as the family farm. Maeve Sullivan did her best, and I don't mean to criticize or say I'd have done any different than Laura's mom, but as the oldest, Laura had to grow up fast and likely too soon."

Trevor pressed a hand to his stomach. He'd always thought he knew Laura as well or better than anyone, but he'd never considered how her family situation might have impacted her life. Or how, even now, it could still impact her choices.

"I'm not saying I'm right." His mom touched Trevor's shoulder, and Mabel woke up and hopped off his lap to sprawl on the bedroom carpet. "And I don't mean you shouldn't tell Laura how you feel about her. Maybe she's not as opposed to marriage and family life as she used to be. It's all to say she might not react as you'd expect."

"I know and I get it." He rubbed a hand across his face. Was Laura *so* independent she didn't need anyone, not even him? When she used to say she didn't want to marry or have a family, because Laura was only Trevor's friend it hadn't really registered. But now, when he finally wanted to settle down and couldn't imagine sharing his life with anyone else, those words returned to haunt him.

"SORRY I'M LATE." On an evening in the first week of March, Laura met Trevor outside the middle school's gym, where the science fair was underway. "Being born and bred in New Hampshire, I should be used to March snowstorms, but somehow I never am." She took off her coat, hat and scarf and hung them on a hook in the hallway.

"I'm glad you're here safe." Trevor kissed her cheek. Since they were in public, it was almost a peck, the kind of kiss he could've greeted anyone with, but it still made Laura's senses tingle. "I worry about you driving in bad weather, and that road across the mountain can be treacherous."

Warmth curled in her tummy and spread up through her chest. Her family and friends worried about her, but with Trevor, that concern was different. Better. "I took it slow, and luckily for most of the way I was behind a snowplow. The listing's fantastic, though, and I expect the property will sell quickly." She returned Trevor's kiss and looped her arm through his. "What did I miss?"

"Only the principal's welcome, and Fred Sinclair taking pictures for the newspaper. I told Danny you were running late and would be here as soon as you could. He knows you'd never let him down."

She would always try her best, but what if she did disappoint him? Would it take her back to square one with Danny despite the connection they'd made? It was partly why she'd avoided a larger family of her own. Could she face that fear and, if she did fall short of Danny's expectations, what would it do to her new relationship with Trevor? As they walked into the gym, Laura glanced around at the various exhibits. From a boy demonstrating what looked like a small wind turbine, to a girl who'd built a robot and many more, the projects ranged from simple to elaborate. All, though, were colorful, engaging and had clearly taken lots of time and dedicated effort.

A chill spread inside her, its icy tentacles tightening around her throat. Trevor had taken part in every school science fair, but Laura never had. Even before her dad died, farm chores meant there hadn't been much time for extracurriculars. Those extracurriculars also cost money, and with a large family depending on a farming income, funds were spread thin and had to go to essentials. However, tonight was about Danny, and being at the school she and Trevor had also attended brought back memories both good and bad.

She pasted a smile on her face. "I swear this gym still smells the same."

"You mean the combination of sweaty clothes and puberty?" Trevor laughed. "I half expect to hear Mr. Gustafson yelling 'let's keep that energy going, boys,' as we were on our umpteenth circuit around this place. I was always thankful when he finally blew his whistle, and I could collapse on one of the mats."

"Unlike me, you were athletic." Laura shuddered. "To me, he said things like 'I appreciate your positive attitude' and 'great effort.' He was always upbeat and encouraging, even when I missed the net in basketball, accidentally scored a goal for the opposite team in soccer and was picked last for most activities."

"Although I didn't recognize it at the time, that's one of the signs of a good teacher. He didn't focus so much on winning as us having fun, taking part and trying our best." Trevor gave Laura's arm a consoling squeeze. "If we'd been in the same gym class back then, I'd have picked you first no matter what. I'd still pick you."

"Aww." Laura briefly rested her head on his shoulder. "That's sweet."

She'd always been competitive, measuring her life in accomplishments more than savoring small moments along the way, but the past few months had shown her she needed to take a different approach. She'd still try her best, but she'd already proven herself and didn't need any more professional awards. But, by spending time with Trevor and Danny she was learning how to have fun, be spontaneous and enjoy the moment more and more.

The thought of Trevor wanting several kids of his own once again bobbed to the top of her mind. She had to find a way to ask him, but this was the first time she'd seen him in a few days and as was so often the case, they were with others.

"Hi, Danny… DJ." As they reached his exhibit

in front of the stage used for school plays and choir and band performances, Laura corrected herself and gave him a high five. "Your project looks great."

"Thanks." His grin stretched from ear to ear. "I appreciate you helping me. Uncle Trevor, too."

"Apart from some gluing and setting out a few animal track stations, I didn't do much." Laura looked at his project board. Divided into three sections, each one was clearly labeled and small sections of text were interspersed with pictures and drawings.

"Nor me." Trevor clapped Danny on one shoulder. "You did a fantastic job. I'm proud of you, like your mom and dad would be." His voice roughened and he cleared his throat.

As Danny told them about the different parts of his project, raising his voice to include several other parents and kids who'd stopped at his exhibit to take a look, Laura's smile widened to match his. Seeing Danny interested and invested in work he'd done, especially so soon after losing his mom, was both heartwarming and reassuring. Of course, there'd be bumps along the way, but tonight Danny's bright face and glowing eyes told her that Trevor, his mom, teachers and maybe even her, were all giving the grieving boy what he needed.

"See here, Laura?" Danny pointed to a long,

narrow set of tracks. "That's a raccoon from behind your barn. Maybe if I set track boxes out there in summer, there'd be a black bear, but they're hibernating now 'cause it's winter." He beamed. "I even got Tootsie's print here in my notebook." He flipped to a page in a book on the display table. "She's a domestic horse, not a wild animal, so she's not in the main part of the project but she still counts. I know she was walking since the prints are shallow and closer together. If she'd been galloping, they'd be deeper with more space between them."

"Wow." Laura's throat clogged with unexpected emotion. From kindergarten graduations to literacy nights and hockey games, she often went to school and other events her nieces and nephews took part in. And yet, this ordinary middle school science fair seemed more than just that. She didn't only feel pride, but also joy in being part of Danny's development and seeing him learn and discover new interests. "Your project's really something. *You're* really something."

"My science teacher said I could maybe be a park ranger someday." Danny's face was still pink with pleasure. "I'd probably have to go to college, but it'd be worth it to have a job at the end where I could spend lots of time outdoors and work to protect animals and nature."

"I'll support you in whatever you choose," Trevor said. "Me and Laura both." Over Danny's head, Trevor's gaze caught Laura's and held it.

She drew in a breath at the expression in his eyes, which held all the love she hadn't known she'd needed or even wanted.

Maybe tonight wasn't just about making a memory for Danny, but a *family* memory the three of them would one day look back on and cherish.

CHAPTER SEVENTEEN

ALTHOUGH HE LOVED spending time with his mom and Danny, it'd been too long since Trevor had been alone with Laura. The day after Danny's science fair, he kept stealing glances at her as they walked along a trail to a local waterfall, their boots sinking into soft, wet snow. With Trevor not scheduled to work, and Danny having the afternoon off school and spending a few hours at Landon's house, this gentle hike was last-minute. While Laura wasn't usually one for impromptu plans, this time she'd been free.

"It's a gorgeous sky. Despite that big snowstorm, spring is sure on its way. As is the deadline to save the rescue." The brightness in her voice dimmed. "I keep worrying we won't make it. The rescue has taken in three more dogs this week alone."

"I'm worried, too, but everyone is doing their best, including you. That's all any of us can ask. I bet the animals at the shelter would tell you the same if they could." Trevor tried to reassure

Laura, hoping the joke would make her smile and lighten her load at least a little.

"You're right but still..." Her voice trailed away and she tilted her face to the sun. Her eyes were shaded by oversize, tortoise-framed sunglasses, so Trevor couldn't see her expression, but he hoped she was as happy for this time together as him.

Every day was like spring for Trevor, full of the hope and promise the season of renewal brought. He tucked one of her mitten-clad hands into his. "You remember that veterinary conference in Las Vegas I mentioned?"

Laura nodded, the cream-colored pom-pom on her beanie hat bouncing. "It's coming up really soon."

"Well, Danny was supposed to stay with my mom, but now, Mom has a chance to go on a maple syrup farm bus tour to Vermont. There's been a cancellation so a spot opened up. Martha Ryan and several others from the knitting group are going, and they'd like Mom to go with them." Trevor took a deep breath. "I know it's a big ask, but could Danny stay with you instead? It'd only be for three nights, four days in total."

"Sure he can." Laura's engaging smile popped out. "That tour would be fun for your mom. Seeing a new place with friends would also be good for her and a nice break." She squeezed his hand, and Trevor's heart filled with more love than he'd ever thought possible. "Danny already spends lots of time at my place, so staying overnight won't be much different. I don't expect he'll be any trouble and there's plenty of space. He can have the guestroom my nieces and nephews use when they sleep over."

"That's great of you, Lulu. Thanks." With her hand in his and walking together side by side, it felt like they were a real team.

"No problem. It'll be fun to have Danny around. Let me know what foods he likes and how much I need to get for him. According to my sister, Courtney, my nephew near his age eats a lot." Laura chuckled.

"Sounds like Danny. Who, by the way, is okay with me calling him Danny, not DJ, at home. You were right."

"When am I not?" Laura gave him a teasing smile and he teased right back, raising his brow.

As they walked closer together on a narrower part of the path, Trevor stopped, glanced around, gently took off Laura's sunglasses and then kissed her. Whenever his lips met hers, Trevor had the sense of everything being right in his world. And as he held her close, the softness of her mouth against his, her sweet scent, a mixture of fresh air and a light floral, infusing his senses, he never wanted to let her go.

Voices rang out nearby, and Laura took a step back. “Too bad.” She adjusted her woolly hat and then held out her hand for her sunglasses as a couple with three kids and a yellow Labrador came around the curve of the path.

“Yeah.” Trevor swallowed and greeted the family whose dog he recognized from the clinic. “Hey, boy.” He bent to pat the dog as Laura spoke to its owners and put her sunglasses back on.

“Shall we?” After the family and their dog had moved on, Laura gestured to the path. “The waterfall’s not far now.” She worried her bottom lip as if she was all of a sudden unsure, their brief moment of intimacy well and truly broken.

“Sure.” Trevor would have taken her hand again, but she’d tucked both hands into her parka pockets. “What’s wrong? Did I say or do something to upset you?”

“No, it’s me.” Laura stared at her boots. “I need to talk to you about something. Ask you a question. I could never find the right time, but to be honest, I’ve been putting it off.”

“O-o-okay.” Trevor drew out the word. Was that the reason for the distance he’d sensed in Laura at the walk-a-thon and even occasionally at the science fair? “You know you can talk to me about anything, right? Like always.”

“Yes, but it’s not like always. Not anymore.” Laura hesitated. “We’re kissing.”

"Which is wonderful." Trevor made his voice firm. He didn't have any doubts. Did she? His stomach knotted as he remembered what his mom had said about Laura being so independent.

"It is but..." Laura stopped in the middle of the path and faced him. "Do you want kids? Of your own, I mean."

Trevor opened his mouth and closed it again. When he was younger he'd expected he'd have a family, but as the years went by, and he hadn't met the right woman, having kids wasn't something he'd given much thought to.

"If I ever loved someone enough to get married, that's speaking hypothetically, of course, I'd need to compromise," Laura continued, the words tumbling out of her faster than she usually spoke. "If my husband, again hypothetically, wanted one child, I guess I could consider trying. But no more than one, and at my age even having a baby could be difficult. So, you see, if you do want lots of children, it'd be better if you dated someone else. Someone younger who'd be able to have a big family. You need to do what's best for you and—"

"Whoa." He raised a hand to stop Laura's torrent of words and tried to catch his own breath. She'd, hypothetically, thought about marriage. She'd also, again hypothetically, be willing to compromise and try to have one child if it was important to that hypothetical husband.

Him. A flood of thoughts and emotions took over. He wanted to climb the nearest tree and shout to the world that this was how much Laura must love him. At the same time, he realized that it would be both a huge compromise and sacrifice for her to try for a child if it was what *he* wanted. Trevor paused. He needed to get these next words right.

"*You're* best for me. I don't have anything against kids, and if I was with a woman who really wanted them, sure, I'd be okay with it. But I'm not okay with dating anyone who isn't you. Please believe that."

"Really?" Laura's voice trembled and, as they began walking again, she scuffed her boots into a snowdrift that edged the trail. "I thought maybe having kids of your own would be important to you. You always said how much you liked my big family."

"I have plenty of family. My mom, for one. Cousins with children who'll carry on the Kaminski name. There's also Danny. He's half Kaminski and now he's not only my nephew but as good as my kid." Trevor hesitated, considering how best to say what was in his heart. "So, yes, really. I want you in my life more than anyone or anything else. It's taken me all these years to realize what and who I want. Why would I look for someone else just to have kids?" As they reached the waterfall, a frothy confection of frozen icicles sparkling like diamonds in the sunshine, he took her arm again. "You're enough for me, Laura. Always, no matter what does or doesn't happen in the future."

He closed his mouth fast. He'd almost said he loved her, but it wasn't the right time. Not stuck in the middle of a conversation about imaginary children. He understood where Laura was coming from, and he appreciated her honesty, but he had to figure out when and where to tell her he wanted to spend the rest of his life with *her*, not some other hypothetical family. And when he shared his feelings, he wanted to make it special and memorable. Maybe over a candlelit dinner when he had a box with the perfect engagement ring in his pocket. He wasn't old, impetuous Trevor. This new Trevor was more measured and patient. He could bide his time.

Laura stared at him for several seconds. "Okay." Her breath hitched. "Of course, Danny's great. He'll always be part of your life. I didn't mean I'd have a problem with him."

"I know you didn't mean any such thing." Trevor kept his expression solemn to hide his inner elation. Laura might not have noticed but he sure had. Before, everything had been maybes and what-ifs, but just now, she'd spoken more freely. She would want to make a life with him and Danny. They were moving forward in their relationship, and soon he'd tell Laura everything that was in his heart. What he truly wanted.

An image of a happy future for them, for all of them, based in Strawberry Pond came into sharp focus as the loose pieces finally clicked into place.

"I'm glad we agree on the kid question." Laura leaned in close. "I was worried."

"No reason to be." As he embraced her again, he knew that everything he'd always wanted, and needed, was right here.

While his mom had been thinking of Trevor's best interests when she'd warned him Laura might not want marriage or a family with him and Danny, she'd been wrong. Laura had changed and, despite vowing to be patient, Trevor couldn't wait to get started on forever with her.

LAURA PUSHED A shopping cart along one of the middle aisles in Strawberry Pond's biggest grocery store. Unlike the smaller, specialty stores downtown, this one was part of a large chain that had been built on the outskirts of town when Laura was in high school. Since she lived alone and usually only cooked for one, she rarely shopped here, so didn't know where anything was.

She turned back to the list she'd made on her phone. Pasta. Bread. Milk. Vegetables. Canned corn but never broccoli. Chicken breasts for herself. Ground beef. Hamburger buns. Cheese. One by one, she'd ticked items off until only a few remained. She'd made Danny's favorite molasses cookies last night and put them in the freezer, along with a batch of homemade granola. She'd also made chili and had the ingredients for burritos and various pizza toppings. What about tortilla chips and a few other snacks? They weren't on her list, but if Danny invited friends over she wanted to make sure she could feed them.

As she turned the cart into the snack aisle, she smiled to herself. Trevor had seemed so nervous when he'd asked if Danny could stay with her while he was at that conference, but she was happy to host the boy. It'd be fun, and since it didn't make sense to add Danny to a bus route for only a few days, it wasn't a big deal for her to take him to school and pick him up.

A much bigger deal was talking with Trevor about children. However, she'd got that conversation out of the way, and since they'd both been honest with each other, she had nothing to worry about. Their future, and not just hers, was bright.

"Laura?"

At Josie's voice, Laura turned away from the shelf where she'd been trying to decide between several brands of potato chips. "Hi," she greeted her friend.

"I don't usually see you here." Josie's strawberry blond hair was pulled up in a high ponytail and, like Laura, she had her phone out with a list.

"No, but Danny's coming to stay with me." As Laura brought Josie up-to-date on Trevor's conference and her own plans, she suppressed a chuckle. For the first time ever, between the contents of her cart and their conversation, she sounded and looked like a mom, and it was okay. In fact, it was great because it was for Danny.

"My grams is thrilled Mrs. Kaminski's coming on the bus trip." While Laura hadn't hesitated in offering to host Danny, Josie's warm smile would have swept away any doubts. "Having gone through losing my dad and understanding how hard it is, Grams has kind of taken Trevor's mom under her wing. The trip will be fun for both of them. If it wasn't a senior citizens tour, I'd like to go along." Josie laughed. "There's something appealing about having everything organized for you and only having to show up at designated times."

"Isn't Heath planning a delayed honeymoon for the two of you?" While the newlyweds had spent a few days in Montréal after their Christmas wedding, at their recent lunch get-together, Josie had mentioned she and Heath wanted to have a week away later in the year.

"He is, and he's being really secretive about

it." Josie rolled her eyes. "It's sweet, but I guess I'm not used to being what he calls 'whisked away.' He assures me he's arranging it with Grams and Gramps to cover farm work and around the girls' schedules, but it's strange not to have to think about anything except packing a suitcase."

"So says the woman who said she liked the idea of having everything organized for her so all she had to do is show up on time." Laura laughed and bumped Josie's cart with her own. "You can't have it both ways." However, she recognized where Josie was coming from. They were both planners who liked their routines.

"True." Josie joined in the laughter. "So what's the latest with Save the Animal Rescue? We only have two weeks left. On my way into town, I checked the thermometer and the fundraising progress seems to have slowed."

"It has, unfortunately. While the car dealership's raffle is still in progress, and there's a few other small things happening, like the nursery school's bake sale, I worry we've exhausted local generosity." Even accounting for the car raffle, Laura had to accept that they'd likely fall short of the funds needed.

Josie's tightened lips and drooping shoulders mirrored Laura's own worry. "Have you talked to Miss Sarah? She made that big donation to launch the fundraiser. If she knew we're desperate, maybe she could—"

"No." Laura shook her head. "Miss Sarah's already been more than generous. We can't ask her for anything else."

"I understand." Josie patted Laura's arm. "I have to get going but I'll try to think if there's any other options. I'll also ask Gramps to give the rescue another shout-out on his next farming video. The last one brought in a few donations."

"It did." However, although welcome, the small amount of money that continued to trickle in wouldn't make much of a difference. In addition to the car raffle, the fund needed another sizable boost if the town was going to be able to buy the rescue's current building. If they didn't raise enough money, they'd also have to either return the donations or, with community agreement, allocate the funds to another local animal-related initiative.

"I'll talk to Heath as well so don't lose hope. We still have a bit of time."

As they said their goodbyes and Josie wheeled her cart away, Laura straightened. Her friend was right. The campaign wasn't over yet so she had to stay optimistic. Thinking about the animal rescue reminded her that she'd forgotten to add dog food to her grocery list. Star and Cooper were running low so she might as well stock up while she was here.

She grabbed several different brands of potato chips so Danny would have a choice, then headed to the pet food section. She'd passed it earlier at the back of the store when she'd picked up laundry detergent.

Walking briskly, she navigated the aisles, saying quick hellos to friends and neighbors as she passed. Many of them had been real estate clients at one time or another, but as much as she'd have liked to, she didn't have time to chat. "Hey, Brent." She waved at him as she approached the pet area. "The house still okay for you?"

"It's wonderful, thanks." He gestured to the plastic basket he held over one arm. "I'm in Strawberry Pond for a few days. Picking up some essentials for when my kids can join me. Cheryl Kaminski's been a lifesaver in getting the place ready. This summer, I'd love to have you and Trevor over for a BBQ."

"That'd be great." With another wave and smile, Laura continued into the pet section. *You and Trevor.* They truly were a couple, and although it hadn't been long since Brent approached their table the night Trevor had taken her out for dinner at that fancy mountain hotel, so much had changed.

She'd sold Brent his vacation home. Although still grieving, Cheryl Kaminski was taking important steps out into the world again. And Laura had let herself love Trevor as more than a friend. She was even thinking about marriage, which, along with the other changes she was making, was the biggest one of all. Laura smiled to herself remembering how she'd been so careful to use the word *hypothetically* when talking to Trevor about marriage and kids. He'd likely seen right through her attempt to make it seem she wasn't talking about them, but that was okay. He hadn't teased or judged. Instead, it had been the same as talking to her best friend but even better.

Scanning the store shelves, she hauled Cooper's food from a low shelf and lifted it into the cart, then then reached for Star's.

"Well, why wouldn't he go back to California?" An unknown female voice came from around the corner of the aisle, hidden from Laura by a display of cat litter topped by a large Special Offer sign. "It's warmer for a start. I've often heard Cheryl say she finds our New Hampshire winters hard."

"But selling her family's home? That'd hurt." A new, higher-pitched voice, one Laura recognized as belonging to a woman near her mom's age who went to their church, joined in. "Besides, Danny's gotten settled here. Why would Trevor uproot him again?"

"True, but mark my words, when the school year ends, I expect Trevor will be off with both his mom and Renée's boy. There's been no signs of Trevor buying a house, has there? If he planned to stay, you'd think he'd at least be looking at places."

The voices faded, and as if by rote Laura made herself put Star's food beside Cooper's. Then, on legs like rubber, she made her way to a self-checkout kiosk. She didn't want to talk to a cashier or anyone else right now.

Trevor would have told her if he had even the slightest idea of moving back to California. It was ridiculous to think otherwise. Of course, he wouldn't uproot Danny again so soon. The two of them had only just gotten settled in Strawberry Pond. Cheryl was also working part-time for Laura. She'd never have taken the job if she'd been planning to leave town in a few months. Lots of people complained about cold weather here, including Laura. It didn't mean they were about to move away, let alone to the other side of the country.

Trevor hadn't come back to her about that list of properties she'd emailed him because he was busy. When Sarah and Jack Fournier returned from Florida after visiting family in Michigan, Trevor and Danny could stay with Cheryl if they needed to. Even when Trevor bought a house, it would take a month or more for the property to close. He might have to move in with his mom for a while, anyway. The only reason Brent McCarthy had taken possession of his house so fast was because it'd been empty and the seller was highly motivated.

Laura tapped the checkout screen and began scanning her groceries. Trevor was different than he used to be. More settled. Stable and less impetuous.

Much as she loved Strawberry Pond, like all small towns, it could be a hotbed of gossip, especially in winter, when there wasn't as much going on. Those two women were talking nonsense, speculating and making something out of nothing.

She'd put what they'd said out of her mind and not even mention it to Trevor. If she did, she'd only sound suspicious and as if she didn't trust him. She had more important things to focus on. Like Danny's visit.

Laura reached for the snacks she'd bought. Dating someone with kids was already complicated so Trevor and Danny's situation was even more complex. She wanted to make sure Danny's stay, another step in forging a blended family, went perfectly.

CHAPTER EIGHTEEN

"DON'T GIVE LAURA any grief, okay?" As Trevor parked his SUV in Laura's driveway, and he and Danny gathered up Danny's luggage and walked to her front door, he tried to think of any last reminders for his nephew. "Remember not to leave your dirty dishes lying around. Put them in the dishwasher right away. As a guest in Laura's home, follow her rules."

"I know." Danny rolled his eyes. "Laura's a neat freak like Grandma."

"Which is a good thing. The two of us should follow their fine examples and learn to be tidier." Trevor rang the doorbell, and inside Star and Cooper barked.

He should also hire a cleaner like he'd had in California, but there always seemed to be something more urgent demanding his attention. Maybe on his flight to Las Vegas he'd have a chance to figure out his priorities and put together a plan of action. At the moment, all he had were various lists online and on scattered scraps of paper.

"Hey, Laura," he greeted her when she opened the door wearing sweats and a matching sweatshirt and covering a yawn with one hand. "Early enough for you?"

"I'm always glad to see you guys." She gave them a bleary-eyed smile and ushered them in. "I shut the dogs in the family room so they wouldn't expect you to stay and play. Coffee's on if you'd like a cup for the road."

"Perfect." He was flying from Boston Logan to Las Vegas and needed to make an early start to get to the airport on time. "Here's an extra set of keys in case Danny loses his and needs something from the Brennan house." He passed them over. "I already emailed you Miss Sarah's phone numbers and contact details for the management company." Gone were the days when all Trevor had to do was lock the door behind him and take off at a moment's notice. Making sure Danny was ready for a short stay with Laura had taken more time than Trevor had needed before several months traveling around Latin America with a backpack in college. "I also emailed you information for Danny's doctor, dentist and school contacts as well as numbers for Landon's parents and their address. Danny's going there for pizza after school tomorrow, so you'll need to pick him up around six thirty."

"I've got the schedule you put together. Everything'll be fine." Laura gave him a reassuring smile. "It's only for a few days." She eyed Danny's suitcase, a large blue roller bag, which, along with a backpack, duffel and box of computer equipment, gave the impression the kid was moving in rather than coming for a brief visit. "Why don't we put your things in the guest room and you can get settled? I'll show you the way and then we'll have breakfast." She glanced at Trevor. "I'll get you your coffee to take with you."

"Great, thanks." He exhaled as he took off his winter boots, slid off his coat, shouldered Danny's backpack and levered the box into his arms. His mom used to jokingly complain about how much stuff Renée took with her on those family summer trips to Maine. Clearly, his sister's son had inherited her need to be prepared for any and all eventualities.

He followed Laura and Danny up a set of carpeted stairs to the second level, decorated in the same muted, earthy tones as the downstairs to showcase the old wood and window views across forest, fields and mountains.

"In here." Laura opened a door partway along a short hall to the left of the stairs. "You have your own attached bath, but if you need it, say after doing chores, there's also a shower off the mudroom." She gestured around the cozy room, painted in calming shades of blue, with a single bed and set of bunk beds as well as a TV, desk, nightstand and two beanbag chairs. "I've left the Wi-Fi password on the desk, and there's a small fridge in the cupboard under the eaves." She showed it to Danny, who looked around, wide-eyed.

"It's great, Lulu." So nice the kid might never want to leave. "You didn't need to go to so much trouble."

"It's no trouble at all." She gave Danny a fond smile. "I keep this room ready for my nieces and nephews, although now they're getting older and busier with school and extracurriculars, they don't come to stay as often as they once did." She picked up a minuscule piece of fluff from the otherwise gleaming desk surface. "If you unpack, I'll have breakfast ready in twenty minutes."

This was it. As Laura discreetly left the room for them to say their goodbyes, Trevor eyed his nephew from across the single bed. "Take care, okay?" His voice rasped and he cleared his throat.

"Sure." Danny opened the backpack Trevor

had set on the carpet at the foot of the bed. "Your conference sounds epic. Have fun."

"I will, but I'll miss you." It was true. Although Danny had only been with him for a short time, it already felt odd to be going somewhere without him. He moved closer and, not wanting to embarrass the kid by hugging him, instead patted Danny's shoulder.

Danny straightened and put a hand on Trevor's arm. "I'll miss you, too."

And then, they were hugging, awkward but nevertheless heartfelt.

"I better get going." Trevor was the first to step back and, as he did, he glimpsed a tattered brown plush ear poking out from the top of Danny's backpack. Bobo. The brown bear his nephew had once carried everywhere and, as a toddler had refused to sleep without. His throat thickened. Although his nephew often appeared almost grown-up, there was still a lot of the kid in him. A kid who needed familiarity, comfort and security. Everything Renée's death had ripped away, and Trevor was trying to haphazardly rebuild. "I love you, kiddo."

"Me, too. I mean, I love you, Uncle Trevor." Danny bent and rummaged in his pack, stuffing Bobo's ear out of sight. "Now, go or you'll miss your flight. I bet you wanna kiss Laura goodbye." His nephew made an "eww" face and laughed.

"Call me if you need anything or, you know, want to talk." Trevor laughed, too. He'd never been good at expressing emotional stuff or even recognizing what he was feeling, which was maybe why it'd taken him so long to understand how he felt about Laura. But it wasn't too late and he was making up for lost time.

With an awkward wave at Danny, more like a flap of his fingers, Trevor made his way back downstairs, where Laura met him in the front hall.

"Everything okay?" She held out an insulated travel mug with his coffee along with a brown paper bag.

"I think so." Trevor wasn't sure of anything right now except he didn't want to leave her or Danny. For the first time in his life, he, the guy who usually couldn't wait to explore a new place, would rather stay enveloped in the comfort and familiarity of home. Unlike Danny, he didn't have a Bobo to bring with him for emotional support.

He took the mug and bag. "What's in here?" The top of the bag was folded over and fixed closed with a Do Not Open sticker featuring a green dinosaur.

"I packed you snacks and a few other things

for the trip. Open it once you're on your way." Her smile was sweet and maybe even loving.

"You remembered." He stared at the dinosaur sticker and his throat clogged again. When he was little, he'd loved dinosaurs and had a green one that looked a lot like the one in the picture.

"Sure I did." Laura put both her hands on his shoulders. "Danny will be fine, and you'll be so busy your time away will whiz by. Go and enjoy a few days of freedom from responsibility." She kissed him, all too briefly, leaving a lingering warmth where her soft lips had pressed against Trevor's.

"This trip's for work, you know. Although Dr. Berner's now working part-time and has been travelling a lot, he's counting on me to come back with news about the latest advancements in veterinary medicine. He said so before he and his wife left for their niece's wedding. I'll also take part in workshops and practice new surgical techniques." Trevor kissed Laura again, savoring her sweetness and the imprint of her arms around his shoulders. "It's not all fun." Right now, it didn't seem like fun at all.

"Despite being for work, you'll have a chance to catch up with old friends and colleagues. You also get to stay in a hotel and not have to clean up after yourself or make meals for a ravenous teenager." Laura grinned as Trevor put his coat and boots back on. "You'll get a break from everyday life."

"I guess." Except, Trevor's everyday life was pretty good, if he discounted the cleaning up and feeding the bottomless-pit teenager. But when all was said and done, he was getting more used to those parts. "Call me if there's a problem or you want to talk." Almost exactly what he'd said to Danny and he meant it. Trevor and Laura talked daily but with a three-hour time difference it wouldn't be as straightforward.

"I will. Now, go or you'll miss your flight." Laura made a shooing motion. "Danny and me will be here waiting when you get back."

"Sounds good." Trevor gave her a final kiss and then, reluctantly, opened the door to go out to his vehicle.

He usually traveled solo so this trip was no different. However, now he wished he could take Laura and Danny with him.

As he started his SUV and turned around to head back down Laura's driveway, he glimpsed her still standing in the half-open doorway.

She waved and smiled, and he did the same.

Maybe the best part of travel wasn't heading off on an adventure. Instead, it could be coming home to one that although not as exciting on the surface, was solid, deeper and better than he'd ever imagined.

"OKAY, SINCE NOBODY else has any other questions or concerns, let's wrap up. Thanks and good night, everyone." Laura checked the time on her computer. It was after nine, and the "Save the Animal Rescue" organizing committee meeting had run late.

Although more donations had come in thanks to Tom Ryan's second social media appeal, the town still needed to find a way to make up what was projected to be a financial shortfall. Since the weather wasn't yet warm enough for a community yard sale, the mayor, Anne Sullivan and several others had agreed to organize a last-minute indoor one and hold it at the community center.

Would it be enough to put them over the finish line? As Laura left the online meeting and powered down her computer, she rubbed a hand against her forehead. The town was used to pulling together at short notice. The date also aligned with a maple event at a nearby sugar bush so they'd attract out-of-town visitors. She had to keep thinking positively. There was no other option, and neither Laura nor the other committee members were about to quit.

As she made her way from her home office to the kitchen, the quiet house wrapped around her like a blanket. Had Danny gone to bed early? Unlikely, because yesterday she'd had to coax him to turn in. Even if he was in his bedroom, she should have heard noise from the shower, TV or his computer given it was above the kitchen and the old house, despite all its modern upgrades, wasn't highly soundproof.

She took out a teapot, mug and her favorite chamomile tea, filled the kettle with water and set it to boil, still listening for any noises from overhead. Like she'd told Trevor when he'd called and texted, Danny was doing fine. He'd gone to Landon's yesterday after school as planned and then came home and did his homework. Tonight, he'd done chores and then said he had homework to keep him busy while Laura had her committee meeting.

Still, she couldn't quite suppress a niggle of worry. "Star, Cooper?" She called to the dogs sprawled in their beds in the family room off the kitchen. "Come." She was used to being in the house with only the dogs for company so tonight shouldn't be any different, even though she somehow felt more alone.

On her way upstairs, she picked up one of Danny's sweatshirts hung haphazardly over the banister, and a math textbook from the floor near the main bathroom. "DJ?" It wasn't easy, but she was trying to use the nickname. She rapped softly on his bedroom door. Maybe he *had* gone to bed.

Star whined and nosed the door.

"What's up, girl?" Laura knocked again, harder this time, and Cooper joined Star, snuffling at the threshold.

Okay, this was ridiculous. Danny deserved his privacy, but Laura also had to make sure he was all right. With a deep breath, she eased open the door. The curtains were open, and in the dim light, Laura put a hand to her mouth.

Despite the tumbled covers and comforter halfway onto the floor, the bed was empty, as was the en suite bath.

And Danny was nowhere to be seen.

Laura flipped on the overhead light as if it might make him suddenly appear. She scanned the room and then darted along the upstairs hall, calling Danny's name, and then went back downstairs, the dogs at her heels.

She pulled her phone from her hoodie pocket. She couldn't call Trevor, not yet. There was likely a logical explanation for Danny's disappearance. She couldn't call Cheryl, either. Mrs. Kamiński was having a much-needed break, and it wasn't as if in Vermont she could do anything practical. It was also too soon to call the police.

Think. Breathe. Call Danny. Of course. Laura wasn't usually one to panic, and if she thought things through in her usual logical way, everything would be fine. She scrolled to Danny's number and listened as the phone rang and went to voice mail.

"Danny. It's Laura. Where are you? Call me. Please. I'm not mad. Only worried." She gulped, ended the call and put her phone back in her pocket, then made another, more thorough search of the house. In the front hall, the hook that usually held Danny's parka was empty, and his boots weren't in their place on the tray. As she put on her own outdoor gear and grabbed a powerful flashlight, her heart seemed to drop into her stomach.

Had Danny run away? If so, why? Nothing had seemed off with him when she'd picked him up at school or over supper.

Landon. Isaac. He often played online games with the two boys. She found her phone again and scrolled to the numbers Trevor had given her for Landon's parents. "Hi, it's Laura Sullivan. I'm sorry to bother you so late." When Landon's mom answered, Laura started to explain herself. "What?" She pressed a hand to her chest. "Landon's missing? And Isaac? You've called the police?" All of a sudden, it was hard to breathe. "Okay, I'll search more here. You'll let the police know about Danny? Yes, thanks. I'll wait for an officer to call me."

After getting a number for Isaac's parents and promising to keep in touch, Laura clipped a leash to Star's collar and, leaving Cooper, a more nervous and excitable dog inside, she set off to make a circuit around the house and outbuildings, the beam from the flashlight cutting through the night. Three thirteen-year-old boys couldn't simply vanish. But it was dark, cold and, as she looked for any signs of footprints in the hard-packed snow, the wind picked up and ice pellets stung her cheeks.

She stopped at the front door of the house again, then set off at a jog on the path to the barn and other outbuildings. "Do you know where Danny went, Star?" While basset hounds were exceptional scent trackers, and often used in search-and-rescue missions, she'd never done any formal training with either of her two. Still, it didn't hurt to try to enlist the dog's help. "Danny? DJ?" Laura continued calling the boy's name, and Star kept her nose to the ground.

Buffeted by the wind, Laura tugged open the barn door and then closed it behind them and turned on the main lights. Horses in nearby stalls nickered as she passed, both in greeting and as if to ask why all of a sudden it was so bright.

"It's okay." Even as her voice and body shook, Laura made soothing noises. It wouldn't do any good if the horses got upset. Attuned to human emotions, they'd pick up on her stress and anxiety. At Laura's side as they neared the end of the central aisle, Star stopped and whined. "What is it, girl?" She glanced around but didn't spot anything unusual. All the horses, both her own and those she boarded were where they should be, and the stable was clean and tidy. "Hey, Tootsie." She scratched the horse's ears as the animal tossed her head and whinnied. Then, Tootsie nudged Laura's arm with her nose and stared at her, dark brown eyes intent.

Star whined again and tugged Laura to an empty stall beyond Tootsie's and barked.

"What are you—" Laura peered over the stall door, then yanked it open. "Danny."

Sprawled in a nest of straw, Danny opened his eyes and blinked at her like a sleepy owl.

Star dashed past Laura, tail wagging and tumbled on top of the boy, licking his face.

"Good girl, Star, but no jumping around." Laura grabbed the dog's collar and sat in the straw beside Danny. "Are you hurt? What happened?" Her heart pounded, and her palms were slick with sweat. She had to call the police. Maybe an ambulance. "Why are you out here?" Her voice rose, its shrill sound almost unrecognizable.

"I'm sorry." Danny curled into a ball as if to make himself smaller. "I fell off your bike. Lost my phone." His words came out half in a sob. "Hurt my ankle. Don't tell Uncle Trevor? Isaac wanted to… Supposed to meet him and Landon in town." Sobs overtook him, and he buried his face in Laura's shoulder.

"Hey, hey, it's all right." Laura wrapped her arms around Danny's heaving body while Star stood, as if on guard, at the open stall door. "You're safe, that's all that matters."

Except for alerting the police, getting Danny to the local hospital and calling Landon's and Isaac's parents, everything else could wait. But even as she held Danny and tried to reassure him, the prickle of unease Laura had tried to suppress over these past weeks could no longer be denied.

This situation, right here, was why she'd never wanted a family of her own. She loved Danny almost like he was her own child. But with that love came worry, stress, feelings of inadequacy and responsibility. So much responsibility. Her hand shook even harder as she fumbled for her phone in her coat pocket to call the police. If she hadn't been in that meeting… If it hadn't gone on longer… If she'd checked on Danny earlier… The thoughts whirled in her head, faster and faster on repeat.

Danny had made a mistake and, although Laura still didn't know the full extent, hopefully it was one he'd learn from.

But she'd also made a mistake, and before tonight she'd been deluding herself. Now that she knew what the mistake was, she needed to fix it. If she didn't, if she tried to convince herself she could make a forever family with Danny and Trevor, she'd be setting all of them up for heartache.

Herself, most of all.

CHAPTER NINETEEN

LATE THE FOLLOWING AFTERNOON, Trevor sat in the cheery, red-covered armchair in Laura's living room. Despite the warmth from the fire crackling in the grate, and mug of hot coffee in front of him, his body was chilled. As soon as Laura had called him the night before, he'd booked a seat on the earliest available flight to Boston and left the conference early.

Now, he was here, still half on Nevada time and half New Hampshire. And with a chastened and remorseful Danny sleeping in Laura's guest room, Trevor had to get to the bottom of what exactly had happened.

"That was a client." Laura came back into the living room holding her cell phone. "Thankfully, they were okay with me rescheduling their house showing." She crossed the room and sat on the sofa. "Before you got here, I spoke to Landon's mom and Isaac's dad, and the police community liaison officer as well as Danny's school to let them know he'd be absent and won't be able to take part in gym class when he's back. He'll be assigned other work instead." She raised a hand as Trevor was about to speak. "I didn't want to leave Danny alone to do morning chores, so Alana, who's not working at the library today, came over to help. She found my bike behind the barn and put it in the tool shed. I also talked to your mom because news of what happened had reached the bus tour group. She said she'd come right home. Tom Ryan was ready to drive over to Vermont and pick up your mom and Martha, but I convinced her to stay and return tomorrow with the group as planned."

"I'm so sorry." When Trevor could get a word in edgewise, he apologized yet again. Although Danny sneaking out of Laura's house and borrowing her bike to ride to town to hang out with Landon and Isaac wasn't Trevor's fault, he nevertheless felt responsible. In all his last-minute reminders to his nephew, he'd never thought to mention not leaving the house without asking Laura first, or the dangers of riding a bike in the dark in winter. What had the kid been thinking? He hadn't been thinking, that was obvious. "Tell me again what the doctor said." When Laura had called him from the hospital, he'd been too rattled to take in the details, and since then he'd mostly been in transit. A frantic dash to the airport followed by the flight, and then the drive from Boston to Strawberry Pond in freezing rain, which had turned into heavy snow when he reached the White Mountains.

"Danny's ankle is badly sprained, not broken, but he'll still need to be on crutches for a few weeks until it heals. Also the usual—rest, elevate and ice, and he has to wear that compression bandage for the next forty-eight hours." Laura grimaced. "He'll need physical therapy as well." In jeans and a faded sweatshirt advertising the Strawberry Pond Strikers, the local baseball team, her face was pale, her eyes dark-shadowed and her usually sleek and groomed hair had mostly fallen out of its ponytail. "All said, though, Danny's lucky. If he'd hit his head on ice when he fell off my bike in the dark, things could've been much worse. He couldn't make it as far as the house, but at least he got into the shelter of the barn. Alana looked in the area where she found my bike, but there's no sign of Danny's phone. It must've fallen out of his parka somewhere. That's why he couldn't call for help."

Trevor rubbed a hand through his hair. The whole thing was a mess. A preventable one, too, if his nephew hadn't been so foolish. And now, he had to deal with Laura, who didn't look angry but rather somehow defeated. Almost broken. "Danny's apologized, and I've grounded him for a few weeks and given him extra chores. I also talked to him about risk taking and trust. He could've been hit by a car or…" Trevor paused. Strawberry Pond was generally safe but, like anywhere else, bad things could still happen. "As you said, he's going to be okay and it could've been worse. I'll call Landon's and Isaac's folks later and the police, too. After that, there's nothing more to be said."

"Not to Danny, no." Laura eyed him over her own coffee mug. "Sneaking out wasn't his idea, but I understand why he followed along. He wanted to fit in and have friends. Peer pressure can be powerful. I gather Isaac was the instigator. Like before, when school let out early, and Danny went home with Isaac without letting anyone know. Isaac was behind that escapade as well." Her shoulders slumped. "I'm not saying Isaac's a bad influence, or Danny's easily led, but sneaking out's serious. It never crossed my mind Danny would do such a thing."

"Me, neither." From what Danny had said, the boys thought it'd be a harmless prank. They'd never thought they'd be caught or that they could've ended up in big trouble. "After Danny was bullied in his last school, it must have felt good to be one of the guys and have what he thought would be fun. I get it. He doesn't have the maturity to always make good choices."

Trevor rubbed the back of his neck, trying to loosen the bunched muscles. "I guess we're getting a crash course in parenting a teenager. We have to set rules and expectations, and Danny needs to know they're to keep him safe and we want to help him learn to make better decisions." He sipped coffee, savoring the fragrant brew.

"*You*, not we." Laura's voice was tight.

"Well, yes, but..." His voice trailed away. Trevor wanted it to be *them* parenting Danny, but after they'd both had a sleepless night, it wasn't the right time to tell Laura about his hopes and dreams for them. "That's family life for you. Like any relationship, it sure comes with a lot of unexpected things you can't control." He chuckled and reached out to pat Star, who was lying near Trevor's feet. "Keeps you on your toes trying to stay one step ahead of kids."

Laura set her mug on the coffee table with a dull thud. "I handled everything last night. I coped with the crisis, including finding Danny, taking him to the hospital and waiting there with him for hours while he had tests. Comforting him. Caring for him. I don't think I could've been any more 'on my toes.' As for staying 'one step ahead,' Danny hadn't given me any reason not to trust him. I couldn't know he'd leave the house soon after my meeting started."

"Agreed, and I really appreciate everything

you did. I'm not blaming you for anything. It's all on Danny, and he knows he has to take responsibility for his actions." Trevor blinked and sucked in a quick breath. He'd evidently said something wrong, but what? "He understands he needs to make it up to you. Regain your trust. Mine as well."

"He does." Laura's voice was icy.

"So what's the problem?" Laura wasn't one to hold grudges, and while she must've been terrified when she discovered Danny was missing, like she said, she'd coped with the crisis. He cleared his throat. "I know why you were upset last night, but why now? Danny's going to be okay."

"It's not about Danny, not really." Laura stared at her tightly clasped hands and then at Star. "What happened last night was totally unexpected. If Star and Tootsie hadn't helped me find Danny, he could still be missing."

"I doubt it. Sure, the animals were great, but someone would've found Danny when they did morning chores. That part of the barn's heated, and he was wearing winter gear. He'd have been okay there for one night. Another part of the adventure."

"The adventure?" Laura's eyes widened as she looked at him. "That's how you see it? Boys will be boys?"

"No, of course not." Trevor tried to placate her. "But you have to admit, we might have done the same as Danny back in the day."

"You, not me."

"Come on, Lulu. If we're going to make any kind of life together, you need to be more adventurous. Don't fear the unexpected. Embrace it. You can be kind of rigid in how you think, and I understand it, but maybe that's why you get stressed." He leaned toward her across the coffee table that separated them. "I still want excitement and adventure, but now with Danny and you. The three of us. What do you think?"

"I think you should leave." Laura stood, and two red patches bloomed on her cheeks.

"What? Why?" Trevor got to his feet as well and held out his arms. "Come on. I was joking. I'm sorry." He'd apologized a lot in the past few hours, but instead of making things better, so far he'd only seemed to make them worse.

"We never should've crossed the line from friendship to romance." Laura folded her arms over her chest and hugged herself. "It was a mistake but now...it's over. Like I said, you need to leave."

"But what about Danny?" He gestured upward to where the kid slept.

"You can either wake him and take him with

you, or I'll drive him home later." Laura moved toward the front hall.

"But—"

"You need to go, Trevor. And not come back." Laura's voice shook.

"Laura? Uncle Trevor? What's going on?" Maneuvering awkwardly on his new crutches, Danny appeared at the living room door.

"Nothing." Laura gave the boy a too-bright smile. "It's time for you to go home. If you sleep all day, you won't sleep tonight. I'll gather your things from down here. Your uncle can pack up the stuff in your room."

Trevor stared after her retreating back and made himself shut his half-open mouth. She didn't mean what she'd said. That it was over. She couldn't. Laura would calm down. She always did.

But what if she didn't? And what if he'd not only lost his best friend, but also the woman he wanted to spend the rest of his life with?

THE FRONT DOOR closed behind Trevor and Danny, and Laura went to the stairs and sat on the bottom step.

"Hey, Star. Come here, Coop."

The dogs sat on either side of her, and Star rested her chin on Laura's knee.

Outside, Trevor's SUV started up and then the vehicle noise faded into the distance.

They were gone. For good. It was for the best, wasn't it? It had to be. Laura dropped her head into her hands, and the tears she'd held back by sheer force of will rolled down her cheeks. She hardly ever cried and she'd vowed she wouldn't this time, either. And she hadn't. Not while Trevor had gone upstairs to organize and bring down Danny's luggage. Not while the two of them were putting on their outdoor clothing. Not even when Danny had hugged her, and Trevor had given her a beseeching look more poignant than anything he could've said.

She'd kept control of emotions until now. Until she no longer could.

As she sobbed, and the dogs whimpered and tried to lick her face, she hugged herself. What had Trevor said? That she was "kind of rigid" in her thinking. That she should "embrace" the unexpected and family life came with things you couldn't control.

Laura sniffed and went to the kitchen for a box of tissues, Star and Cooper at her heels. She knew all about the unpredictability of family life. That's why she'd never wanted it for herself. Last night with Danny had been a rerun of her teenage years. Like the time her middle brother decided to play rodeo cowboy and fell off a friend's horse and broke his arm. Since their mom was at work it'd been Laura who, a day after passing her driving test, had taken him to the hospital in their dad's old pickup. And when one of her sisters had snuck out after curfew to meet a boyfriend, it'd been Laura who'd noticed she wasn't in bed and gone after her.

And almost every day during her middle and high school years, she'd had to rush through her homework to do farm chores, make meals and look after her younger brothers and sisters until her mom, who'd always had off-farm jobs, got home. Most days, it hardly seemed like Laura had gone to bed before she got up again for early chores before catching the school bus.

She didn't blame her mom. Laura stared out the kitchen window in the dusk without truly seeing the familiar view of snow-covered fields bracketed by distant mountains. Her mom had been grieving too and, in retrospect, had likely been even more overwhelmed than Laura. She couldn't blame her dad for having had a heart attack and dying, either.

Life happened and, more than some families, they'd been unlucky. Still, they'd come through. She had come through.

Laura closed the kitchen curtains. The house was quiet, exactly how she liked it, but the silence seemed to press in on her. Suffocating. Stifling.

It was when Trevor talked about them parenting Danny that she'd panicked. It was as if in that instant she saw the independent life she'd fought so hard to build evaporating like mist on a lake. Losing control of her identity. Getting caught up in caring for Danny like she'd had to do with her siblings for all those years. Never feeling like she had her own identity in the family apart from "eldest child" and the "responsible" one. Her mom's right hand. Trustworthy and dependable Laura. Always good in a crisis.

She took a forgotten sweatshirt Danny had left draped over a kitchen chair, and sat at the table, hugging the shirt, and cried harder. What was she going to do? She'd told Trevor to leave and not come back and she'd meant it. But he was also her best friend, and she didn't want to imagine her world without him.

The ringing of her cell phone broke into her tears and she gulped, reaching for the phone in her pocket. Recognizing Anne Sullivan's number, she hit Answer. "Hello? Oh, yes, Aunt Anne." She tried to keep her voice steady.

"I'm sorry to bother you, dear, but I thought you'd want to hear it from me rather than anyone else." Anne paused. "I'm afraid it's not good news. I've added up the numbers several times, and basing projections on what we've raised, even with the funds from the car raffle included, I doubt we'll make enough to buy the animal rescue building. If I'm estimating correctly, we'll still be between ten and fifteen thousand dollars short."

Just when Laura thought her life couldn't get any worse came this new blow. "Oh."

"Yes, and with the lease up so soon..." Anne's voice trailed away. "We did our best, but maybe it wasn't meant to be. We'll still go ahead with the yard sale, it's too late to cancel, but I wanted to let you know where we're at."

"What'll happen to the animals?" Laura rubbed Star's silky ears.

"I don't know, but perhaps the veterinary clinic could take some of them in temporarily. Various farms might also have space but that's only a stopgap. Maybe other rescues, both in New Hampshire and out of state, as well as in Canada? We can reach out to them but, like ours, most rescues are already full to bursting. We'll also have to return donations or, if there's agreement, put the funds toward some other animal-related cause. However, that's a problem for another day."

Laura had been foolish to be so optimistic. Trevor was right all along. How could they have expected to raise the money needed? The short time frame had only compounded the difficulty.

As she said goodbye to her aunt, she rested her head on the kitchen table atop Danny's sweatshirt, emotionally numb and, for the moment, all cried out. She could take several cats or dogs here. Star and Cooper were fine with other pets and she had plenty of space.

Moments or maybe half an hour later, her phone rang again, and she answered without looking at call display. "Yes?"

"Laura?" Josie's voice was tinged with concern.

"It's me." Still with her head half-resting on the table, Laura couldn't be bothered to sound upbeat for her friend.

"Anne Sullivan called Grams in Vermont about the fundraising problem and Grams called me. It's such a shame and… Something else is wrong, isn't it?"

"Trevor and I broke up." Laura was too tired to try to lie.

"Oh, honey." Josie's voice was soft and soothing, as if she was speaking to one of her daughters. "I'll be at your place in twenty minutes. I'll pick up Alana and chocolate on my way. This is a Farm-Hers emergency." The name for their friendship group, which had initially linked them as women working in agriculture, but now they rarely used. "The girls are at school, but Heath's here to meet them from the bus." She brushed away Laura's half-hearted attempt at an objection. "Sit tight but maybe… Have you ever thought about talking to your mom?"

"No." Why would Laura talk to her mom? They only ever chatted about unimportant things, not feelings or relationships.

As Josie ended the call, Laura finally raised her head and began to collect the scattered tissues. Then, a new thought hit her.

What if those women she'd overheard at the grocery store were right? She'd dismissed the idea of Trevor moving back to California at the end of the school year and taking his mom and Danny with him as gossip. But what if it wasn't? What if that's one of the things Trevor meant by still wanting to have adventures?

If he'd been planning it all along, on top of everything else, she'd been duped.

CHAPTER TWENTY

"CAN WE ORDER PIZZA?" In the family room at the Brennan house, sitting on the sofa with his sprained ankle resting on a large ottoman, Danny paused the movie he'd been watching and darted a glance at Trevor.

"I guess." The kid had hardly looked at him since returning from Laura's, and Trevor didn't know how to get through to him. He picked up his phone to scroll to the online menu. He didn't feel like cooking or eating, but Danny needed to be fed, and the fridge was pretty much empty. It'd been more than twenty-four hours and he hadn't heard anything from Laura. On the rare occasions they'd argued before, it had never gone on this long. They could both be hotheaded, and certain each one was in the right, but they were also both quick to forgive and forget. "The usual?" He scanned the menu options.

Danny shrugged. "Sure, but it won't be the same without Laura."

As if Trevor needed the reminder. He placed

the order for delivery and set his phone aside. Usually on a weekend, Laura would come over and the three of them would get a pizza, watch a movie and play a board game. Although Trevor hadn't recognized it then, he'd come to count on that routine and it was a highlight of his week.

"Why won't you tell me what happened between you and Laura?" Danny clicked off the movie and the TV screen went dark.

"It's nothing." Trevor picked up last week's issue of *The Strawberry Pond Gazette* and flipped through it. A piece about the chamber of commerce's upcoming chili cook-off included a picture of Laura and the mayor at the previous year's event. His gaze lingered on her beaming smile, as always like a burst of sunshine, even though the photo was in grainy black and white. Would she ever smile at him like that again?

"It's not nothing. Laura hasn't called or dropped by, and even I could tell things were weird when we left her place." Danny reached over and took the newspaper from Trevor's hands. "Maybe I can help."

"Thanks, but it's between me and Laura." How could a thirteen-year-old understand the complexities of adult relationships? Trevor didn't understand them himself. Before he went to the conference, everything had been fine. But now, when he'd thought they could put what Danny had done behind them, everything with Laura had blown up in his face.

"Yeah, right." Danny's voice was heavy with sarcasm and he gave Trevor what was becoming a signature eye roll. "You're handling it just fine. Not." He grasped his crutches and pushed himself to stand. "When the pizza gets here, I'll eat in my room."

"No, you'll eat with me in the kitchen like always. Family meals are important." Trevor's mom had insisted their family gather together for food at the end of the day, and it was a tradition he'd resurrected with Danny.

"If you say so." Danny balanced on the crutches. "Landon's mom said she'll pick me up and take me to school with Landon this week. She'll bring me home, too. So you don't have to bother."

"It's not a bother." Trevor suppressed a huff of irritation. Ever since returning from Laura's, Danny had been acting out. Either like now, verging on rude, or sullen and uncommunicative. The common denominator was unpredictable, and Trevor had no idea how to handle his nephew's behavior. "I also don't want you being home alone after school while I'm at work."

"It's not like I can go anywhere, is it?" Danny gestured to the crutches.

"That's not what I meant." Trevor pressed a finger to his temple where a headache throbbed.

"You need someone to handle practical stuff like making a snack. You shouldn't be putting weight on that ankle yet. That's why I suggested you could hang out at the clinic until I finish work."

"Whatever." Danny clumped to the patio window and looked out at the melting snow dripping from the eaves.

"Laura said she called your school but do you need a doctor's note or anything else to be officially excused from gym class?" Trevor spoke to Danny's back.

"Already taken care of. Laura asked the doctor at the hospital for one. She was really great. Almost like Mom."

"I'm sure she was." Trevor tamped down more irritation. If he'd been here, he'd have coped. Was Danny implying he wouldn't have?

"I heard about the animal rescue having to close. Can we take some of the animals here?"

Rap music blared from the Danny's phone, making Trevor jump. "No, we can't take any of the animals. It's not our house. And turn that music down."

"So where will the animals go?" Danny silenced his phone, turned away from the window and fixed Trevor with a hard stare.

"I don't know." Despite being organized in a rush, this morning's indoor yard sale had raised a good sum. However, news about the fundraising effort likely falling short had spread around town, more due to folks talking than the official announcement posted on Strawberry Pond's website and various social media accounts.

Laura must be devastated, and Trevor's heart hurt for her and the other committee members. So many times, he'd picked up his phone to call or text her and then decided he couldn't. After all, she'd told him to leave and not come back, so it was up to her to make the first move.

"You don't care, either."

"Don't care about what?" Trevor tried to focus on Danny.

"About the animals." Danny stuck his bottom lip out like a petulant toddler. "I heard Laura's taking a cat and her kittens."

"Absolutely, I care." For whatever reason, Danny considered Trevor the "bad guy" in this Laura situation. It wasn't fair, but the kid missed Laura and was only seeing things from one biased perspective. However, despite his best efforts, Trevor's patience was wearing thin. "Look, do you want to go stay with Grandma for a few days?" After what had happened, maybe some time apart would be good for them both, and his mom always said that if Trevor ever needed a break, she'd be happy to have Danny visit.

"I guess." Danny paused. "It's not like I need *you.*"

Trevor gasped and put a hand to his chest. “Danny. That’s not—”

“Forget it.” Danny interjected and muttered something unintelligible under his breath.

“You might not think you need me, but I need you. Besides, your mom left you in my care.”

On his way toward the family room door, Danny stopped and half turned. “Yeah, she did. She *left* me, and I hate it. And just when things were getting better, like with Laura, and I had friends, you went and ruined everything.”

“I didn’t mean to. How did I—”

But Danny was gone, only the thump of his crutches reverberating on the wooden floor.

As Trevor reached for his phone again, this time to call his mom and ask her to have Danny to stay, he’d never felt more alone or unhappy.

He’d let his nephew down. He’d let Renée down. He’d also let Laura down, although he didn’t know how or why.

And he had no idea how to make any of it right.

HAVE YOU EVER thought about talking to your mom? As she turned off the country road into the familiar farm lane, Josie’s voice echoed in Laura’s ears. The snowbanks on either side of the lane were lower than on Laura’s last visit, and bare spots of gravel poked through the vehicle ruts. Overhead, the sky was a softer blue, and when Laura had done early chores, she'd heard birdsong, and spotted several ducks by the open water on the pond near the barn. However, even the changing season couldn't take the chill from her heart.

She'd argued with Trevor before, but this time it felt different. Had she overreacted? He'd said he'd been joking so after her initial anger faded, other thoughts came to the fore. Josie and Alana had been there for her with the comfort, support and chocolate Josie had promised. But this next bit was on Laura, and she needed to face some uncomfortable truths about herself.

Taking a deep breath, she parked in a cleared space outside what had once been the summer kitchen in the old farmhouse where she'd grown up. There wasn't anything special about this visit. If they didn't speak by phone, it was when she usually dropped by to see her mom. Yet, like with Trevor, today felt different. For the first time in years, she needed to stop avoiding and talk to her mom about things that truly mattered.

Walking around to the side door, she noted that the pasture fence had been repaired and a new chicken coop installed. Why hadn't her mom mentioned having work done? Laura rapped on the door and then opened it. "Hey, Mom. It's me."

"I'm in the front room. Come on through."

Her mom sounded the same as always and why wouldn't she? Unlike Laura, her world hadn't been turned upside down.

Laura slipped out of her coat and boots and padded through the kitchen and along the hall. There were differences here as well. The family pictures that lined the hall and up the staircase were gone, with only lighter patches on the wallpaper to show where they'd been.

"Mom?" Laura's heartbeat sped up as she came into the living room and saw her mother sitting on the floor, surrounded by open boxes. "What're you doing?"

"What I should have done a few years ago. What you've been ever so politely suggesting I think about for those few years as well." Her mom paused with a book in one hand. "After gathering donations for the town yard sale in such a hurry, somehow I kept going with the decluttering." She gave Laura a faltering smile. "It's long overdue, don't you think?"

"I guess but..." Laura stopped and scrutinized the room more closely. It looked like her mom wasn't only decluttering but preparing to move. "What are you doing with the family bible?" It sat open on an end table instead of in its usual place on a bookshelf near the sofa. A shelf that had been emptied.

"I'm taking it with me." Her mom got to

her feet, grimacing as her knees creaked. "I'm moving into that new fifty-five-plus community, where the town roller rink used to be. Your brothers are taking over the farm full-time, and Mike and his family decided to live here."

"But—but…you never said anything to me." Torn between relief and worry, Laura said the first thing that came into her head.

"No." Her mom sat on the sofa and patted the space at her side. "I've been thinking about it for a while, but the apartment I'll be moving into only became available last week. I planned to tell you today. I didn't want you fretting and fussing before the decision was made, or take on what you'd likely see as your responsibility. You have your own life."

"I do." Laura closed her mouth. It was great to see her mom taking the initiative so why did Laura feel left out? "Are you looking forward to your new place?"

"I sure am." This time when her mom smiled, dimples in her cheeks that Laura couldn't remember seeing in years appeared. "Having everything new and convenient will be wonderful, but more than that, I'll be closer to friends and your sisters and their families, especially in winter. Although I love this old place, it's time to leave. If your dad was still here it'd be different, but since he's not, I've hung on out here too long."

Her mom wasn't saying anything beyond what Laura had often thought, but it was still a shock.

"How are things with you?" Her mom pulled a nearby box closer. "If you don't mind, I'll keep on packing. Mike and his family want to do some redecorating so I'm getting as many things out of the way as I can."

"Tell me what you need and I'll help." Laura was used to taking the lead with her mom and, although welcome, this sudden role reversal was still startling.

"Maybe you should do the same." Her mom paused. "Tell *me* what you need."

There was the opening Laura wanted, and it wasn't as difficult as she'd feared. "I broke up with Trevor." There, the words she'd dreaded saying were out.

"I see." Her mom busied herself cutting a length of packing tape. "You never told me you two were dating, but you didn't have to. I guessed there was something more than friendship between you. Likely always was, except you'd never admit it. So, what happens now?"

"I don't know." As someone who usually finished her holiday shopping in September, the idea of having no clear idea where she'd go from here should have been terrifying. Except it wasn't. Instead, it felt oddly liberating. "I was in the wrong. Trevor's always been so easygoing whereas I'm more structured. That's why we clashed." It wasn't about Danny at all, not really. Only what Danny represented. What Laura thought family meant. "It's a mess, Mom, and now I've lost everything."

"Oh, honey." Her mom turned away from the box and put one arm around Laura's shoulders. "It's hard but that's when you can start over fresh."

"Like you did after Dad passed?"

"In a way." Her mom exhaled. "Despite the awfulness and pain of losing him so early, I wouldn't trade my life with your dad for anything. But my grief meant I relied on you too much. I didn't see it at the time, but I do now. And I'm sorry."

"You don't need to apologize." Laura's eyes burned. "I guess I should've said something before. Even though you relied on me, it sometimes felt like I was forgotten in the family."

"Never." Her mom's eyes widened and she gaped at Laura. "Oh, my dear. I never knew. You were a kid. Older than the others but still so young." She let out a shaky breath. "I can't change what happened back then, but what can I do now?"

A sprig of hope bloomed in Laura's heart. If it

wasn't too late with her mom, maybe it wouldn't be too late with Trevor, either. "Listen, I suppose. It'll take time, but I'd like to get to know you. Who you are now." With her short silver hair and brown eyes, her mom didn't look any different, but there'd been lots of changes inside. Changes Laura would never have expected. "You and Dad were always together. I guess I never thought about you being your own person." Instead, she'd assumed her mom had gotten lost in her marriage but perhaps she'd been mistaken.

"Although it might not have seemed like it, I've always been very much my own person. Before I married your dad, during our marriage and all these years since I was widowed." What might have been amusement sparked in her mom's eyes. "I had off-farm jobs. I've also always had my own friends. Which was lucky because after your dad passed, I no longer fit with that 'couple' group we used to pal around with. We had shared interests, but your dad and me had different ones as well. Don't you remember him going off to the curling rink and me having my book club and aerobics?"

"Not really." Although now her mom mentioned it, Laura had a vague memory of a celebrity workout her mom used to watch, jumping up and down in front of their old TV, her big, bouncy hair held back by a pink headband.

"Like all you kids, you never asked or took the time to think about me as anyone but a wife and mom. It's natural. I never thought about my own mother that way, either." Her mom patted Laura's hand. "I'd like to get to know you, too. Not only as my daughter, but, I hope, my friend. You've always been so smart, capable and independent. To be truthful, sometimes I've thought you didn't need me."

"Never. You're my mother. Of course, I need you." The tightness in Laura's chest eased. In all those phone calls and weekly visits, although well meant, she'd never made an effort to truly get to know her mother. That would change, starting now. What would it be like to rely on her mom when she needed to, instead of always trying to take charge? Yes, she'd indeed been too independent. While the thought seemed to come out of nowhere, it had been percolating beneath the surface for weeks.

"It's like I've been drifting out here," her mom continued. "At first, I had you children and keeping us all afloat financially to focus on. But as everyone left home and money wasn't so tight, these past years have given me space to think. While this move may seem sudden, I've spent a lot of time reassessing my life. It was at Courtney's baby shower things truly crystallized. When I looked at my family, I realized you were all happy and secure in the paths you'd chosen." She paused. "Except, now possibly, you?"

"There's nothing wrong in staying single. Or not having children. They're personal choices." Laura bit her lip. "Sorry, I didn't mean to be defensive." It was almost exactly how she'd reacted with Trevor.

Her mom nodded. "There isn't anything wrong with either of those things if they're what you truly want. And if you haven't chosen them out of fear."

Laura's breath caught as her mom's words hung between them.

"Loss is part of loving someone." Her mom ran a finger over her plain yellow-gold wedding band. A ring Laura had never known her to remove. "But when you lost your dad, it was as if you closed a part of yourself off."

"I—I did." Laura scrubbed a hand across her face as more realization dawned. She hadn't wanted to be hurt, but she'd taken independence and self-sufficiency to an extreme. It was as if she'd been on autopilot all these years, never deviating from what she'd thought was the right path when, in some ways, it had been entirely the wrong one.

While she'd reached the point of considering getting married and trying to have a child with Trevor if it was important to him, as soon as

Danny made a bad choice Laura had retreated into her old, familiar pattern. She'd closed herself off again, thinking it was safer to be on her own. But everyone made bad choices, not just teenagers. Loving someone meant accepting who they were, including forgiving their mistakes if they were willing to learn from them. Loving someone also didn't mean sacrificing herself or her happiness, but listening to what the other person thought and needed and then figuring out how to find a middle ground.

Even though Trevor wasn't set on having children, if they were to make a life together, lots of other important issues would come up. Issues they'd have to work through together and resolve.

"I've made a big mistake, Mom." Laura's stomach lurched.

While financial security was important, she'd never let herself consider any other kind. The type of security that meant truly opening her heart to someone else whether a husband *or* a child. Making herself vulnerable. Being part of a family while still being herself. She'd always looked at her life as "either or" as if she couldn't have "both," but maybe she could.

"Most mistakes can be fixed." Her mom's soft smile and gentle squeeze on Laura's hand gave her both comfort and hope. "And if it's Trevor you're talking about, it's not too late."

"You think so?"

"I know so. Trevor's been part of your life too long for him to give up on you because of one disagreement. He gets you, Laura, all of you." She chuckled. "He probably wants to talk to you as much as you want to talk to him."

"I told him to leave and never come back." Laura pressed a hand to her mouth and her face burned. "I've been so wrong." At her age, she should've been smarter, but she'd hung on to old ways of thinking even when they no longer fit or were based on false assumptions.

"Then you're the one who'll have to take the first step, won't you?" Her mom wrapped Laura in a hug. "But if you love him, it'll be worth it."

She *did* love Trevor in all the ways a woman could love a man. There was no doubt about it. And while she'd be stepping into the unexpected, like Trevor had said, she had to embrace it.

There was no other way. Not if she wanted to truly live her life. Not the once-familiar life she'd outgrown, but a new one that could be better than she'd ever let herself imagine. A life she'd share with Trevor, her best friend and so much more. Whether in California or anywhere else, they belonged together.

But first, she had to tell him she'd been wrong.

CHAPTER TWENTY-ONE

"I SHOULDN'T HAVE said what I did. It was mean."

"What? When? Are you okay, Danny?" On Monday afternoon, Trevor looked up from a veterinary journal and stared at his nephew, who hovered in the front hall at the Brennan house. "I thought you were still at Grandma's, and she was picking you up after school."

"I am and she did, but I asked her to bring me here. She's waiting in her car." Danny clomped into the dining room on his crutches, then sat across the polished table from Trevor. "If it's okay, I'd like to come home. Here. With you."

"Of course, it's okay. I missed you." More than Trevor could say. He closed his laptop on the article about cat behavior problems, having read the first few paragraphs three times and not taken in any of the information. On his day off, instead of relishing what should've felt like freedom from responsibilities, he'd been aimless and unfocused. Lonely.

In California, Trevor had never had a problem

living alone, but now, it was too quiet. He even missed not seeing Danny's stuff around everywhere. How things had changed. "I miss you, too. And it *was* mean when I said everything was your fault. I'm sorry." Danny ducked his head but then looked at Trevor full-on, not quite man-to-man but close. "Mom getting sick and dying wasn't anything to do with you. You didn't ruin stuff with my friends, either. Landon's great, but Isaac… I knew it was a bad idea when he said I should sneak out of Laura's house and meet him and Landon, but I did it, anyway. Isaac always wants to do stuff like that, but I don't and now I know Landon doesn't, either. Maybe Isaac's not a good friend for me."

"He doesn't sound like it, but it also sounds like you won't make the same mistake again." Trevor hesitated. He didn't have to reference one of those grief books still stacked on his nightstand. All he needed, truly needed, was to speak from his heart. "With your mom, don't beat yourself up for being mad. I've been pretty mad, too. Your mom got sick so fast and then she was gone." Trevor hadn't even begun to process his sister's illness when he'd had to face her death. Then he'd moved here and been thrown headfirst into parenting a teenager. Along with a new job, trying to support his mom and then his unexpected feelings for Laura, it was a lot under any circumstances, but especially in such a short time. "We've both been dealing with a pile of things so we're bound to make missteps."

An image of the heap of snow the plows had left in a corner of the clinic's parking lot popped into Trevor's mind. It towered over the surrounding buildings and, at the end of winter, it was old and filled with the season's grit. That snow pile looked much like he'd been feeling with grief, responsibilities and worry all pressed on top of each other. Now, he wanted to start fresh—hold on to the best of the old and treasure his memories, but welcome the new. *Laura.* His heart sank. More than anything, he wanted her to be part of that fresh start.

"That's kinda like what Grandma said about mistakes." Danny worried his bottom lip.

"You're grandma's a smart woman." And Trevor's mom had also given him good advice about Laura. He'd thought he'd understood it but had he really?

No, even when Laura had talked to him about whether he wanted children, he'd been so focused on all those "hypotheticals," and caught up in the idea that like him she'd been thinking about marriage and a family, he'd ignored everything else. He should have asked more questions, like when she'd mentioned missing out on skating and other activities because of her family responsibilities.

Instead, he'd joked about family life and relationships. His stomach clenched. He could hardly have said anything worse, but he'd kept on. Telling her to embrace the unexpected. That she was rigid in her thinking. The fear of the unexpected had been forged with her dad's death. As for being rigid, she'd had to be looking after her younger siblings alongside school and working on the farm. She'd needed a fixed schedule to get through it all. He pressed a palm to his mouth to hold back a groan at how insensitive he'd been.

"Uncle Trevor?" Danny's voice was tentative, and Trevor forced himself to focus on his nephew. One thing at a time. "You know when you asked if I wanted to play hockey?"

"Yes?" Trevor stopped himself from saying anything more.

"Well, I was also kinda mean then. I guess you wanted to do something nice for me, but see, I don't want to play hockey."

"That's okay. It was only an idea, but you're a good skater and—"

"Wait. I need to finish." Danny raised a hand. "I want to learn how to figure skate." Danny looked at Trevor as if he expected him to automatically say no. "Like one of Josie's daughters.

I heard Lottie talking at the walk-a-thon, and she's taking summer classes in Conway. She said they're for skaters of all levels. I know you and Grandma really want to go to Maine, but maybe I could work more at Laura's barn to earn extra money to pay for lessons."

"Don't you worry about money." Guilt punched Trevor's chest. He'd landed on hockey because it seemed the obvious choice. But going forward, he needed to look beyond the obvious and listen more than he talked. Not only with Danny, but Laura too, if only he could convince her to make up with him. "We can do both, that vacation in Maine and figure skating for you. Maybe I could share the driving with Josie and Heath."

"Great." Danny's smile was like the sun coming out after rain. "I also want to learn to ride a horse. Laura said she'd teach me if you were okay with it, but..." His smile disappeared. "So what about Laura? Are you gonna fix things with her?"

Trevor had never been a quitter, and if he loved Laura, which he did, he wouldn't give up. He straightened. "I sure am." That commitment was the most important thing, and he'd figure out the details later. Just like he'd keep figuring things out with Danny. His nephew liked to build things so maybe instead of those art classes he'd tried to push, there were other options. A robotics club, perhaps. But first things first. "You said your grandma's in her car?"

"She is. To keep warm. She's not doing anything else for the rest of the afternoon, so I bet she could stay here with me if you need to go somewhere." A small smile tugged at the corners of Danny's mouth.

"I do need to go somewhere. Stay here, and I'll talk to your grandma on my way out." He pushed back his chair. "And maybe we *could* take a dog in from the animal rescue." Miss Sarah was a dog lover, and Buttons lived here. There were numerous chew marks on the wooden baseboards to prove it. "But I won't give up on Laura *or* trying to save the rescue. While I go find Laura, you and your grandma put your thinking caps on. We still have a few days until the deadline, and we need a miracle."

After Danny gave him a thumbs-up, Trevor tugged on his boots, grabbed his jacket and went out to speak to his mom.

Then, he got into his SUV, and five minutes later, parked in the lot behind the high school and set off across the snow-covered football field. The drifts weren't as deep as they'd have been earlier in the winter so he could get to what he still thought of as his thinking place.

Yes, there it was, half-hidden by trees several hundred yards beyond the school property. The ruins of an old woolen mill abandoned since the nineteen forties wasn't just Trevor's thinking place. It was also a special place for him and Laura. In spring, summer and fall, as kids they used to play in the ruins and, as they'd grown older, it was where they'd talked about life, school and the future. Now, it was where he needed to go to marshal his thoughts before he drove out to Laura's farm, or wherever else she might be, to make amends and tell her what was in his heart.

After leaving the field, he walked along the river that had once powered the mill, still mostly frozen but with a trickle of water flowing down the middle shining bright in the slanting sunshine. In a tree still bare of leaves, a blue jay chattered as if urging Trevor on.

He wouldn't let Laura brush him off. He'd assemble his reasons why they should be together forever and start by—

"Laura?" As he rounded the corner that led into the mill ruins, he stopped.

"Trevor?" She spoke at the same time as him.

"What are you doing here?" Laughter bubbled up and he tried to suppress it.

"I could ask you the same thing." She got up from where she sat on a rocky outcrop covered with a tartan picnic blanket.

That blanket was typical Laura, and she probably had snacks with her, too, but Trevor wouldn't tease. Instead, he wanted to celebrate her being the most prepared person he knew. That organization balanced his more haphazard approach to life. Then, he looked at her more closely. Was she trying not to laugh as well? "We must be pretty good friends if we independently come to the same place at the same time. No doubt for the same reason." The laugh he'd been trying to hold back erupted.

Her laughter joined his, and then somehow they were hugging with no more awkwardness between them.

"I guess we are." Laura sobered. "I was on my way to look for you. I made up a reason to call the clinic, and the receptionist said today's your day off so I was headed for the Brennan house. But I came here first to plan what I wanted to say. I'm so sorry, Trevor. I was wrong, and I overreacted and oh, everything." Now, her voice held unshed tears.

"I'm sorry, too. I was wrong to joke. I didn't think. I charged ahead like I always do. I may seem like this happy-go-lucky guy, but that's only on the outside. If you'll give me another chance, I know we can work things out because I love you, Laura. The adventure I want most is to build a life in Strawberry Pond with you." He put a hand to his face. "There I go again. I didn't mean to tell you right away. I meant to make it special so you'd—"

"I love you, too." She put a finger to his lips. "Life's short and we shouldn't waste it. And where better than right here? This place is more special than anywhere, at least to me. I even have tea and cookies. The cookies are for you."

"You made me cookies?"

Her smile broadened and became teasing. "Chocolate chip, your favorite. Another way of apologizing."

"Not needed but, oh, Lulu." Trevor knew his heart was hers. For the first time in his adult life, he didn't feel the need to rush off anywhere. Being with her was calm, peaceful, and bone-deep solid and right. "I've always loved you, but I never recognized it until coming back here."

"Me neither but…" She looked at him with all the love he'd ever needed and more. "I need to talk to you. Really talk. We can't move forward if I don't."

LAURA TOOK A deep breath. Trevor loved her like she loved him. With that love, they'd work everything else out.

"I was scared of getting lost in a relationship. Whether with a family or with a man. The guy who asked me to marry him might not have been right for me, but I didn't even consider getting engaged because of what I thought making that commitment meant."

"And now?" Trevor's expression was hopeful, expectant.

"I'm not scared anymore. I mean, of course, I'm frightened, but not like I was. Now, I realize that to truly live my life, I have to face my fears and move ahead and make choices despite being scared. It'll take time, but I'm determined."

"When have you not reached any goal you set?" Trevor must have noticed her slight shiver. He indicated her backpack, and she nodded. Inside, there was a thermos and two travel mugs. He poured tea from her thermos into one of the cups and handed it to her. Then he opened the tin of cookies, took one and bit into it. "These are even better than my mom's."

"They can't be. I used your mom's recipe to make them." Laura gave him a small smile. "I called her last night to ask for it, and we ended up talking. She didn't interfere, but she listened." And while Cheryl hadn't said much, she'd been the same wise and caring older friend she'd been since Laura's childhood. Her second mom.

"Well, these cookies are still better because you made them for me." Trevor returned Laura's smile, his chin smeared with chocolate and crumbs.

Focus on what she needed to say, not how endearing Trevor was. "Anyway, that getting lost in a relationship fear built on how lost I often felt in my family. Like I was only the oldest and not my own, independent person." Now, for the hardest bit. "A part of me I didn't even want to acknowledge also thought if I let myself truly fall in love with a man and have children with him, I'd lose myself. I thought my mom didn't have an independent life without my dad and all us kids. I was wrong. Now, I know it doesn't have to be that way." In part thanks to Becca and Evan, for whom she'd found the perfect house. One that suited them as individuals as well as a couple and their kids. "After buying my horse farm, which was all I thought I ever wanted, there was still something missing. I wondered if there was more to life and when I finally listened to my heart, I know there is. That more is you. And Danny. You said you wanted us to build a life in Strawberry Pond, but I heard…well, it was probably gossip, but if you want to move back to California with your mom and Danny, I'll come with you. I could get a real estate license there. For you, I'll make it work."

Laura stopped. That was likely the most she'd ever said about her feelings to anyone. It was also likely the most she'd ever said to Trevor without him interrupting her.

"Is it my turn?" Trevor set aside the cookies.

"Yes." Laura sipped some tea to moisten her dry mouth.

"For a start, I want to tell you I heard what you said. All of it. Any talk about me going back to California is wrong. Folks putting two and two together and making ten instead of four. Somebody likely heard me say I missed San Diego weather, which I do, but not enough to return. I wouldn't uproot my mom, Danny or you, and Strawberry Pond is home for me as well. And the rest? I need to think about it more, but it makes sense." His gaze never wavered from hers. "I talked to my mom a while ago, and if I'd truly listened to her then, I wouldn't have been so insensitive with you about Danny. I can't promise I won't interrupt or joke again, but it's something I want to change so I need you to call me out on it, okay?"

"Okay." The word was almost a whisper. She wasn't the only one who'd done some serious thinking over the past few days.

"And now..." He set Laura's mug aside and, clasping her hands in his, he kneeled in front of her. "I love you, Lulu, and it'll be forever. So will you marry me?"

"Yes, I will marry you, Tuna." She didn't have to think it through, or try to plan logistics. For now, making the promise was enough. "I'll love you forever, and I always have. I just didn't recognize when the love I had for you as a friend turned into one that's bigger, deeper."

"Me, neither." He leaned closer. "I expect you'll want to choose your own engagement ring so—"

"Nope." She grinned as happiness bubbled up inside her. "Surprise me."

"Really?" Trevor's eyes widened.

"Sure." She squeezed his hands. " I trust you know me well enough to choose something I'd like. I still have the locket you gave me for high school graduation. It's the most special piece of jewelry I own. I keep it in the box it came in from Stella's Jewelers on Main Street."

"You do?"

She nodded and scooted closer to him. "I do." Which sounded an awful lot like a wedding vow, but they'd get there soon enough. For now, she wanted to savor this moment.

"I also wanted to say I'm so sorry about the animal rescue—"

"That's the one goal I didn't meet."

"Hang on. We're so close, and I haven't given up. There's got to be a way of getting that last bit of money. I'm saving for Danny's college, but I could even loan—" A muffled ringing stopped him.

"Is that your phone?" It must be, as Laura had

turned hers off. Something she never did, but she hadn't wanted to be distracted or disturbed.

"It doesn't matter." Trevor moved closer. "I could put up some money and—"

"But the call could be to do with Danny or your mom." Although the new more easygoing Laura wanted to kiss Trevor, responsible Laura still held sway and likely always would.

"You're right." He dug in his jacket pocket and pulled out his phone. "It's Miss Sarah. It must be urgent if she's calling me on my cell. Hello? What? Of course." Trevor's eyebrows raised almost to his hairline and his breath kept catching as he listened, only interjecting with an occasional surprised gasp. "Thank you so much. Truly, that's amazing. Yes, I'll tell Laura right away." He grinned and said goodbye. "You'll never guess."

"I won't so you better tell me." She knew it was good news, though.

"You remember that painting of the field and sheep with the sheepdog Miss Sarah loaned to display at the art show and sale?"

"The ugly one?" Laura shuddered. "I kept wanting to move it to a less prominent position but out of respect for Miss Sarah I didn't."

"Thank goodness. A Boston art dealer who came to the event saw it, got in touch with Miss Sarah and has now bought that painting for fifteen thousand dollars. A famous artist painted it before he became famous. Miss Sarah asked me to ship the painting to her in Florida. I did and didn't think about it again. The reason she asked me to send it to her was because the art dealer wanted to see it again and planned to fly to Florida to talk to her about it."

"That's great for Miss Sarah, but why are you so excited?"

"Because Miss Sarah is donating the money from the painting to Save the Animal Rescue. She never liked the painting, either, but felt obliged to keep it because it was a family heirloom. However, she said it wasn't doing any good in the attic, she has lots of links with her family history, and she wants to sell it and use the money to benefit Strawberry Pond." Trevor flung his arms around Laura. "We did it. We met the fundraising goal, and the town can buy the rescue building!"

"We… You… Miss Sarah." Laura could hardly speak. "We better rename that building after Miss Sarah, Buttons or both of them." But all of that, including Laura taking the naming idea to the fundraising committee, could wait because she had something much more important on her mind. Something that couldn't wait. "Kiss me, Trevor, because while the animal rescue news is great, you, us, is what I really care about."

"My love." As his lips met hers, all Laura could think about was how nothing had ever sounded so right.

Trevor, Tuna, was her love, too, and they were each other's. Now, always and forever.

EPILOGUE

"APART FROM MY OWN, I can't remember when I last attended such a beautiful wedding. It was truly intimate and joyful." At Cheryl's side near the bottom of the church steps, Sarah Fournier's smile was as bright as the breezy June day. "Right from when they were walking to and from school together, I expected Laura and Trevor to marry one day and now they have."

Cheryl dabbed at her eyes with a tissue. She'd never been far from tears today, but they were happy ones. Seeing her son and Laura get married was something she'd never let herself dream of, but was nevertheless a dream come true. "And to think they're staying right here in Strawberry Pond. Well, it couldn't be any better." With her family nearby, Cheryl could look to the future with hope instead of fear. And despite her grief over losing her husband and daughter, she'd learned to hold joy and loss together in her heart as well as in her life.

Sarah nodded. "When Trevor and Laura come

back from their honeymoon, Jack and I will have a party for them at the Brennan house. Perhaps in the garden? We'll invite the whole town."

"That'd be wonderful." Cheryl smoothed the front of the elegant blue "mother of the groom" dress she and Laura had shopped for together.

"It's decided then." Sarah darted a fond glance at her husband talking with Fred Sinclair, Tom Ryan, Josie's daughters and her husband, Heath. "You and dear Laura's mother must plan it with me. Florida was wonderful, and I enjoyed meeting Jack's extended family in Michigan, but I'm glad to be back in Strawberry Pond. As the saying goes, there's no place like home, is there?"

"That's the truth." Although home wasn't only a place but a feeling, and that feeling came from a nurturing community with family and friends who cared about you. "Did you hear that Trevor, Laura, Danny and me are going to Maine in August? Old Orchard Beach, where James and I used to take the children was like our home away from home." The trip would be bittersweet, but it was also a time to forge new traditions and memories.

"That will be lovely for you. I always find ocean air so invigorating. Oh, there's the photographer. The bridal party must be coming out soon." Sarah waved the small sachet of birdseed, which, along with a bubble-blowing kit, each guest had been given at the end of the wedding ceremony. "Laura looked so beautiful in her mother's dress, and my goodness, isn't Danny growing into a handsome young man?" She gestured to Cheryl's grandson as he came out through the open double doors of the church, his blond hair gleaming in the sunshine. "He reminds me so much of Trevor as a boy."

Cheryl sniffed and patted her eyes once more. Danny *was* like Trevor, and in the new suit, crisp white shirt and tie he'd worn as Trevor's best man, he looked much more grown up than thirteen. However, he was also, as he should be, his own person and still a boy. She smiled as he held on to Star and Cooper at the end of flower-bedecked leashes, Star wearing a floral collar and Cooper with a bow tie.

Like the rest of them, Danny had grown and changed so much in the past months. And while today especially Cheryl's husband and daughter had never been far from her thoughts, along with Laura's dad, she truly believed their loved ones were with them in spirit.

"Cheryl?" Martha Ryan's soft voice was close to her ear. "All right?"

"Yes." Cheryl made herself smile. Martha had been there for her in ways Cheryl hadn't known she'd needed and would continue to be there for the ebbs and flows of life. "I know it's a happy day but still…" She stopped and swallowed a lump of emotion.

"The empty spaces where folks you're missing should be get to you. I know." Martha looped an arm with Cheryl's. "But you find new purpose and go on."

"You do and I am." Cheryl still had lots to be thankful for. Her life wasn't over, and instead, through Trevor and Laura, she was part of a wonderful new beginning. "As well as those figure-skating classes, Danny can hardly stop talking about going to live with Laura at the farm, especially because Trevor's bought Tootsie for him. Danny loves that horse, and when Tootsie's owner was transferred for work and had to sell, Danny was heartbroken at the thought of Tootsie going away."

"According to Josie, Danny has a real knack with horses," Martha said.

"He does, and he bonded with Tootsie because of taking care of her." Cheryl nodded. "I offered to chip in some money toward buying her, but Trevor said no, it was something he wanted to do for Danny." Another part of keeping his promise to Renée to give her son whatever he needed. "Danny's staying with me while Laura and Trevor are away, but I expect he'll have me out at the farm most days. Wants to keep an eye on things for Laura, he says." Cheryl chuckled. "If it was up to him, he'd be half-moved-in by the time the newlyweds get back. Between Trevor and Danny moving out of the Brennan house when Sarah and Jack came home and in with me for a few weeks, the boy mustn't know whether he's coming or going. He's been a good sport about it all, though, and Laura's made sure to include him in the wedding plans."

"She's good for that boy like Heath is to Josie's girls." Martha's voice was warm with approval. "It takes all kinds to make a family, but what matters most is that sense of belonging and connection. Trevor and Laura give that to Danny as well as each other."

"And unconditional love," Cheryl added. Another change for her in the last six months was Mabel. The poodle had given her that love, companionship and, on the worst days, a reason to get out of bed in the morning.

Clapping broke out around them, and Cheryl looked up to where Trevor stood beside Laura at the top of the church steps. Had she ever seen her son look so happy? No, she hadn't. Laura looked happy, too, almost as if she couldn't quite believe she was now a married woman. It was how she kept darting glances at Trevor, and the loving way she brushed what must be a speck of lint from his suit jacket. Laura wasn't only good for Danny, but she was good for Trevor and now, as his wife, she was Cheryl's daughter for real. A daughter-in-love.

With the other guests, she tossed birdseed as Trevor and Laura came down the stairs, followed by Danny, as well as Josie and Alana as bridesmaids, and one of Laura's brothers as a groomsman.

Amid the shower of birdseed, bubbles drifted on the breeze, floating upward into the sailor-blue sky.

The wedding party smiled for everyone taking photos, and then Laura and Trevor gestured to her and Laura's mom to join them.

A dog barked.

From where she now stood between Trevor and Danny, Cheryl glanced around. Star or Cooper? No, the two basset hounds sat quietly at Danny's feet, still playing their parts in the wedding to perfection.

The barking came closer and then a brown-and-white blur of fur barreled through the gathered guests.

A woman shrieked, and other voices raised up in a babble of sound.

"Buttons!" Sarah Fournier spoke above the mayhem. "How did you ever get out? Jack, do something. I can't… My dress—Buttons, stop! Come here, baby."

"It's fine." Trevor ran across the church lawn,

grabbed Buttons by her collar and then scooped her into his arms.

"Oh, my word." Cheryl put a hand to her mouth and gestured to Laura.

"It's okay, Mom, Cheryl. Truly." Laura laughed as Trevor rejoined them. "Buttons is being Buttons. You wanted to join the fun, didn't you?" She rubbed the basenji's ears as the curious canine sniffed the roses in her bouquet. "Family, friends, even dogs. We're surrounded by love. As it should be." When she kissed Trevor, the guests, led by Danny, cheered and Star and Cooper thumped their tails.

A lifetime of love. Cheryl's eyes misted again. What she'd had and wished for Trevor and Laura. And for this unexpected family. One she was so lucky to be part of.

* * * * *